**Praise for Naomi Bellis
and *Step into Darkness***

"With lovely writing and high adventure, *Step into Darkness* marks the debut of a sparkling new voice in romance."
—*New York Times* bestselling author Jo Beverley

"Romance, adventure . . . and a touch of magic. A spellbinding combination."
—*USA Today* bestselling author Kelley Armstrong

"A high-adventure romance . . . powerful conflict and a unique plot tinged with magic. Strong characters play out their roles against a tumultuous and dangerous backdrop. This book is for all adventure lovers."
—*Romantic Times BOOKclub*

"*Step into Darkness* is an action-packed Georgian espionage romantic intrigue. . . . Fans will enjoy this enchanting historical."
—The Best Reviews

"This fast-paced adventure has something for almost every historical fan: romance, adventure, a trace of magic, secrets, and espionage."
—Huntress Book Reviews

"Naomi Bellis's writing is a joy—well paced, with likable and memorable characters."
—*Parkersburg News and Sentinel* (West Virginia)

"Ms. Bellis has created a story that is at once an epic tale and a passionate roma___ A story that will captivate from the first page ___ _r a thrilling read."
___day

"A breathtaking deb___ ___gic combine effortless___ ___ular read."
___tion

OTHER BOOKS BY NAOMI BELLIS

Step into Darkness

Draw Down the Darkness

Naomi Bellis

A SIGNET ECLIPSE BOOK

SIGNET ECLIPSE
Published by New American Library, a division of
Penguin Group (USA) Inc., 375 Hudson Street,
New York, New York 10014, USA
Penguin Group (Canada), 90 Eglinton Avenue East, Suite 700, Toronto,
Ontario M4P 2Y3, Canada (a division of Pearson Penguin Canada Inc.)
Penguin Books Ltd., 80 Strand, London WC2R 0RL, England
Penguin Ireland, 25 St. Stephen's Green, Dublin 2,
Ireland (a division of Penguin Books Ltd.)
Penguin Group (Australia), 250 Camberwell Road, Camberwell, Victoria 3124,
Australia (a division of Pearson Australia Group Pty. Ltd.)
Penguin Books India Pvt. Ltd., 11 Community Centre, Panchsheel Park,
New Delhi - 110 017, India
Penguin Group (NZ), 67 Apollo Drive, Mairangi Bay,
Auckland 1311, New Zealand (a division of Pearson New Zealand Ltd.)
Penguin Books (South Africa) (Pty.) Ltd., 24 Sturdee Avenue,
Rosebank, Johannesburg 2196, South Africa

Penguin Books Ltd., Registered Offices:
80 Strand, London WC2R 0RL, England

First published by Signet Eclipse, an imprint of New American Library, a division of
Penguin Group (USA) Inc.

First Printing, April 2007
10 9 8 7 6 5 4 3 2 1

Copyright © Naomi Lester, 2007
All rights reserved

This book is for those trusty souls who have been with me from the start. They still read everything I send them, no matter how raw or silly it is or how short the time frame. I am eternally grateful for their gentle reality (and sanity) checks, virtual hugs, and relentless encouragement. Without them, this book would never have made it to paper.

Chapter 1

Prelude—April 1798

The courier, puffing and dripping with rain, brought the papers at five minutes past midnight. For Sir Alaric Fitzwilliam, master of spies, the delivery meant a long night of work got even longer.

The damp leather of the correspondence bag smelled of horse and tobacco. Sitting down at the desk in his study, Sir Alaric pulled out the bag's contents: one letter wrapped around a second. He unfolded the outer page first. The thick paper was expensive, obviously from Lord Bedford's own stock.

A single line of writing: *It is as you suspected.*

The Hellfire League had returned. This was grave news.

As Sir Alaric fingered the edge of the page, rain spattered against the windows with a forlorn sound. Stillness hung over London's soaking streets.

The second letter lay on the desk before him. The seal was red, stamped with the outline of a moth. Despite his experience, despite his own considerable power, Sir

Alaric felt a tremor of fear. The seal confirmed the League was active. They used the moth as their signature.

The League cannot win this war. I am the Master. I will fight them. He picked up the letter. The wax seal, already lifted from the paper by Bedford's knife, crumbled as he unfolded the page. Scarlet specks of wax sprinkled the desk and the white of his cuffs.

Sir Alaric pulled his candle closer. It did little to dispel the heavy shadows that blurred the cluttered corners of the room. The only comforting touch was the light snoring of Lady, the greyhound, sprawled on the carpet before the fire.

She was the one creature who saw all of his secret faces. His role as the Master was but the first. He was also a member of the Circle, a handful of ancient families who carried the gift of magic in their blood. That heritage gave him a frightening perspective on the letter Bedford had intercepted:

> *Warmest greetings.*
> *The French are agreeable to our price for assistance with the Irish plan. We will draw down the darkness. Send the word to meet in the usual place at the time of the Lion.*

Draw down the darkness. It was the blackest of the League's canon of foul sorceries. The time of the Lion, when the sun was in Leo, was high summer. It was a good, dry time of year for the French to mount a military invasion.

It is beyond what I dreaded. Sir Alaric sat a moment, swallowing down his anxiety. *Fear garners nothing. Action gains results.*

He flipped the paper over. Who wrote this letter? To whom was it written? There was neither salutation nor signature. Bedford did not indicate whether or not he knew the identity of the author.

There was good reason for caution. The Circle had its hidden malcontents, those who privately pursued unscrupulous aims. They formed the Hellfire League. No one was certain who made up its ranks, and they were dangerous foes.

The Master pondered, listening to the rain on the window. If he was reading the message correctly, the League had just agreed to help the French attack England. That was treason.

And the best thing he could do was let the plot unfold. When the Hellfire League gathered, there would be a unique opportunity to capture all of its elusive members. The question was how. The Circle—the ones he knew could be trusted—would not be able to accomplish the task alone. Gifted though they were, most were not warriors. They had none of the skills necessary to smoke out a conclave of villains.

The Master leaned his elbows on the desk, resting his chin in his hands. Not many men, even amongst his spies, would survive a confrontation with the League. Even subtle Lord Bedford was not enough of a fighter. The right agent would have to be both clever and deadly.

July 1798

By the time the hands of the gold-mounted clock in the entrance reached midnight, Redfern would be triumphant or dead. He had work to do, and his quarry would likely object.

Nights like this—fraught with daring and intrigue—

came far too often. In the last five years, he had been shipwrecked, pursued by both French and Austrian armies, and frozen in the icy wastelands of Canada. By comparison, an evening at London's fashionable Apollonian Rooms was soft work. Nevertheless, the cold breath of treachery might whisper through even the dullest social occasion.

One can but hope, or my night is wasted, he thought, full of weary resignation as the footman took his card with a courteous nod. An impeccably dressed gentleman of fashion, Redfern would easily gain entry. The cut of his coat hid the garrote, the pistol, and both knives. It paid to hire a good tailor. The footman read the card and bowed slightly. The son of an earl and the grandson of the cantankerous Marquess of Bavington, Redfern was welcome everywhere that mattered.

Redfern approached the top of the marble stairs that swept into the rooms. The décor was elegant, with ivory silk draperies and gold sconces. Despite the cool night, the women were dressed in filmy gowns *à la grecque.* It was said the finest gowns were so sheer a lady could draw them through her wedding band. Being of manly and mortal flesh, he hoped the style would linger.

At least two hundred members of England's aristocracy filled the rooms, their numbers fleshed out by wealthy merchants and the usual smattering of hangers-on. They were the cream of London, hot with discussion about the corn markets, the upcoming elections, and that French General Bonaparte. What these men said mattered. Many had the ear of the king, or at least that of the dissolute heir apparent.

That morning, Redfern had received a coded—and rather vague—letter ordering him to this elegant gathering. Sir Alaric required his presence and his expertise. Somewhere in the throng of wine-swilling, pastry-crunching *ton* lurked a traitor. The Master had questions of an urgent nature for this turncoat.

And which one will it be? Redfern wondered, looking out over the crowd. In an hour, he would meet with the spymaster and, like a relentless hound, he would be set upon the traitor's scent. Weariness settled over his heart. He was good at his work, but he did not relish it. He was a spy of necessity, his half of a bargain to save his family from ruin.

"Nicholas Saville, Viscount Redfern."

So announced, he descended the stairs, recognizing a duke here, a marchioness over there. Making his way to an ornately carved archway, he allowed the undertow of the crowd to pull him along. Before he met the Master, he would have a look around, learn who of interest was here and, just as significantly, who was absent. To the right was a salon dotted with gaming tables, and he turned in that direction. Where there was money, there was power. Where there was power, there were villains.

Someone passed by, brushing close. With a fighter's instincts, Redfern drew back, his eyes widening, muscles tight, but the man merely walked on.

Lord Bedford, he thought. He had met him before, but long ago, probably in some gaming hell both would like to forget. Curiosity piqued, Redfern followed the man for a few steps, watching him disappear into a room set with card tables.

Redfern stopped in the doorway, his hand on the frame. Bedford paused to talk to someone, a red-haired man Redfern did not know. There was nothing remarkable in their expressions, so he noted the incident for later consideration. There were other claims on his attention.

Somewhere, there was a traitor. One by one, he searched the tables, looking for something, someone out of place. A gesture or a posture would give away his quarry. He would know it as surely as a musician could pick out a sour note. That certain sensitivity, that nose for a lie, was his gift.

"I don't recall seeing your name on the guest list."

Redfern felt himself go still at the sound of *her* voice. Very slowly, he took his hand from the door frame and turned. His body felt sluggish, as if his mind were moving faster than the physical world around him.

"Hello, Helen," he said, feeling every nerve in his skin grow white hot. This was a meeting he both craved and dreaded.

Helen Barrett was as tall as he, but slight, elflike. When Redfern first met her, he had been attending Oxford with her brother and she had been a pretty schoolgirl ten years their junior. Now a woman in her early twenties, Helen was stunning. She wore one of the Grecian-style gowns, the sheer drapery caught at the waist with a belt of twisted gold. The soft fabric seemed to melt into her flesh, leaving little to his imagination.

"I heard rumors that you were alive. I heard rumors that you were dead. I did not know which to believe." She tilted her head slightly to one side, looking him up and down.

"Helen," he said again, pulling breath back into his lungs. Here, now, was the worst possible time to meet her. He was surrounded by danger, enmeshed in espionage.

"I'm glad you remember my name," she replied, her voice thick with sudden emotion. She stopped, clearing her throat. "And, apparently, you recall my face. I thought perhaps one or both had slipped your mind. It has been three years since I last saw you. That is a long time."

Redfern took a few steps away from the doorway, toward an alcove sheltered by a potted orange tree. Helen followed, her movements slow and automatic.

"I was detained abroad," he said. "You know that. I had business interests to look after."

"And this business took three years?" Her eyes, the soft gray of old silver, were wide and bright. Redfern reached for her arm, but she pulled back, her expression growing distant, as if her soul were in retreat.

"Please, Helen," he said softly. There had been no safe way to put in a letter that he was a spy, only that he must make journey after journey, always with the hope he would return soon to England. "I need to explain so much, but not here. This is a terrible night for such a discussion."

"Nicholas, what do you want of me? Do you want me to wait yet again?" She pressed her lips together. "No. I am done waiting."

He had made a mistake. Something in her tone made him push all other matters from his mind. The fate of nations could wait a quarter hour. His voice dropped yet lower, careful of eavesdroppers. "I want you as my wife."

"So you said. When, precisely, is this supposed union to take place? I would have liked some hint of it—perhaps in a Christmas letter—perhaps Christmas of last year, or the year before that. I've lost track of how long I have been"—she hesitated, as if searching her thoughts—"pining. Pining. Such a strange word, as if I were a tree." She closed her eyes. "I'm sorry. I'm so . . . I do not mean to sound shrewish. I . . ."

"Oh, my love," he said, forcing down a smile. Even in her distress, there was something of her imaginative spirit. "I wrote as often as I could."

"So you did, with great wit and elegance. You were most decidedly in your element. Your enjoyment in a turn of phrase, a descriptive passage, was abundantly clear. I began to think you had more use for me as a correspondent than as a lover." Helen looked away, the clear, strong lines of her face as still as a portrait carved in ivory. "Your punctuation was impeccable."

Redfern reached out again, picking up her hand. He could feel her quick, faint pulse. "My last letter received no answer. Your reply was lost."

A flush crept over her cheeks. "There was no answer."

He had thought to raise her fingers to his lips. Instead, he let her hand slide from his grasp. "Why not?"

She turned those dark silver eyes on him. "There would always be another delay, another reason to stay abroad. It was clear you were never coming back."

Redfern flushed. "Not so clear as that. You see—I am here."

"How long have you been in London?"

"A week only."

"A week, and not one of your celebrated letters. Not a visit. Not a card." She smiled and lifted her shoulder in a delicate, ironic shrug. "What am I to think? Your devotion has curdled like last Sunday's milk."

"I have duties awaiting me here." His excuse limped even in his own ears.

"Am I not a duty? Believe me, I was waiting."

Redfern frowned, frustrated by her words and manner. And yet, it was true, circumstances had been unfair to her. He would atone, however she liked. All he wanted was to feast on her—first with his eyes, and then with every other faculty.

"Tell me, Nicholas," she asked softly, "when do I receive the same attention as a duty?"

He took a step closer. "You have always received my consideration. I love you."

She put the flat of her hands on his chest to stop him. "I grow old and wither under the cold blast of your consideration."

"There were dragons to slay, my dear."

Redfern watched the flush of temper rise up her throat to her cheeks. His own chest ached with wanting her, and wanting to shake her. *If she would only wait until we are alone!* he thought. *I will explain it all.* But which secrets would be safe to tell? Perhaps none.

"If not a dragon," she said in a low, tight voice, "there was a hydra; if not a hydra, a hippogriff. You wrote time and again to say you would come once you had done this or that. Yet you always found one more reason to linger. You shamed me with your absence. You broke me with waiting."

There was something she did not say, some subtle message that shot a bolt of panic through his gut. Reaching out again, he caught her by the shoulders. She stiffened, but still he brushed his lips against hers, the merest suggestion of a kiss. True, it was uninvited and, yes, utterly inappropriate in such a setting. He did not care. He was losing her.

He could feel the catch of her breath against his skin as she stifled her first response. For the briefest moment, he felt the soft, scented brush of her cheek, the velvet of her lips, hot and tender. Her mouth was sweet, as if she had been eating strawberries. He began to ache in places almost forgotten. There were other women in the broad world, but only one Helen. He cared only for her.

Falling close behind the first kiss, his second probed deeper, his tongue finding the edge of her teeth. Finally, she responded, her own kiss drawing him in. Like a call to his deepest instincts, her sigh filled him with fire.

"I love you," he said. "I'm here now, and I love you."

He felt her hands stiffen against him. Pushing him back, Helen looked into his face, her eyes round with shock and desire. The air between them felt thick, magnetic, and fraught with misfortune.

"Do you not feel my love?" he asked softly. "Is there shame in my caress?"

Helen blinked, and tears blurred her lashes. Redfern reached forward to brush them away, but she turned, shrugging him off.

"I am back; here, you see me, you feel me," he protested, his voice rising.

"Hush!" She touched his mouth with her fingers, the touch of her nails against his skin provocative. "It is too late. You have left too often. There is nothing you can say that will make me believe you will stay."

"Helen, you are unjust!"

"Unjust? I thought you were oceans away, yet here you are in your best finery, just in time for the meal."

"There are reasons . . ."

"I release you." Her voice was barely audible.

"Helen?"

"Nicholas, farewell." Her hand fell away, leaving him without the touch of her flesh.

"Helen!"

She took a step backward, the tendrils of her golden hair swinging against her neck. "I'm going to marry someone else. Someone who hates to travel." The tears on her face reflected the candles like some strange, quicksilver mask. She turned and was gone.

He was stunned, an utter numbness flowing over him. A long moment passed before he could close his mouth and swallow thickly. A sudden, deep lassitude overtook him. He knew the night could only grow worse, and Helen had just stolen his nerve.

Chapter 2

Helen pushed past the knot of people standing in the archway to the main room. Crowded and hot, the larger space afforded some privacy simply because it was noisy and congested. The loud gabble of the crowd discouraged any but the most determined conversationalists. She frowned, slipping farther into the crush.

Wiping her face with her fingers, she forced herself to appear calm. Disbelief stole over her, a thick wall that kept the last ten minutes at a distance. Events felt unreal, as if some other Helen had just seen Nicholas. Touched him. Kissed him. Pausing, she looked back over her shoulder. Of course, Nicholas was not there. He never was, not when it mattered. As always, he had priorities above and beyond Helen Barrett.

She had recognized him immediately, even though he was the last man she expected to see. She had not seen his face at first, just a glimpse of his dark hair and tall, straight back. What was so remarkable about him? Why did he stand out? He was young and handsome, but so were many men.

Perhaps it was the set of his shoulders, the almost insolent air that kept people at a distance, as if he knew a joke no one else shared. He was never cruel, or mean, or sly, just . . . contained. That had been what first attracted her, as if he had been a puzzle to solve.

Apparently, she hadn't found the answer.

Did I do the right thing?

Biting her lip, Helen forced herself to turn and keep moving, putting one foot in front of the other as she crossed the room. Grief barely left her room to breathe, as if it had lodged under her heart like a child. *Walking away is for the best. If he wanted me, he would have stayed.*

He had sworn to love her. His promise was a beautiful, exquisite gift she had never been allowed to unwrap. Something was always more important to Nicholas than his waiting bride. As the years dragged on, her spirit had begun to fade.

No man was worth that feeling of neglect, not even a dashing, dark-eyed viscount. As much as she loved Nicholas, he would never make her feel cherished and secure. Helen stopped, suddenly exhausted. She wanted to go home before she gave in and started to bawl with the abandon of a baby. She needed to find her brother.

As a rule, James Barrett was not hard to locate. One had only to look for the powerful parliamentarians, and he would be at the edge of the group, hanging on every word. Helen scanned the crowd and, sure enough, he was deep in conversation with one of his fellow members of the Commons, not ten feet from the prime minister. Now that James was elected to serve as the Honorable Member from Widgley-on-Thornton, he cultivated his career with the anxious care of a gardener with a rare orchid.

Helen had just started forward to catch his attention

when William Pitt, the prime minister, turned and said something to James. She saw her brother's broad face turn pink with pleasure. Pitt placed his hand on James's shoulder and smiled. The latter said something that made Pitt laugh. Despite herself, Helen felt a flash of pride. It was good to see her brother's hard work and ambition succeeding so well of late. No doubt he would write a long letter to his wife that night, relating his witty conversation with Pitt in minute detail.

The herd of political men began drifting toward the doors, going outside to smoke, get a breath of fresh air, or retire en masse to one of their clubs. James was in tow, and obviously happy to be included.

Helen stopped in her tracks, a wave of resentment welling up. Apparently she was expected to cool her heels until James saw fit to return and take her home. That held no attraction. She would leave on her own. To her annoyance, she felt tears well up once more. She lifted up her hand to wipe her eyes yet again, and saw the fingertips of her gloves were soaked.

I'm being ridiculous. As James's sister, she could bear a little inconvenience if that meant he could further his career. She was just upset tonight. *Of course, it would have been nice if James had spared a thought for me. Just once, I'd like to be first in someone's plans.*

"Helen!"

A hand caught her arm, strong but gentle. Helen felt herself pulled to her left. She shook herself free of the importunate grasp, instinctively turning her face away. She did not want to be seen weeping.

"Why do you look so grim? Oh, Miss Barrett, what is the matter?"

The voice made her raise her eyes. It was not, as her

treacherous heart had hoped, Nicholas. Instead, it was the Earl of Waring.

"My lord," she said, forcing pleasure she did not feel into her voice. There was something about the man, something she could not pinpoint, that made her uneasy.

The earl studied her face, his expression furrowed with concern. He gestured to a spindly, gold-painted table nestled between two potted orange trees. "Come, sit with me. It is quieter over there."

Politeness, and the fact he was an earl, demanded Helen acquiesce. At her nod, he drew her to where the seats were sheltered by the wall. "You look as if you would be glad to rest a moment. May I get you some refreshment?"

"Thank you, but no." Helen sat. It did feel good to let the chair take her weight; her limbs felt weak and heavy from spent emotion.

"What troubles you, Miss Barrett?"

"My lord, I beg you, do not ask me that."

He studied her, running a hand through his curling chestnut hair, hesitating for a long moment. "Then let me distract you," he said. "I can do at least that much." The earl put a box on the small, dainty table. "Open it."

"What's this?" Helen asked, confused.

"Open it," he repeated, flashing a sudden grin. "I am hoping it will bring a smile."

Helen eyed the rose satin jewel case that lurked on the table before her, the moment charged with meaning.

I can't hesitate forever.

With a gut-twisting lurch of apprehension, she lifted the shell-shaped lid. She prayed against all reason the case would be empty because, polite and attentive as he was, she wanted nothing from him.

Please make this box vanish, she urged silently. *If that's not possible, please make me vanish.* But any spare miracles had already been used that night at the gaming tables. Helen was doomed.

"Oh!" She gave an involuntary gasp at the pink sapphires that glinted against the silky white lining of the box. The necklace was beautiful and perfect—and came from the wrong man.

"My lord, this is far too much," she said, appalled. "One would think I had done something scandalous to merit such a gift."

As she looked up, Helen could feel her heart racing, blood flushing her cheeks. She hoped he would take the hint. To accept such a gift was only a step or two away from accepting him, and she would not make such a promise. She waited a heartbeat, the hot, perfume-soaked air robbing her of breath. There were too many partygoers in this room. Why had nobody opened the windows?

"Too much? This? This is just a trifle for your birthday," the Earl of Waring replied, sitting down in the chair next to hers. He leaned toward her confidentially, his glove-tight suit showing off the line of his strong shoulders. "A day late, to my shame, but I did not return to London until this morning."

Even though he was in London, Nicholas had forgotten her birthday, Helen suddenly realized. The thought struck her, cold and sharp.

"I hope you forgive my tardiness," the earl went on, fingering the buttons of his waistcoat. The quick movement of his fingers belied a slight nervousness. "I thought pink sapphires would best suit your fair-haired beauty."

The compliment—and gift—was flattering. "It is

lovely, my lord. But is not pink a color for younger girls?"

"Pink is the color of roses, and you are a gray-eyed Athena of a rose."

"Flowery praise is sweet, but beware of horticultural metaphors, my lord, lest our conversation stray to pruning and manure."

He smiled, and it really was a handsome smile, crinkly around his clear blue eyes. Lord Waring was not a young man, but he was elegant and smart. He was also a powerful politician and her brother's mentor.

Marrying him, Helen admitted, would be convenient. James would be overjoyed to see his sister become a countess—even better than the wife of Viscount Redfern.

Her pulse beat in her ears, faint and quick. Unfortunately, loving the earl was not possible. However unwisely, her heart still yearned for a man who was not, and would never be, by her side.

Did I do the right thing, sending Nicholas away?

Embarrassment and grief made her temper simmer, giving new life to the headache pulsing at the back of her skull. The chandeliers glittered on the glasses and silver. She was hot, prickling where the silver-edged lace at her neckline touched skin. More wine was being served, making the noise level creep up still further.

"This gift is anything but a trifle," Helen began, keeping a smile in her words for her brother's sake.

"You are correct; you are not a woman for trifles."

"Trifling is a dangerous game."

"I do not propose to play it. I prefer higher stakes."

The earl put one hand, just the fingertips, on her gloved wrist. The gesture was at once polite and sensual, a mix few men could achieve. Piercing blue, his eyes met hers, seduction lurking in his solemn expression.

She licked her lips, treading carefully. "Indeed, I will not play any games with you, whatever the stakes. I'm sorry, Lord Waring, but it would be improper for me to accept your present."

He leaned back, eyes narrowing, mouth quirking in a half smile. "You're a grown woman, Miss Barrett. You don't need permission to accept my courtship."

She bowed her head, resigned to an unpleasant discussion. Of course it would never occur to a rich and titled widower that she, a woman well past her first Season, did not automatically desire him for a husband. No, he was a Catch, and he knew it.

Once more, she thought of her brother. Much of his success depended on the backing of the Earl of Waring. Much of the earl's favor, she knew, depended on her.

There were truths she had to face. Even if she were content to sit by the window, waiting forever for Nicholas to return, there was James to consider. The Earl of Waring could hand James his career. Duty forbid her to close that door, and yet showing favor to the earl would be a sacrifice. She did not like the man.

"However, if you need your brother's blessing to accept my attentions, I'm sure Barrett would be pleased to give it," Waring said with a sly smile.

Helen sat back in her chair, her resolve to be polite straining under the weight of his self-assurance. "This conversation is nonsense. You know I am engaged to be married."

No, that was not true. She had just broken it off. A feeling of loss knifed through her, making her breath catch in her throat.

He gestured around the room with his hand. "But where is the mysterious Redfern? I begin to think you have invented him as an excuse to avoid unwanted suitors."

Helen ducked her head, blinking back fresh tears. "You are quizzing me. I hardly have hordes of young bucks breaking down my door!"

"Yet you have turned away a number of eligible offers." He lifted an eyebrow. "I would lay money you would turn me down flat if I asked for your hand."

"Lord Waring, a public party is no place for such words, much less for such a gift! For you to give this to me here is—" She stalled, seeking a less inflammatory word than "addlepated." She gulped air. "It is *indelicate.*"

"Yes, but every man who sees us together will know where my desires lie. Not a one will think to cross me by paying you court himself." He leaned forward. Helen noticed his cravat was so well starched, the movement did not disturb it in the least. "You cannot cling to your absent love forever. You will choose to live in the present someday, Miss Barrett—Helen."

The earl narrowed his eyes. "I will fight for what I want. I will make you want me." After a heartbeat, Lord Waring colored, as if he had betrayed himself. "I'm sorry, I did not mean to press you."

Closing her eyes, Helen wished herself away from the conversation. She opened them only to find the earl staring at her with great earnestness. She needed a brandy the size of a birdbath.

His questions about you have merit, Nicholas, she thought grimly. *Where were you all this time?*

She had understood when her lover had gone traveling to oversee some business venture for the first time, five years ago. Precisely what business it was, she never knew. He would be gone for months, then appear for a week, two weeks, two months only to unexpectedly vanish again. The last absence had lasted three years. The unknown adventures of the handsome, aloof viscount had spurred the imagination of the *ton*. Rumors had risen like mist over a swamp, ranging from gothic to plainly ridiculous. Someone even suggested he was kidnapping English ladies and selling them to the sheikhs of Araby. Yet, he would not discuss his "business." Was he protecting her—or did he just not trust her?

"Where has your wandering love been, Helen?"

"My fiancé has been in the Americas," she replied, her voice stiff. She had not given the earl permission to use her Christian name.

The earl was no longer smiling. "Tell me, just how long has he been gone?"

She swallowed. "He has been coming and going for five years." Handing Lord Waring his pink box, she lowered her eyes, refusing to look at him. "Thank you, but as I said, it would not do for me to accept this."

He took the jewels, the muscles in his jaw working. "I honor you, Helen, so I must speak the truth. If a man is stricken with wanderlust, he may return home, but he will not stay by your side. Even if Redfern returns to claim your hand, you will lose him again. Men like that cannot be still."

Pain squeezed Helen's throat, presaging a storm of emotion she could not, *would not,* indulge. His words were too close to her private thoughts.

"You may well be correct, Lord Waring. Tonight I have ended my engagement." The moment the words left her lips, she knew she had spoken unwisely.

He looked up, his lips parting. In a rush of regret, Helen held up her hand, stopping his reply.

This cannot be. I'm sorry, James, but I do not want this man near me.

"Then you are free," said the earl, ignoring the gesture. "I am pleased to hear it."

"I will not discuss this with you further." Helen swallowed hard, feeling as tired as if she had died and simply waited to lie down.

He lifted the gold-plated catch of the jewel box.

"I do not want your gift, my lord," she said, but his gaze held hers. The color of his eyes was so clear, she could see every gradation of blue in their bright depths. The effect was mesmeric.

"Accept this necklace simply as a token of my regard, and as acknowledgement that not all the doors between us are firmly closed."

Strange, the words held an echo of her thoughts. The earl lifted the jewels from the box and, before she could protest, fastened the clasp at the nape of her neck.

The sapphires felt hot against her skin, like chips of captive fire. She touched the stones, feeling their smooth planes and the filigreed goldwork between them. The muscles in her neck and shoulders began to relax.

It must be the heat, she thought. *I feel a trifle light-headed.*

Chapter 3

After speaking to Helen, Redfern wandered from room to room, his thoughts scattered like sand in the wind. There was no defense, no weapon in his arsenal against his anchorless feeling of loss.

He drifted among the gaming tables for several minutes before returning to where he had last seen Helen. Of course, she was not in sight.

Helen's dismissal had blasted him, a lightning bolt of surprise. He had not seen it coming—but he should have. No woman should wait so long. He was the one at fault, and somehow he must make amends. *How?* he wondered. *How can I give her back five years of her life?*

There was no answer. Miserable, Redfern turned and walked toward the main room. His eyes automatically searched the crowd.

There, across the room. She sat beside a man with curling chestnut hair. He searched his memory.

"That is the Earl of Waring," said a voice in his ear.

Redfern caught his breath. The man standing next to him was tall and thin, with straight white hair that fell past his shoulders. Sir Alaric Fitzwilliam, known only to a select few as the king's master of spies or, more simply, the Master.

Redfern's eyes darted back to Helen. The earl was giving her something. Redfern squinted. A jewel case. Alarm and anger flooded through him. What gave Waring the right to give her gifts? Surely she would not accept it! He took a step forward, but Sir Alaric caught his arm.

"The earl is well connected," said the Master. "Her brother relies on Waring to usher him into the halls of power."

Redfern swallowed, realization dawning. "Far better for Barrett if Helen became the Countess of Waring than . . ."

"Than Lady Redfern," the Master finished.

Across the room Waring reached over and touched Helen's wrist. Redfern looked away, jealousy rising like bile.

The Master raised one eyebrow. "She still waits for you?"

Redfern turned back, his gaze feasting on Helen's face, her intelligent eyes and achingly vulnerable mouth.

"No." He licked his lips, as if the word had parched them. "No. She could not forgive me for leaving her alone so long." His voice held all his disappointment.

In a room behind them, a fiddler played a snatch of a country dance. "Oranges and Lemons." It was one of his sister's favorites. After the emotions of the night, the small, domestic detail stung him. He could not afford softer feelings right now, not in front of Sir Alaric. He forced all emotion from his face, ruthlessly pushing the surge of nostalgia away.

"Hmm." The Master looked over at Waring and Helen with mild interest. "I do not see you as the marrying kind.

I've been married, and I loved my wife, God rest her. But marriage is a demanding and time-consuming business and does not mix with the work we do."

Distracted, Redfern said nothing. Helen was talking, and he could not get a direct enough view to read her lips.

The Master gave him a long, appraising look. "You and I struck a bargain," said the Master, his voice the barest whisper in Redfern's ear. The tone of the statement was typical of Sir Alaric, companionable on the surface, the inexorable menace of an iceberg beneath.

"We have struck several bargains over the years," Redfern said. His words were tinged with bitterness.

Sir Alaric leaned in, dropping his voice still lower. "I would remind you, before we proceed further, that you are still in my service." His dark eyes met Redfern's. "You and your family remain in my debt. I am about to ask you for the next payment on that debt."

The other frowned. "I have not, and I will not renege on my word. I have fulfilled your commissions to the letter. In India. In Canada. In Louisiana." An edge of temper tinged Redfern's tone.

"Remember," Sir Alaric said softly, watching Redfern's face, "it was at your request that I took you into my service. Remember your brother gambled away all his expectations and more before he blew out his brains. I covered up the suicide; I discharged his atrocious debts so that you and your siblings had a future. You owe me your service for keeping your family's reputation clean. I did not undertake such an extensive rehabilitation for nothing."

Redfern's lip curled. Of course he remembered. It was not the sort of thing one forgot. "You would ruin my family? My brother and sister are innocents barely out of the schoolroom."

"If I thought it would help England, I would bring them all to their knees, including your grandfather, the marquess. Protecting the throne is what I do, Redfern; that is why I exist."

He rested his fingers on Redfern's sleeve, the gesture casual, friendly. "You are mine as much as my dog is mine. You will do whatever I ask."

Redfern looked across at Helen, his anger bright but fruitless. Every word from the Master put her further beyond his reach. "When is my debt paid? After this conspiracy? Or the next?" Sarcasm crept into his voice.

A footman paused, offering them wine. The Master accepted for both of them, handing Redfern a glass of claret. He waited to speak until the servant bowed and moved on.

"I understand you desire your freedom, but I rely on the fact that you want to protect your family even more." Sir Alaric sighed, volumes of fatigue in the single breath. "Redfern, I do not blame you for wanting quit of me, but I am not done with you yet."

"It is not just my life. Time weighs heavily on a woman."

The Master shrugged. "You had to choose: Marry Miss Barrett, or protect your family."

"I have lost her," Redfern said quietly. Helen was opening the jewel case, her mouth forming an "oh!" of surprise. His stomach twisted with jealousy and regret. "In her eyes, I have broken my promise to marry her."

"Better that than the alternative."

"Which is?"

"Do you really think marriage to you would be fair?"

Sir Alaric's voice was sharp. "You do not know from one day to the next where I will ask you to go, and still less if you will ever return. She is better off this way. She should marry another and be happy."

"I'm not an oath-breaker."

"We are all liars. It is our profession."

Redfern was silent, his gut tight with fury. It was true, Helen was better off. She deserved a home. But then . . . he could not put words to the feeling. Without Helen he would be alone. There was no one else. He had never quite been able to let her go.

It had been up to her to take that final step.

"Let us go upstairs," said the Master. "As long as that woman is in sight, I will not command your full attention."

Redfern hesitated. Helen still had the jewel case in her lap. Feeling his gorge rise with resentment, he turned to follow Sir Alaric. Their engagement had been over less than an hour, and she was already receiving another man's jewels.

A sense of betrayal jarred him, the same sick vertigo as when tumbling from a jumping horse. As soon as he stopped falling, as soon as the hard truth crashed into him, he knew the pain would be terrible.

The clock struck ten as Redfern walked up the narrow stairs at the back of the Apollonian Rooms. As he climbed to the second floor, Redfern broke into a chill sweat, his heart pounding with delayed emotion. In the last few minutes, his body had finally realized what his intellect already knew: He would never touch Helen Barrett again. He paused, reaching the top of the staircase, unaccountably winded by the short climb. He stood there for a moment. Below, the din of the assembled guests roared, a distant sea.

The Master stopped at one of the doors in the short hallway and unlocked it. "Come," he said in a voice that brooked no delays.

Redfern entered, every nerve alert. While he gave rich rewards for excellence and loyalty, the Master was not a man tolerant of mistakes. One could know too much, or too little, or simply make the wrong move.

"Sit down," said the Master, and Redfern sat, taking one of the two armchairs drawn up to the fire. The Master's greyhound, Lady, lay by his chair. She raised her delicate head, watching him with dark, liquid eyes, as he sat.

Redfern watched as Sir Alaric bent to stroke Lady's head. It was the one creature he seemed to love. The hound pushed against the man's hand, licking his fingers. The Master's long, thin face was drawn, made paler still by his flowing white hair. He looked fatigued.

Without preamble, the Master began. "I have received confirmation. The French Republic proposes to invade Ireland in support of the rebels."

Redfern stared, momentarily shocked out of his personal turmoil. "Why would the French involve themselves now? The rebels in Ireland have clearly lost!"

The Master shrugged. "Not that I believe France truly cares whether the Irish are ruled by London or Dublin or the Druids of old, but Ireland is a step away from our shores. The French will use this opportunity to create a staging ground for a war against Britain. The dispatch alludes to a French proposal to attack England from two sides, catching us in a pincer from both coasts."

"The French plan is ill-advised," Redfern said. "They

tried this same invasion in ninety-six and it did not succeed."

"It was only a December storm that drove the French ships out of Bantry Bay." Sir Alaric sat back in his chair, crossing one long, elegant leg over the other. "A fair wind would have changed everything."

Another awkward silence fell in the small, lushly appointed room. The fire was hot at Redfern's left, chasing out the damp of the fine rain falling outside. By now, it was late, and the candles burned low in their ornate silver holders. The two men sat perfectly still, the tension between them nearly solid.

Here it comes, thought Redfern. *He does not give me this information for nothing. Now he will tell me what he wants.*

The Master shifted position again, as if he had grown stiff. Lady got to her feet in one fluid motion, pushing her flank against Sir Alaric's leg.

"This is why I have called you back to London."

Redfern did not reply.

"We have intercepted correspondence that shows someone in England is in communication with the French." Sir Alaric turned his eyes on Redfern. "It is my surmise the head of this conspiracy is highly placed. For that reason alone, utmost secrecy is essential. I foresee a great family of the realm crashing to the dust."

"There will be scandal."

"There cannot be, in particular because there is another wrinkle to this affair that must be kept from the public eye. The Hellfire League is involved."

"The Hellfire League?"

"The League is made up of devotees of the dark arts. After years of silence, I am receiving reports of them once more. They are no mere drinking club; they dabble in black magic and the members are from the top echelons of society. I have reliable information they have agreed to help the French."

Redfern was silent, struck dumb with bemusement.

"You look incredulous," said the Master. "I suppose that is to be expected.

Redfern cleared his throat, acutely embarrassed. "Everyone has heard rumors of the League and the Circle, but no one credits them any more than one would a— a lake monster or an honest politician. I concede magic is possible, but not likely."

Sir Alaric's smile was wintery. "You think that I am working too many late nights. Consider that France's General Bonaparte, among many others, has often employed occult forces. If a foul wind upset French plans before, why not ensure victory through supernatural means?"

Redfern frowned. He thought it more likely there was simply a French spy at Horse Guards, the army headquarters in Whitehall.

The Master shrugged at his doubtful expression. "The Hellfire League exists. Do not discount it in your researches. They are planning to gather later this month or early next. I want to catch the lot of them when that occurs."

Redfern wondered if he had crossed the Atlantic for a fool's errand. "I will be thorough," he said evenly.

"Be watchful as well. They are dangerous." Rising, the Master moved to a side table, Lady at his heels. He filled two crystal glasses with ruby-colored port.

"I need you to make contact with another of our agents," Sir Alaric went on. "He is here tonight."

"His name?" Redfern's tone was businesslike, hiding his disgruntlement.

"Lord Bedford. He uncovered the League's involvement through a series of intercepted correspondence. He has been trying for some months to trace the identity of the League's members, but they have proven to be elusive. He will give you what assistance he can."

"Bedford?" Redfern remembered literally bumping into the man when he arrived. The touch had been a signal to draw his attention, and he had failed to follow it through. Irritation at his oversight needled him.

"Redfern," Sir Alaric said, turning and offering a glass. "Here is a new bargain, one with the potential to please us both. Perhaps it will even solve your difficulties with the lovely Miss Barrett. Find out who proposes to unlock England's back door. Bring me the head of the Hellfire League. Do it in time for me to stop the French and, if you live, perhaps I shall set you free."

Chapter 4

Helen was alone, waiting for the earl. When she had complained of the heat, he had insisted on finding her refreshment. Spirits low, she sat fanning herself and watching the crowd while he went hunting for something to drink. More than wine, water, or ices, she wanted to escape, but good manners required her to stay and be polite to Waring. It was hard. The overbearing man had far too good an opinion of his own merits.

Wearily, she looked around, fingering the pink sapphires of the necklace. It felt heavy and strangely hot against her skin.

It is not right to keep his gift. I will have to give it back. But not now. She was too weary to withstand another debate, as if the conversation with the earl had tapped the last of her energy.

She sat without moving. From here, she could see most of the crowd. Between the clumps of milling guests, the floor was dotted with quasi-Grecian statuary, copies of plundered originals brought home from the Grand Tour. *It is a wonder any stones still stand in Athens,* Helen mused. Even the ceiling followed the theme: A pastel fresco floated above, showing the loves of Zeus painted in the Italian style.

The sight of Leda and the Swan, Europa and the Bull, made her wince. Zeus was a great deceiver of his lady loves, and she was in no mood to smile at his romantic misdemeanors. The god's careless attitude to love reminded her too much of her own plight.

Nicholas had come back but not, it seemed, for her. He had been in town a week without sending word. That was damning behavior for a lover. Still, should she have given him more of a chance to explain himself? Had she rushed to the wrong conclusions? The thought roamed around and around her head like the refrain of a particularly irritating song.

Waring seemed to be taking his time. The room was thinning out by degrees as guests, mostly the men, escaped outside to enjoy the cool of the night. The opening and closing of the doors created a pleasant current of air sweetened by a light rain. It was the most relief she had known all evening. Something, probably the heat, was making her feel thickheaded and fatigued.

From the corner of her eye, she saw the earl walking toward her, a servant bearing a tray of food and drink trotting at his heels.

Lord Waring would be a handsome man if he were anyone else, she thought idly.

"I am sorry I took so long," said Waring, the skirts of his coat swinging with his eager step. "It is hard to move a dozen paces without meeting someone, and there were two or three annoying creatures who would not be put off with a polite sentence or two."

The servant set a plate of dainties on the table and then filled two glasses with iced champagne. The wine bubbled with the promise of cool, sweet pleasure. The earl picked up a glass and passed it to Helen. The touch of it was moist, the cold surface already fogged from the heat of the room.

"I expect we'll spoil our dinner," said Waring as he waved the servant off, "but that is one of the prerogatives of adulthood. Another is being able to stay up far too late for one's own good." His eyes studied hers with hypnotic intensity.

Helen drank, the gesture hiding her distraction. She was still thinking of Nicholas, and her pulse felt quick, unsettled. She set the wineglass on the table, forcing her mind to form coherent ideas. The champagne was already making her dizzy. "You allow me late hours and a poor diet. I can see you have my best interests at heart."

"Always," he laughed.

"Next you will permit me to climb trees in my Sunday clothes and skip my lessons whenever I see fit."

"Why not? You would look delightful dangling from an apple bough in your best silks, and I doubt there is much anyone could teach you that you do not already know."

"If I were in fact so universally wise, life would be devoid of surprise. I would be a complete bore."

The earl leaned forward, a bold smile dawning in his expression. "You are hardly a bore, so perhaps I can still teach you a thing or two."

Helen blinked slowly, resisting the force of his gaze. "My lord, I violently contest that conclusion." She said it in a light tone, but his innuendo annoyed her.

Nicholas had never once embarrassed her this way.

Pressing her fingers to her temple, she tried to bring her thoughts into focus. Surely the earl had not meant to be insinuating. She was being harsh. The man had just given her a fine gift.

Her common sense rebelled against her attempt to put a good face on the situation. *I don't care if he gives me all the rubies of India, he is a toad.*

"Ah!" Helen started, spilling her champagne. The necklace had caught on her skin, stabbing her painfully. She set her wine down and unhooked the clasp.

"What are you doing?" Waring asked, clearly annoyed.

"It pricked me. There must be a sharp edge." The wretched thing was as annoying as the man who gave it. "It felt like a bite."

Just then, Helen saw Nicholas cross the room toward the door. Loss and regret subsumed her, blasting thoughts of the earl and his horrid gift from her mind.

"I have done the wrong thing," she murmured to herself.

"What's that?" asked Waring, his voice alert.

Nicholas turned, his movement slow. As his eyes found hers, his expression changed. For a moment, his face was filled with grief, his composure shredding in the space of a breath.

Icy shock tingled in Helen's hands and feet. That look held all the feeling she had so desperately wanted from him.

He loves me! She drew air into her lungs, all at once feeling unaccountably free.

"I made a terrible error!" she exclaimed. One glance at Waring's haughty displeasure confirmed the statement.

"What are you saying?" the earl asked again.

Without thinking, succumbing to the instincts of her long love for Nicholas, she jumped up from her chair and ran after him. She felt an overwhelming desire to be near him, to feel his breath on her skin. She felt fully alert and alive.

"Nicholas, wait!"

Nicholas stopped, turning, his shoulders stiff. "Helen?" he replied, his expression closing over, growing guarded.

"I have a bargain for you," she said, panting from her haste.

He looked at her sharply, the color draining from his already pale face. His dark eyes seemed huge with apprehension.

"I have grown shy of bargains," he said softly, the low tones of his voice bringing back memories of desire.

Helen touched his arm, once more regretting everything that had happened so far that night. The logic of her heart demanded she take back her dismissal, give him one last chance. The logic of her head could go hang.

At that moment, a tall, lean man, his brown hair streaked with gray, came up to them.

"A thousand pardons for my interruption." He bowed to Helen, then to Nicholas. "I have been called away suddenly and desperately wanted to pass this on to you."

After a long moment, Helen remembered the man was Lord Bedford, though she could not recall where she had met him. He had an anonymous, forgettable quality. She wanted him gone.

He handed Nicholas a note. It looked hastily folded. "It is just my compliments to your mother. How is the countess?"

Nicholas looked unaccountably grim. "Perfectly well, thank you."

"I have not seen her for months and hoped to call on her."

"I'm sure she will be delighted."

"Very well then." He bowed again. "Miss Barrett. My greetings to your brother." He turned to Nicholas. "Good night."

With that, he turned and left. Nicholas looked at the letter in his hand, his expression cautious. Then his gaze loomed over the nearby guests. Helen could not begin to guess what he was looking for.

"Your bargain?" he said after a silence.

Her breath caught in her throat a moment before she spoke. The interruption had scattered her thoughts, making it hard to remember what she had been saying. The force of Nicholas's presence didn't help her concentration, either. "I might have been too severe in my judgment of you."

Helen suddenly realized she saw him clearly now, without the veil of memory or surprise to cloud her vision. Nicholas looked weary, the lines around his aquiline features deeper than she remembered. He looked like a man who had not slept well for some time.

Emotion thickened in her throat. "I need to explain myself. You have been gone so long I thought you could not possibly care for me. I require more"—she cast about, desperate to find exactly the right words—"tangible signs of affection."

His brows drew together, forming a vertical crease. Anger flashed, lightning-quick—a glimpse of his private emotional storm. He glanced down at the necklace still clutched in her hand. "Yes, I see the tangible affection the Earl of Waring presented to you tonight."

Helen felt her cheeks grow hot. Nicholas had seen her with Waring. A sharp stab of guilt and doubt roused

Helen's temper. "How dare you!" she shot back, her voice barely above a whisper.

"I not only dare, I applaud you," he said, growing paler still. "He is most worthy of consideration. He is reputed to be very rich. My fortune is pin money by comparison. He is an earl, whereas I shall not inherit my father's title for many years to come. His lands are vast. He has power and influence. He is a logical choice." Smooth, calm, his words were a model of iron self-control, but the air around him seemed suffused with pain.

Helen looked away, tears filling her eyes. "There is nothing between me and Lord Waring. These sapphires are . . . they are a mistake."

Nicholas gave a small, brief smile, his eyes on the jewels. "Of course."

"Nicholas, I am speaking the truth."

He ran a hand over his thick, black hair. He had cut it shorter with the changing fashion, and she wasn't sure she approved. Glancing at the letter, he put it in his pocket.

"What does my belief matter, now? You have dismissed me. Good-bye, Helen."

As he turned to go, she was filled with a sudden panic. Nicholas was about to walk away. She clutched at his arm. "Listen to me! Nicholas, you are deaf with jealousy."

He stopped, frozen. Helen felt the tension in his muscles. His eyes, the irises so dark they were almost black, searched her face. Nicholas covered her free hand with his own, gentle strength in the gesture. She threaded her fingers through his, pulling his hand close to her side.

His voice was low, meant only for her ears. "I have

always valued your ability to arrive at the meat of the matter."

She laughed. The tears caught in her lashes slipped down her face. "And you always make my blunt manner sound like virtue."

"What do you want me to do, Helen?" Direct, intense, his gaze lingered over every detail of her face. He leaned toward her, closing the space between them.

Her fingers curled tight around his. "Remain with me tonight? Just for this one evening. Stay with me until James returns to take me home." She squeezed his hand again, feeling the warmth of him against her palm. "That is my bargain. All I ask is your company for a few hours. Let me know I truly have your regard, and I will be content to wait for you a while longer. It is not so very much for you to give, and it would go a long way in restoring my faith in our future."

She knew she was begging, but the cost to her pride was slight when so much was at risk. Helen waited a handful of heartbeats, but Nicholas did not reply at once. Instead, his lips pressed tight together, he released his hand from hers and slipped Bedford's letter from his pocket. Unfolding it, he glanced at the words.

What is he doing? Helen wondered, furious at his wandering attention. She could barely stop herself from slapping the note out of his hand.

Nicholas closed his eyes, the dark lashes stark against his pale skin. "No. Not now. Not yet."

She could hear regret in his voice, but still his denial smothered her, a blanketing, crushing weight. Waring was right. He would never stay. Her new hope, scarcely born, withered.

"Then go," she said, drawing back a step. "You will always be saying good-bye, and I cannot bear it any longer. One night is not such a dire test, and yet you cannot even give that much."

Nicholas opened his eyes, his expression bleak. "Love is not a matter of proofs. It cannot be tested like an equation. If you do that, you will only find failures."

Helen bit her lip, tears now flowing freely down her cheeks. "The fact that I am still not your wife is all the mathematics necessary. Put us together and it amounts to nothing!"

Nicholas looked away, the crease between his eyebrows deepening. His fingers crushed the letter still in his hand. "You do not understand."

"Then explain yourself."

Angry, she fastened Waring's necklace around her throat once more. Let Nicholas see he had lost her to another! "Explain why you can find time for everything and everyone but me. It is the least you can do after I groveled before you."

"Not now." Nicholas's voice was flat with anger. "We have a new interruption."

"Your tête-à-tête will be fodder for every breakfast table in London." The Earl of Waring bore down on them, his blue eyes bright with irritation. "What are you thinking of?"

Startled, Helen stepped back. She did not think their conversation had been loud or obvious. Glancing around, she did not see any other guests looking their way. The charge was groundless.

Confused, she turned back to Waring, who was devouring her with his eyes. "Helen, you are distraught," he said.

Waring's look almost frightened her for a moment.

The earl turned to Nicholas. "Have you no shame?"

After a frozen look at Waring, Nicholas gave a slight bow. "If I have distressed you, Miss Barrett, I am deeply sorry."

The words held all the love and sorrow of their long liaison. They almost undid her there and then. How could he rebuff her and then draw her back in almost the same instant? He would drive her mad!

"There is no cause for concern," she said to the earl, voice shaking.

Neither man gave any sign she had spoken. She might as well have been mute. Frustrated, she felt her fatigue and headache seeping back. *Why do I feel so ill?* Was it simply dealing with these two men?

Waring's spine was rigid. "It is time you left," he said to Nicholas.

The latter, by contrast, appeared relaxed to the point of insolence. "Perhaps, but that is not your decision."

Waring stepped closer, his face but inches from Nicholas's. "A gentleman would not need to be told when his welcome had lapsed."

Waring reached for the other man's arm. The latter jerked back, but Waring held on, stepping into the small space between them. The move was aggressive, invasive. Nicholas drew away, but the earl followed with the smooth grace of an athlete.

"I think it would be best if you allowed me to escort you outside," Waring spoke through gritted teeth. "We can conclude our discussion there."

"I have nothing to discuss with you."

Waring tried to move one foot behind Nicholas, an effort to put him off balance. A look of surprise and anger flashed in Nicholas's eyes.

Faster than Helen's eyes could follow, he grabbed the earl's wrist hard enough to make Waring wince. The move forced Waring's hand down and stopped him in his tracks. Bedford's letter fluttered to the floor.

Automatically, Helen bent to pick it up. Without meaning to, she saw there were two lines of writing. This was no letter to the countess.

It read: *Discovered. Beacon Park. One hour.*

Cold shock hit her. Bedford was discovered? By whom? Why, and how did that involve Nicholas? She looked up, mouth open, about to speak, but her eye caught a glint of steel. Nicholas held a knife in his free hand, hidden in the narrow space between his body and the earl's. Words choked in her throat. Where had *that* come from? Despite her growing headache, Helen's vision grew sharp, as if her survival hung on every detail.

Slowly Nicholas raised the point of the knife to the middle button of Waring's waistcoat. "Pray, my lord, take a step back and keep your hands to yourself. I refuse to fight like a schoolboy in a public place. As you pointed out, it breeds unwelcome speculation."

"Gentlemen!" Helen stammered, appalled.

With a filthy look, Waring complied. Nicholas dropped his hand and, with a smooth gesture, made the knife disappear into his sleeve.

"Much better," he said in a perfectly calm tone. "I believe you are holding my correspondence, Miss Barrett."

Overtaken by shock, Helen's hands began to tremble. She folded her arms to hide their shaking. He had asked for the letter, but she was too beside herself to respond.

"Helen?" he asked, a world of concern in the one word.

"What are you involved in?" she said, her voice barely above a whisper. "Do I even know you anymore?"

Turmoil filled his face. Some decision, hard and painful, darkened his eyes. In a swift movement, he cupped her face in his hands and pressed his lips to hers. His breath was hot in her mouth, a heat that reached deep into her. Her own heart seemed to stop, a reeling, unruly yearning taking the strength from her limbs. The brush of her clothes, the weight of the jewels around her throat chafed her flaming skin. Tender but sure, the touch of his fingers on her face was too much, as if he drank her will and she would surely perish the moment he withdrew. Yet this aching was what she craved most, and part of her rejoiced.

It was her reason that went wild with protest. An abyss of public shame threatened. Such a display of affection was scandalous. Nicholas was destroying her reputation. The thought was like a dousing with cold water. Recovering, with both palms on his shoulders, she pushed him away.

"What are you doing?" she snapped, her voice an angry whisper.

Waring started for Nicholas again, but the latter raised one admonishing finger. Waring jerked to a halt, his eyes murderous.

"Patience, Lord Waring," Nicholas said, his voice cold as slate. "One moment more, and I shall trouble you no longer."

Waring snorted, but did not move a muscle.

Nicholas turned to Helen, waiting a long moment before he spoke. She thought she heard the faintest tremor in his words. "Earlier this evening, you ordered me from your life," he said. "Although you later offered me a reprieve, your first assessment was right. My life is not my own. I can't stay with you a single night, much less give you the affection and security you deserve. You are well rid of me."

His face was calm, but his eyes were filled with loss. Still confounded by the knife and the note, Helen was silent.

"As for the kiss, well, even a condemned man has one last opportunity for prayer. Good night, Miss Barrett, Lord Waring." With the barest nod, Nicholas turned and walked away, his tall form relaxed and easy, as if nothing in the world was amiss.

Helen knew better. The kiss still burned on her lips. She thought of the note, and then realized he had taken it from her.

Waring took a deep, angry breath and blew it out. "The insolent dog!" He dusted his sleeve vigorously where Nicholas had touched him.

Deep in thought, Helen barely heard him. *Discovered. Beacon Park. One hour.*

She touched the necklace at her throat, curiously fingering its stones. The sapphires felt far too heavy for their dainty size.

Meaning to say something, she met Waring's eyes, but her thought died before it was fully formed. *How odd.* Waring's gaze seemed to burn hot, the blue like the heart of a flame.

"That man is a villain!" exclaimed Waring. "Do you understand that, Helen?"

The earl's exclamation struck her with the force of an arrow, a shaft tipped with spellcrafted poison. Helen gasped, her will shuddering beneath his stare. Her frantic heart, like a fairy-tale princess, began a gentle slide into a long sleep.

And then Helen was no longer troubled. Over the years she had wondered what business kept Nicholas from her side. She had been a fool not to give the rumors surrounding her fiancé more serious thought. But, where moments ago she had been doubtful, now she was certain.

Nicholas was distant, evasive, and often away on secret business. He kept mysterious meetings. He carried hidden weapons and was quick to use them. The only possible explanation for his behavior was the simplest. The man she had promised to marry, the man for whom she still—regrettably—had feelings, was a criminal. She had made a fortunate escape. Lord Waring was a much better match.

Deep inside, the part of Helen that was still herself knew there were far too many unanswered questions. Alas, that small voice had been choked to silence by the dark magic of the earl's necklace.

Chapter 5

Gripped in the talons of a night that would not end, Redfern walked to Beacon Park. The merciful dark gave him anonymity, allowing his blood to cool.

He had let his emotions rule his head. He had not been prepared for Helen to come after him, to offer him a bargain that proved everything the Master had said to be true: If he could not even stay with Helen for the course of the evening, marrying her would be folly. He had to let her go.

A safer course, Redfern thought, *but not an acceptable one.*

He had made the grand gesture, kissed her, and walked away. It had been the lordly, heroic thing to do.

He ached to turn around and walk right back. Decency alone kept him from storming into her home and claiming her—his bargain with the Master, his family, and the fate of nations be damned. There was no future without Helen.

He had to find a way to have Helen without hurting her. And quickly. Time was against him and Waring was circling like a predator.

Redfern stood on the pathway just inside the border of the park. In the darkness, he could barely make out the footpath that led toward the lake, the pale stripe of gravel like a seam in the lawn. The rain had stopped, the wispy gray clouds torn apart and drifting as if shredded by nervous fingers. Behind him, a carriage rolled by, jingling harness and clopping hoofbeats fading to silence. Nothing was left but the shushing of the wind in the high trees. Uneasy, he started down the path toward the water.

Do I deserve to have Helen? He had been a poor brother to Michael. What sort of husband would he be?

His conversation with the Master had stirred the embers of old guilt. Everything had changed when Michael had killed himself. They had argued just hours before, and Redfern had not been kind. The timing of the suicide haunted him. All Redfern could do was atone by restoring the family fortunes. So, he had offered the Master his freedom.

He walked on. The ornamental lake lay close to the carriage route that looped around the park. Rolling lawns and a miniature pagoda made the spot a favorite with amateur painters and sightseers, and during the day it was teeming with humanity. At night, especially on a rainy night, it was deserted. In the high branches of the oaks, a nightjar shrieked, raising the hairs on Redfern's neck.

The footpath ended where it met the wider road circling the water. Reflections on the lake shivered, tremulous silver beneath the slender moon. Clouds came and went, dimming the light, then sailing away.

Redfern stopped at the water's edge. The long grass at his feet whispered in the breeze, heavy and wet from the recent rain. Beyond his line of sight, there was a plonk and a splash in the water, the whistling beat of wings.

Some unseen creature had caught its meal. Ripples drifted slowly across the water, glistening in the path of the wavering moonlight.

Redfern's senses strained to catch some sign his informant was near. He could barely make out the empty pathways and lawns. All was quiet. There was only the wind, laden with the muddy tang of fresh rain. He was alone. Taking out his watch, he angled the face to catch what moonlight he could. It was getting close to midnight. How long should he stay?

Just as that question formed in his mind, he heard the thunder of an approaching vehicle. A large one, Redfern thought as he listened to the growing rumble. Large and traveling fast. He walked from the shore to the road that ran beside the lake, finding a better vantage point.

The great black coach, heavy and ornate, appeared on the left-hand arc of the carriage path. Four black horses, their mouths flecked with foam, strained to pull the lurching vehicle around the curve of the lake. The conveyance looked old, antique even, the boxy frame long out of fashion. Yet, the monstrosity was gilt and polished, its trim shining in the fugitive light. As it got closer, Redfern saw a crest on the doors. It was a device he had never seen before: the stark, black wings of a moth against gold-painted panels washed gray by the darkness. Black plumes rose from the heads of the horses, nodding and tossing as the beasts galloped straight toward him.

The driver's caped coat blew around him. The man's face was invisible, his hat pulled low. He did not seem to notice Redfern standing on the road.

Redfern stepped back from the road, not trusting the driver to slow or stop before he was crushed to pulp beneath the horses' hooves. As the coach careened by,

Redfern suddenly understood why the thing looked vaguely familiar. It was a funeral coach.

When it was some distance past him, the vehicle slowed, not quite coming to a full stop. One door flung open and something fell out, landing heavily in the grass. Before the door was shut again, the coach was gathering speed. In a matter of seconds, the grim equipage was swallowed by the lakeside shadows, only the rumble of its passage lingering like a phantom.

After waiting a dozen heartbeats, Redfern cautiously approached the spot where the vehicle had paused. The object—and he was sure it was a person—that had been pushed from the coach door lay in the long grass, a shapeless heap. The figure did not move or make a sound. Still, Redfern pulled the knife from his wrist sheath, balancing it lightly in his hand. Even in the dark, he could throw a knife with more accuracy than most could fire a pistol, and a knife had the advantage of silence. He walked slowly forward, working hard to keep his nerves in check.

Redfern knelt beside the heap, feeling the damp of the grass through his breeches. The huddled shape was indeed the form of a man—a tall, lean man of middle years. Bending closer, Redfern listened for the sound of breathing. For a long moment, he waited, hearing nothing but the lonely chirrup of a frog. Grim dread formed like frost in Redfern's veins. He checked at the throat for a pulse and found nothing. The skin was warm, but the man was quite dead. Swallowing hard, Redfern grabbed the body at the hip and shoulder and rolled it faceup.

It was Lord Bedford. Redfern caught his breath in surprise. Dread crept down Redfern's spine, turning his fingers to ice. What had happened?

He positioned Bedford's head so the light caught his

face. His eyes were wide open, shot scarlet, as if he had wept blood. The dilated pupils made him look blind, eerily reflecting the moon. A thin red line, still wet, snaked under his chin. His face was red, his mouth open and slack.

Garroted. A neat job. A professional job.

A faint nausea came over Redfern, a cold, damp revulsion. Why had Bedford's body been thrown here? Who had been driving the funeral coach? He could not resist glancing over his shoulder, searching the shadows for signs of an unseen enemy.

A dozen questions rose up, but he pushed them away. Speculation could wait. Biting his lip, Redfern turned his eyes from the man's face, forcing his attention to other details.

Bedford was dressed as he had last seen him, in formal velvets and laces. The scent of the Assembly rooms—a mix of perfumes and candle wax—still clung to him. The man's clothes were dry, though they were fast soaking up the dampness from the ground where he had landed. On the other hand, Bedford's knees were filthy with mud and grit. It looked as if he had knelt in dirt.

He was struck with a vision of Bedford falling to his knees, begging for his life. Redfern's stomach turned sour.

Bedford's pockets were turned out, but his gold watch was undisturbed. The murderer was also a robber, but he took something specific. In all probability, it was whatever information Bedford was going to turn over that night.

The man's breeches were half-undone, the buttons gaping. Perhaps he had been caught relieving himself in the relative quiet of an alley. Or, could a woman have been involved? He said he had been called away. For what reason?

In any case, it was likely the murderer had lain in wait. Silently Redfern shook his head as he lifted Bedford's hands in his own, searching them for wounds. Darkness made it difficult to see, but he could tell the skin was scraped, the nails broken. Bedford had fought, but not hard enough. Then again, if he were being strangled, he most likely lost consciousness before he could struggle free from his attacker.

Again, Redfern's mind painted the scene in unwelcome detail. It was easy. He had seen death too often and in too many variations. It was one of the chief hazards of working for the Master, and it was hard on the soul.

A smear ran along the forearm of Bedford's jacket. It was too dark to see clearly, but it matted the velvet in a greasy mass. Redfern took out his pocket handkerchief, wiped at the smear to pick up a bit of the substance, and folded it inside the square of silk.

He scanned Bedford's form one last time, running his hands along the edge of the body. He felt a small piece of heavy paper, perhaps a calling card, underneath Bedford's hip where it had fallen from his clothes. It was too dark to read the print, so Redfern put it in his pocket.

He knelt for a moment more and then closed the dead man's eyes. There was no dignity in this kind of death. Heart heavy, Redfern rose, backing away until he reached the carriage road.

The park was still completely empty. Nevertheless, he walked quickly, his head down, his hands in his coat pockets. The vision of the dead man sprawled on the wet ground spread like a film over his thoughts, blotting out everything else. He wanted to put distance between him-

self and that horrific sight. He would send word to the
Master to have Bedford's remains collected and given the
respect he deserved.

Redfern left the park, walking into the streets beyond.
It was a good neighborhood, its well-tended, orderly
houses a balm for the chaos of his thoughts. He stopped
at the corner. The scene was gray on black, the ornate lattice of the wrought-iron fences stark against a moody sky.
He could hear a horse and carriage roll past, a door open
and shut, but all else was silent. The quiet held him, kept
his nerves from crumbling completely.

Instead of meeting his informant, Redfern had just discovered his murder. Someone had known where Bedford
was going. That someone had killed him—not by magic,
but by brutal human force.

Redfern took some satisfaction in the last point. He
could not quite follow the Master's fascination with the
Hellfire League, but murderers he understood. Murderers
he could—and would—catch.

It took half an hour to find his way home. The house
he had rented was one of the dozen new homes built on
Sparrow Street, on the edge of the fashionable St. James
area. The facades were elegant, with all the columns and
pediments demanded by the current Greco-mania.

Expecting he would be late, Redfern had told the servants not to wait up. Locking the front door behind him,
he started up the stairs, steps muffled by a thick, red-
patterned carpet. Even though the fires had burned low,
the air felt hot and stuffy after the cool night. Below, he
could hear the low-voiced tick of the clock in the drawing room, the romping of the housekeeper's mouser as it
chased something down the hall.

He reached the top of the stairs and stopped before a

lunette table that stood opposite the landing. He could see just well enough in the dark to find the candle there and light it. The glow bloomed over the mahogany table, spilling over a jardinière of flowers and the fine lace at Redfern's cuffs. He picked up the candle, shielding the flame with his hand, and walked into his dressing room. It was dim, the uncertain light revealing a round table and the foot of a chaise longue to his right.

He set the candle down and went to build up the fire. His room, for some reason, always felt cold. The ritual of reviving the embers soothed him. When he stood, rattling the grate into place, new warmth caressed his legs like a cat. He remained there, warming his hands, for a few minutes. Gradually, the events of the evening flowed through his thoughts, from Sir Alaric to the murder and finally to Helen. The sight of her, face frozen with dismay at the sight of his knife, played across his inner vision. Deep helplessness dragged at his heart. He wanted to reach into that moment, catch her shoulder, and make her listen to his story. Anger played in his gut, at the back of his throat, like something volcanic.

He was not a ruffian. Nevertheless, Redfern's instincts had been trained to the point where another man making a threatening move would cause him to reach for a weapon. His life had depended on that reflex more than once.

Years of living in danger had put a gulf between him and the rest of London society. By the look on Helen's face, he was no longer fit for polite company.

Warmed now by temper, Redfern pulled off his coat, throwing it over the back of a chair. The card he had taken from beneath Bedford's body fluttered to the floor, a white exclamation on the carpet. He scooped it up and then fished in his pocket for his handkerchief.

He sat down, pulling the candle close. Starting with the handkerchief, he opened it carefully. The substance on Bedford's sleeve was a grayish white, soft and greasy but thick enough to be opaque. The smell was very faint because there was not much more than a smudge of the oily matter, but it reminded him a bit of linseed oil. Could it be an artist's paint?

There was a fleck in the paint. Redfern ran his fingernail under the handkerchief, making the fleck stand out from the grease. It was a copper-colored bristle. Perhaps the hair from a paintbrush? It looked too short, but then a bristle might break.

Setting the handkerchief aside, Redfern picked up the card from where it lay, facedown, in the puddle of candlelight. He turned the card over, and grunted his surprise. A long moment passed before he lowered the card, mind racing.

The inscription read: JAMES BARRETT.

What had Helen's brother to do with a spy like Bedford? And where had Barrett been all evening?

Redfern nearly started from his chair as a thought struck him. He knew James Barrett's history. After all, they had been friends together at school. After Oxford, Barrett had bought a commission in the infantry. He had taken a ball to the shoulder and sold out a mere two years later, but his brief military career had opened certain doors once he had won a seat in the Commons. Barrett's past connections took him frequently to the army headquarters in Whitehall.

Whitehall was where military secrets of interest to the French were to be found. This was a much more likely source of treachery than a sorcerer's club. If Bedford had Barrett's card, could that possibly mean he suspected Barrett of some connection to this French/Irish plot?

Redfern put his face in his hands, grinding his palms against his tired eyes. As much as the circumstances fit neatly together, could James Barrett be a traitor? A killer? It didn't seem possible. James was ambitious, even power-hungry, but not ruthless.

Nothing was ever simple.

So much, Redfern thought ruefully, for mending his relationship with Helen. Tomorrow would find him on her doorstep, questioning her brother for Lord Bedford's murder.

Chapter 6

The next afternoon, Redfern set out for the Barretts' house on Rithet Lane. The large, Palladian-style home had a high brick wall on either side that sheltered the private gardens beyond. The house dated from the time of King Charles II, but Helen's father had bought it for James Barrett only a dozen years before. Their father, a wealthy banker, also had a country house south of London. A low, wrought-iron fence ran along the front of the property, a rose-covered archway framing the entrance. The greenery was pretty, softening the rigid regularity of the architecture.

Redfern left his carriage and driver in the street and walked through the open gate. He walked up the white, scrubbed steps and rapped with the heavy brass knocker. A bee rumbled in the hollyhocks as he waited, the air smelling of sun-warmed earth.

The door opened and the Barretts' young footman looked out. "Lord Redfern," he said as he bowed. "Good afternoon."

"I have come to see Mr. Barrett." He handed the footman

his card. "If the garden is unoccupied, I will wait for him there. I do not wish to disturb Miss Barrett."

"The family is all in the house," the servant replied. "You will have the garden completely to yourself."

Relieved, Redfern went down the steps and around the house, taking his time. There was much to admire in the spacious grounds. He had known James Barrett since Eton, and had always been astonished by his family's knack for accumulating wealth.

The beds close to the back of the house were filled with herbs and greens, plants useful to the cook. From there, a short flight of steps led down to a lawn surrounded by pear trees and graced with a summerhouse. The small building held a table and chairs, and Redfern sat down to wait in the shade.

The merciless sun was directly overhead. Bleached by the bright light, the flowers in the border beds looked pale and fragile as the light breeze rippled through them. The garden had a midday quiet, as if even the birds were napping in the heat. Only the rustle of the dry breeze broke the silence.

Redfern had nearly begun to doze when a maid brought refreshments, putting the tray on the small, round table at the center of the summerhouse. At the sight of the glasses, Redfern realized he was thirsty. As the young girl turned to go, he saw James Barrett, the Honorable Member from Widgley-on-Thornton, emerge from the back of the house and cross the lawn toward him. Without a topcoat, vest unbuttoned, Barrett looked relaxed. In contrast, tension wormed through Redfern's gut, making him realize how little he wanted to question Helen's brother. He was, after all, the closest thing he had to an old friend.

"Redfern," Barrett said by way of greeting. He sank

onto a chair and loosened his cravat, puffing out flushed cheeks. Prosperity had thickened his already stocky body. Sweat was glistening along his temples where the fair hair was thinning. "Demme, it's hot. Too early and too hot to go about paying social calls. Still, it's a rare pleasure to see you. It's been a long time. Have you come about Helen?"

It was a natural question, but it still irritated Redfern. What had passed between him and Helen was too raw for discussion.

"No, not that," he replied, and watched Barrett's surprise with satisfaction.

"About your appalling and public attack on Lord Waring, then?" Barrett leaned forward. "He told me all about how you pulled some bloody great knife out in front of half of London."

"An interesting topic but, no, I came to ask you about this." He placed the card he had taken from Bedford's body on the table between them.

Barrett looked blank. "What about it?"

Redfern let some of his anger leak into his voice. "Lord Bedford was murdered last night, garroted with a wire. I found your card on his body."

"My God, what happened?"

Redfern narrowed his eyes, gauging the man's reaction. Barrett was turning pale, something not easy to do on command. "I'm wondering what your connection was to the man," said Redfern.

Barrett took in a long, steadying breath. His eyes, gray like Helen's, took on a flinty look. "I'm not sure what right you have to ask."

"Bedford was my friend," Redfern lied, taking the decanter from the tray the maid had left. The gesture was

deliberate; he wanted control of the moment, so he took
the initiative from his host. After pouring wine into two
glasses, he pushed one toward Barrett. "I need to know
why he died."

"Your questions are unofficial?" Barrett replied, wrinkling his brow. He looked at the glass as if it might leap
up and bite him.

"Purely." That was nearly true.

"You can understand, as a member of the Commons, I
need to be cautious." Barrett smiled his apology, but it
was insincere. "Bedford's death is a sensitive matter. He
was, after all, a peer. I could not answer in any official ca-
pacity without being properly briefed."

Redfern sat back, feeling slightly sick. This was unlike
his friend, who had always had a decent, open character.
Did it matter to Barrett that a man was dead? Apparently
not, or at least not as much as his career.

Barrett sighed. "Why are you always involved whenever there is trouble? It's been that way since we were
boys. It's been worse since your brother died."

Redfern flinched, but took care that it did not show on
his face. The Barretts, like everyone else, assumed
Michael's death had been an accident. The risk of scandal had been too great to tell even his best friends. "I am
just a bird of ill omen."

Barrett's expression soured. "So it seems."

Redfern took a sip of the wine. It was cool and
delicious.

Barrett shrugged, a touch surly. "I barely knew Bedford. I had been introduced to him three or four nights
ago at a private club."

"The Hellfire League?" Redfern asked casually. Mentioning the League was worth a try, just to see Barrett's reaction.

"No." The man's brow furrowed in confusion. "I don't know that one. At the Hollingshead Club."

Redfern had never been in the Hollingshead, but he knew it as a gentlemen's club devoted to serious political talk. As there was no gambling, drinking, or sports on offer, he had seen no reason to set foot inside.

"What was the meeting about?" Redfern asked.

Barrett looked around, as if expecting eavesdroppers to be hiding in the forget-me-nots. He looked so unhappy, for a moment Redfern pitied him.

"Ireland," said Barrett.

Redfern raised an eyebrow. "Who else was there?"

"Bridewell. Collingsworth. Waring. Fairmeadow wandered through—I have no idea what he was doing there; the fellow has duck fluff for brains."

Redfern's ears perked at the mention of the Earl of Waring. It would be delightful to catch him in a hanging offense. "Was the discussion heated?"

Barrett finally picked up his glass. "Not really." He drained half the wine in one swallow. His movements were growing jerky, disconnected; his mind was trying to be someplace else and had left his body behind to fend for itself.

What's wrong? Redfern wondered, and then tried again. "Was there no debate?"

"There was no debate, just the usual observations born of hindsight."

"Such as?"

"Mostly speculation as to whether we were too hard on the Irish. Alternately, whether we should have built more garrisons there."

Barrett paused for a long moment, running his hand through his fair hair. The skin around his eyes looked pinched, as if he suffered a bad headache. In fact, thought Redfern, he looked ill.

"The troublemakers are just starving tenant farmers, most of them," said Barrett. "It was not a pleasant discussion. A lot of the talk was cruel."

For an instant, Barrett seemed like the fair-minded boy Redfern had known. Then that boy was gone.

Shaking his head in disgust, Barrett drained the rest of his wine and refilled his glass. "I went to listen. Some of the more important men in the party were there, and I wanted to know their opinions. Comes in useful when one has to say the right thing." He smiled ruefully, but the amusement didn't reach his vacant eyes.

Redfern mulled over his friend's words. Both in looks and manner, Barrett did not seem himself. Decidedly, their meeting was burdened by the events of the previous night. Or, it might mean he was hiding something. "And Bedford?"

"We sat at the same table. Like me, he said little, but was most interested in the opinions of others. He was an agreeable man."

Redfern leaned back in his chair. "Did you talk about anything else?"

"My work."

"At Horse Guards?" Redfern asked, using the popular name for the army headquarters.

"And other things." Barrett looked perplexed, but the expression was a mere shadow, there and gone. "How is that relevant?"

Redfern chose to retreat. He could go no farther without directly accusing Barrett, and so far the man had revealed nothing that implicated him. "I'm not sure. Was that evening at the Club the last time you saw him?"

"I saw Bedford last night. He asked to call on me, so I gave him my card as my address is on it. We did not speak at length, though."

"What time did you see him?"

"I'm not sure about the first time we spoke, but I was standing outside the Apollonian Rooms with some friends when I saw him leave at about eleven o'clock."

His curiosity piqued, Redfern sat up. "Did he leave alone?"

Barrett's expression was satisfied, as if he realized he had shifted Redfern's scrutiny onto another. "He met that red-haired actor, Thomas Hanson. I saw them speaking."

"Did they leave together?"

Barrett shook his head. "To be honest, I didn't notice. I returned inside shortly after that and took Helen home."

Redfern slumped back. Tapping his teeth with his thumbnail, he digested this new scrap of information. "When I examined the body, Bedford had paint—the type of face paint actors use—on his jacket."

Again, he watched for Barrett's reaction, but there was none. His expression was blank.

"You think Hanson is guilty?" Barrett asked.

"I don't know. I have too little information to form an opinion." He had never heard Hanson's name before this.

After a long pause, Barrett shifted on his chair. "Redfern, you know I am your friend. I don't mind telling you what I can, if for no other reason than the pleasure of talking to you. But, given your breach with Helen, you should not have come to our house. I would have been happy to meet you somewhere else."

Redfern did not reply, but felt his expression go hard

with resentment. Despite their supposed friendship, Barrett seemed to show little concern that he had lost his old friend as a potential brother-in-law. There was even less consciousness that he was banning a boyhood friend from his home.

"Helen is not prepared to receive you right now," Barrett said, his tone gentle but firm. "She would not say much about it, but it sounds like your parting did not go easily."

Redfern clenched his teeth, but forced himself to swallow his temper. "Not really."

Barrett's mouth twitched. From his expression, Redfern guessed the blunt reply was not what Barrett had anticipated.

"I am disappointed by your sister's decision," Redfern continued. He could not say Helen's name. It was a struggle to keep the regret from his voice. "However, I will respect her wishes. I will not come here again."

"I am grateful," Barrett replied, the pinched look around his eyes growing more pronounced. His words sounded rehearsed. "What I mean is—for her sake, I'm glad. If you are not going to stay in England long enough to marry, it is best to let her go. She has had other offers and it's time she became mistress of her own house."

What other offers? Redfern wondered with some heat. He cleared his throat. "As I said, I will respect her feelings."

The man's face resumed his curiously blank expression. "Forgive the observation, but that is overdue."

Bridling, Redfern drew himself up, but Barrett placed a placating hand on his arm, nodding toward the house.

Biting back his words, Redfern turned. Helen was walking across the lawn, her white muslin dress rippling with the motion of her strides. Redfern swallowed hard, feeling suddenly adrift. Unconscious grace was one of her great charms, and he was far from immune.

Barrett made a small motion, and Redfern was reminded of the man's presence. His temper prickled. "Despite your reluctance to allow me to breathe the same air as your sister, I trust you will agree it is too late for me to climb over the back fence."

Barrett gave him an expressionless stare. Redfern turned away, his eyes only for Helen.

Chapter 7

Helen wore no hat or gloves, but walked with her face tilted up to the sun, her fair skin looking almost pure white in the bright light. Usually, her stride reminded Redfern of a child, exuberant and unbound. Today, though, she walked as one burdened with fatigue.

In the next breath, he remembered it had been her birthday that week. He gave an inward groan. Forgetting the event was a small sin compared to his others, but it was further proof of how his private life was unraveling. Before this, he had never forgotten anything concerning Helen, no matter where in the world he had been.

He should not have kissed her last night. Like a drug, a taste only made him want her more, and his desire increased in proportion to the impossibility of having her. He felt his heart pound, laboring against the heat of the summer air and the heat of his yearning. The moment felt thick and heavy, like a yoke settling on his shoulders.

As Helen approached, both men stood and stepped out of the summerhouse. Redfern schooled his face, hiding his discomfort.

He bowed. "Miss Barrett, how pleasant to see you."

The statement sounded hollow. They had been through so much, yet that simple sentence was all politeness would allow.

"Lord Redfern, this is unexpected," she said, her tone tight with disapproval. She shaded her eyes against the sun. Stray tendrils of her hair blew in the breeze, the light silvering the fair strands.

Redfern licked his lips, more unbalanced than he had expected by her coldness. "I asked Barrett to meet me in the garden in hopes that I might leave you undisturbed. Nevertheless, since you have found us, let me apologize for last night. I am afraid I abandoned common sense altogether."

Helen looked away, her face turned in profile against a backdrop of blue delphiniums. "Yes, I believe you did. Do you really regret it? And, if so, what portion of your madness do you regret? You're being vague, Nicholas. You had a busy night."

A long silence followed. Barrett shifted impatiently, but Redfern stood still, frozen by her words. He had fought with Waring, kissed Helen, let her slip from his life for her own good. As she said, the night had been eventful, and that was only the part she knew about.

"I regret causing you distress," he said at last. His stomach twisted when he saw she was wearing Waring's damned necklace.

"Still vague, but if it will help you sleep peacefully, I accept your contrition." The words were cool despite a lightening in her voice.

She seemed so weary, he thought, gnawed by guilt. Some of it, at least, was his fault. Barrett was right; he should not be there.

"Thank you," Redfern replied. "It is more than I deserve."

"I will give nothing more than that." Helen lifted her head a little, a small, defiant gesture. "Understand that nothing else changes from where we left it last night."

Redfern blinked slowly, not letting an unexpected wrench of disappointment show on his face. "Of course not."

"Then sit down, Redfern," said Barrett in a heavy voice, returning to his chair in the shade. "Behave like a decent fellow, set aside your gloomy news, and have a drink with me."

"With pleasure," Redfern said, feeling none.

"Helen?" Barrett raised a wineglass toward his sister. "Sit down or go back inside, but please stop hovering. There's no call to stand there like a reproachful ghost out of a bad play."

Redfern had heard brother and sister bicker many times—during his school years, he had been almost a member of the family. Still, Barrett's tone annoyed him. Redfern held a chair for Helen, but she shook her head.

"I will return to the house," she said. "I came out merely to satisfy my curiosity. What brings you here, Nicholas?"

Barrett exchanged glances with Redfern, who shrugged. "I came to tell your brother Lord Bedford died last night."

"Lord Bedford?" Helen exclaimed, suddenly alert. "Did we not see him ourselves? He hurried off. He said he was called away."

"I would not discuss that meeting outside the three of us," said Barrett. "It may save answering inconvenient questions later."

"What do you mean?" she asked.

Barrett grimaced. "He did not die naturally."

"That is horrible!" Helen started back, looking from one man to the other. "What in Heaven's name happened?"

Turning pale, she finally took the chair Redfern offered. Once she had seated herself, he sat as well.

"As yet, that is unknown." He thought about Barrett's card, but decided against mentioning it. Until he knew something certain about Barrett's possible involvement, there was no point in putting unwelcome thoughts in Helen's mind. "Did you know Lord Bedford?"

She shook her head, looking down at her hands in her lap. "I knew him by sight. That is all." She looked up; her gray eyes narrowed. "How well did you know him?"

Her look was filled with meaning, and Redfern remembered she had read Bedford's note.

"He was a friend."

"It is not proper for a gentleman's friends to die by violent means. The rest of his acquaintance is sure to grow uneasy."

Redfern's chin jerked up as if she had struck him.

Barrett sat forward. "Helen, at times your frankness is a liability."

She pressed her lips together in a sullen gesture. "Forgive me, but I find if I am outrageous, then occasionally someone listens to what I have to say. It is difficult, between prime ministers and mysterious appointments abroad, for my voice not to fade away in the clamor of other concerns."

"That is uncalled for," snapped Barrett. "You're being deliberately extreme."

Helen rose, her cheeks flushed. "Excuse me, gentlemen. I shall be in the music room."

Redfern stood. "If you feel your interests are treated lightly, the fault is on our side, not yours."

Barrett sat back, the movement jerky with pique. "Don't encourage her. She just aims to draw attention to herself by being shocking. She has been insufferable all morning."

Redfern studied her, looking for some sign of softness in her guarded expression. He could tell the news of Bedford had shaken her, but she seemed more worn out than anything. If only he could take her in his arms and comfort her!

"I have always valued a forthright nature," he said. "In an age of politics and social consideration, honesty is rare."

"A curious concern for a man of so many secrets," Helen returned. Her eyes yielded nothing. "If you value a forthright nature so highly, could you not aspire to possess such qualities yourself?"

Redfern frowned and hesitated too long. She turned to go, the sun making a halo on her sleek, pale hair. His chest ached with the words he wanted to say, but dared not. Any explanations would be fraught with secrets he dared not tell.

Helen looked back over her shoulder, shading her eyes against the sun. "Good-bye, Nicholas." The words were chill. "I do not expect to meet you here again."

She walked away, her long strides swishing in the grass.

"Damnation," he replied, more under his breath than aloud.

The music room, overlooking the garden, was at the back of the house. By the time Helen reached it and looked out of the window, both Nicholas and her brother had left the summerhouse. They must not have stayed for that last drink of wine. Relieved that Nicholas was gone, she sat down on a lyre-backed chair. This room was her favorite place, a haven of soothing solitude.

Weary, she tilted her head back. The headache that had begun the night before had not abated, and the silence was a relief. The room was cool, high-ceilinged and spacious, decorated with a gold-patterned carpet and two large, landscape paintings her father had brought back from France before the war. There were a fortepiano, a harpsichord, and her harp, as well as enough music stands and chairs for visiting musicians. A glass-fronted cabinet filled with sheet music stood under the window. Whether she was the mistress of the salon or one of the amateur performers, Helen loved nothing better than an evening of song. As she sat, silent and still, the room seemed to whisper the last fading echo of all the notes sounded within its walls.

Nicholas played the harpsichord with taste. Most gentlemen had some musical training, but he had real ability. When they performed together, their parts always neatly intermeshed. There had never been the awkward jostling and false cues one encountered with a new partner. Their ability to anticipate each other had been flawless from the start, their sympathies perfectly aligned. The reserved young Nicholas had said little at first, but nonetheless made himself completely understood. It was not that he was shy, but rather that he disliked meaningless chatter. Instead of compliments or candy, he courted her with subtle music. For months, they had met every Tuesday afternoon to read through a new piece he had found, sometimes with friends, sometimes just the two of them alone. By the time they moved from notes to words and finally to kisses, the job of wooing her was all but done. He had read her like the score, knowing just when to increase the tempo, when to slow and lighten his touch.

All that was over now. Whoever he had been, he was that young man no more. Something went wrong when his brother died. For whatever reason, that loss had wounded him in ways she never understood.

Helen sat, studying the pattern on the carpet. More than anything, she felt numb with grief. Nicholas had apologized for last night and, no doubt, he was truly sorry. Still, he had threatened the earl with a knife. He had compromised her in the middle of a soiree at the Apollonian Rooms with half of the *ton* looking on. His friend had fled the party, only to be murdered within hours. Neither Nicholas's actions nor his acquaintances were those of an honest man.

Sorrow, a slow starburst of pain, seeped into her breast. How could she do anything other than send him away? She bit her lip. In the end, it was Nicholas who had left the room. He had kissed her, and he had left. He always left.

It was for the best, and she was well rid of him. Restless, she stood and walked to the window, looking out at the garden. A butterfly, colorful wings flashing as it passed from shade to sun, was making its giddy way through the flower bed.

She lowered her eyes, wondering how such a fine man could go so far astray. It was a sad, sad waste.

"Helen."

She turned. Barrett was in the doorway. "Yes, James?"

He sat in the chair by the harpsichord, running one finger over the mother-of-pearl inlay on the case. "Helen," he repeated.

She folded her arms. "Yes?"

He shifted uneasily. "Please do not take this amiss, but I cannot say that I am distressed that your betrothal to Redfern is over. He seems always to be in the midst of trouble. Despite his title and connections, I cannot help but feel you can aim higher for a husband."

She blinked. James had been so odd lately, turning on friends, conducting his business with no mercy for old alliances. Had ambition become a disease with him? "I am surprised you are so cold. I thought he was your friend."

"I like him but I don't want him as a family member. There are others who could grace our table with less drama and more advantage."

"You refer to the Earl of Waring?"

Barrett looked abashed, but only for a moment. "Yes."

"And what, besides fortune and power, would recommend him to me? Does he paint well, or play the violoncello?"

Her voice held the slightest edge of sarcasm because she did not like to be pushed. On the whole, she agreed with her brother's preferences. The earl was a good match. Last night, as she waited with him for James to return and take her home, she had seen Waring in a new light. Suddenly, as if by magic, she realized that he was a man of excellent sense.

"Surely you have thought what such a match would do for our family."

"I have." She had lain awake the whole night thinking of it. No wonder she was tired.

"In four generations the Barretts would have risen from blacksmith to banker to countess."

"And what makes you think an earl would want to marry a Barrett?"

He smiled, the picture of satisfaction. "You are beautiful and our father is staggeringly rich."

The persistent ache in her temples made her feel contrary. She wanted to lie down. Perhaps she had caught a chill. "Is it so very important that I marry an earl?"

Barrett blinked in surprise. "We worked hard to raise this family up. You are quite prepared to enjoy the fine dresses, the beautiful house, the music lessons our labors have made possible. You think you may take all this, but owe us nothing?"

"Do you believe that if I am made to feel guilty enough, I will throw myself at whomever you decree?"

Barrett slammed the flat of his hand on the harpsichord, setting the strings humming. "Is Lord Waring that dreadful?"

"No, of course not." Helen gulped in pain at the loud noise. Confusion suddenly swamped her. It seemed the more she argued, the worse she felt. It was less effort to be quiet and agreeable.

She fingered her necklace, the stones hot from her skin. It rubbed unpleasantly against her neck. She wished she could take it off, but for some reason she always forgot. It seemed the necklace wanted to stay right where it was, wound around her throat.

Barrett's eyes were hard. "The earl has been a godsend to me. Think of how much more he could do as my brother-in-law. We would be relations, Helen. Can you not do this much for us? That is the woman's role in furthering the family. Look how hard Constance works for my interests. Why can't you do the same?"

"Constance is your wife, and your life and hers are bound together. By marrying you, she accepted her role in your career."

Perhaps Constance should woo the earl, quipped a small, dry voice in the back of Helen's mind, but the dissenting thought crumbled almost at once.

"By the by," she said, "are you going to go see Constance now that her time is near?"

"Of course." With a sulky air, he traced a crack in the harpsichord lid with his fingernail.

This was a sore point with Helen. He had left his wife and son at their country house. Constance was too close to bearing their second child to be seen in public. She was sickly, but still he stayed away, too careful of his position to spend time anywhere but at the side of his mentor.

Barrett looked up. "Why are you arguing with such vehemence? I thought you liked Waring."

"I do," Helen temporized. "I just want you to spare a thought for my feelings, James. My engagement to Nicholas ended last night, and you are already hounding me to wed another."

Barrett's gray eyes were hard. "An election will come, Helen. I will need Waring's help to keep my seat. I do not have forever for you to mourn that man."

Helen laughed, raising her arms and dropping them in a gesture of surrender. Her brother had changed so much of late, grown so callous. "Well, that is honest, at least. Do you know the election date? Exactly how much time do I have?"

Barrett bit his lip, looking at the floor. "Any woman should be grateful for the earl's attentions."

"I am, but even with so fine a man, a little time is essential for affection to grow, and I believe love is required for any degree of marital happiness."

Her brother furrowed his brow. "I cannot think of one instance where that rule would begin to apply. The world is a concrete place, Helen. I beg of you, be wise. A woman has to get what she can for the sake of her future children. Think about the fact that Waring's sons—your sons—will have the world at their feet."

The conversational leap from courtship to marriage to sons made Helen dizzy. "And motherhood is to comprise the sum and total of my happiness?"

Barrett looked away impatiently. "Things can be arranged to your liking. Waring can do as he pleases." He paused. "Or, as his wife pleases, depending on how persuasive—or clever—she might be."

"There's a rule of thumb," Helen said bitterly. "Make sure you're smarter than your husband so you can rule him."

"It might not work in the earl's case," Barrett said with an apologetic shrug. "But he is a reasonable man."

As long as one agrees with him. At that thought, Helen felt another wave of nausea. She literally didn't have the stomach to continue the argument. "I am sure you are correct. Excuse me, I feel ill and must lie down."

She walked to the door. "A word of advice, brother. I respect your abilities as a politician. I honor the brave service you rendered England as a soldier." She put one hand on her hip, her face flushed with irritation. "Don't ever dream of setting up shop as a matchmaker."

Barrett laughed, uneasy but doing his best to seem amused. "Why not?"

"You know nothing of the hearts of women."

"Nonsense!"

"You'd be over your head standing in a puddle."

"You just want a husband whose world revolves around you," he said derisively.

Helen studied her brother and sighed. "Poor Constance. You're not the man she married, you know."

Barrett stared at the pattern in the carpet and wondered what on earth his sister meant. Then he stood. It didn't matter what Helen wanted. Or his wife. There was an election to worry about, and the earl expected Barrett to hold on to his seat. The earl needed Barrett's vote in the Commons.

He would do whatever the earl required. That was the only thing that mattered.

Chapter 8

Redfern's carriage pulled up in front of the Ash Lane Theater, but he was not able to open his door. A gig was trying to back away to make room for an elegant closed carriage, and another vehicle with a matched pair of grays refused to yield enough to let the gig through. The side of the carriage was too close for Redfern to get out without scraping paint. Everything was a tangle of wheels and hooves, and some time passed before Redfern could alight. Such early evening traffic snarls were usual, but the chaos put him in a foul mood.

There was little wonder the street was bursting with activity. The Ash Lane was one of the newer venues, joining Drury Lane and Covent Garden as one of London's patent theaters. It was fast gaining an audience; the company of actors was first-rate and the clean, new boxes were lushly appointed and comfortable. In a better neighborhood than its competition, the theater had fewer whores and footpads lingering outside. The owner, Mr. Summerville Vine, had set about to attract an exclusive audience, and the *ton* had responded to his overtures. At least, Redfern speculated, until the next novelty came along.

He gave the crowd on the street a cursory glance. A girl was selling violet nosegays from a wicker basket; hired sedan chairs were putting down their passengers. Most of the well-dressed theater patrons he recognized from drawing rooms and gentlemen's clubs. Though busy, not much of note was happening on the street. Only a few young men waited outside, smoking and telling jokes until it was time for the curtain to rise. Losing interest in the scene, Redfern joined the stream of patrons going through the Ash Lane's double doors.

Like all theaters, the seating was divided into distinct areas. The least expensive seats were on the main floor, or pit. Above these, three white-and-gold balconies soared, arcs of ornate plasterwork and richly carved balustrades. These were the galleries. The first and most sought-after level was the haunt of prosperous shopkeepers and minor officials. Each level above that was less costly and less comfortable as one rose to the ceiling. Around the sides of the theater were tiers of boxes, the small, private rooms where wealthy patrons could sit protected from the common rabble. Redfern's was located on the left side, one tier up and close to the stage. Smaller than most, it contained only four velvet-covered chairs, but he had a clear view of the stage and audience.

As he sat, he adjusted the gold-fringed curtain of the box so that he could watch the other patrons unobserved. *Like a hunter behind a blind,* Redfern thought with a wry grimace.

One thing he had learned early on: The spying game was not particularly dignified. It required a great deal of skulking, and much of it made one feel foolish. Mind you, it had its bonuses. Sir Alaric had granted him use of the box for the evening—the Master had spies, and hence seats, in all the theaters. Public entertainments, where folk of all social classes and occupations could mix together without comment, were notorious meeting places for thieves and traitors. In the colorful confusion of a public crowd, it was easy to pass information in what looked like a chance encounter. Hence, the Master had every performance, and its audience, watched.

Wonderful work if one adores modern plays, Redfern mused. *Which I don't.* There were too many vapid comedies for his taste.

He looked around, watching the patrons as they took their seats. A din of conversation and shuffling feet made a steady roar as the audience settled. Colorful paper packages of candy appeared, the ritual passing of treats between friends. Redfern recognized the bright red wrapping from his favorite confectioner and had a sudden, nostalgic flash from boyhood. He remembered fighting with his brother over the last of the sweets. The thought of Michael dimmed his mood.

One of the theater hands was making his way around the small apron of the stage, lighting the wicks of the footlights. Above, the enormous chandeliers were already lit, still swaying slightly from being hoisted to the ceiling. It was early yet, and the uppermost gallery and the pit were still half-empty. Later, once the shops and factories let out their workers around eight o'clock, more of the cheap seats would fill up with patrons coming to see the second half of the evening's entertainment for half price. At that point, the livelier musical entertainments would begin.

Something caught Redfern's eye, and he looked up

sharply. Across the stage and a little to the right, James Barrett entered one of the larger boxes. A moment later, the Earl of Waring ushered in Helen. Narrowing his eyes, Redfern inched a little farther into the shadow of the curtain.

And so my quarry enters. He folded his arms. *I might as well get into the spirit of melodrama—like Hamlet's play within a play, the audience is the real scene of action. Like the poor old Dane, I'm moping about looking for proof of murder.*

Since meeting with Barrett in the garden of the Rithet Lane house three frustrating days earlier, Redfern had kept the man in his sights. Although the calling card barely qualified as a link between Barrett and Lord Bedford, he could not shake the feeling Helen's brother was somehow—even unwittingly—connected to Bedford's death. The Horse Guards connection was too much of a coincidence to ignore, and he had caught no word, not even a sulphurous whiff, of the Hellfire League. Barrett was still his best lead.

Sheltering himself behind the curtain, he lifted his spyglass, a tiny version of the telescoping, brass field glasses military officers used. The box across the way sprang into view as Redfern focused, the circle of his vision playing over Barrett's round visage before centering on Helen.

Swathed in pale green silk, Helen sat between the two men. Her tall, slender form was still, her posture subdued and painfully correct, elbows tucked against her sides. Only the winking of her jewels betrayed movement, the slow rise and fall of her breath.

She is not happy, Redfern thought, lowering the glass.

The Helen he knew loved the theater and would be laughing and chattering, pointing out new faces and

fashions. He looked from Helen to the men beside her,
wondering what was wrong with them. Did they not see
the change in her? He looked at the earl and raised his
glass once more, focusing in on the trio. Waring was
laughing, talking to Barrett over Helen's head.

Swine.

There were so many reasons to despise the earl it was
hard to know where to begin, and he was finding more all
the time. Waring was a political climber, buying and selling favors the way others traded horseflesh. No wonder
he got along with Helen's career-minded brother. They
were the same breed of grasping devils.

Redfern had soon found that following Barrett meant
following Waring. The two were almost constantly in
each other's company, the earl more often at Barrett's
house than his own. One rarely went out without the
other. Whatever Helen's brother was involved with, so
was Waring, and that meant conspiracy.

And Helen is in the middle, he thought, *caught between her ambitious brother and that smooth-tongued
opportunist.*

If catching the Master's traitor meant freeing Helen
from their influence, so much the better. It gratified him
to fix the earl in the crosshairs of his glass, literally and
metaphorically. Redfern already had Waring's boot-boy
in his pay, which was how he knew about this jaunt to the
Ash Lane Theater.

Still, he had proof of nothing. Even though Bedford
carried Barrett's card, no leap of logic could translate that
into Waring betraying England to the French. Redfern
knew he wanted the earl to be guilty, and jealousy was
tying knots in his chain of reasoning.

I need facts. Instinct and judgment are pulling in opposite directions.

Irritated, Redfern lowered his glass. He was trying to save Helen from—what? A brilliant match? Or a disastrous liaison with a murderous villain? Such confusion was not to Redfern's liking. He should just find an excuse to call Waring out and run him through, then take the first ship to the Amazon until the furor died down.

And then you would leave Helen behind one more time, like the fool you are.

A rap came at the door of the box. "Oranges, sir? Would you like to buy an orange?"

He snapped the spyglass closed and put the brass cylinder in his waistcoat pocket. "Yes, please."

The door opened and a girl about twelve appeared with a basket over her arm.

"How much?" he asked, thinking she would grow up to be pretty if disease and poverty spared her. The orange girls of the theater often had to sell more than their fruit before they had enough money to eat.

"A penny for my best orange, sir," she said, mischief in her face.

"That is a high price for an orange, isn't it?" he returned, falling into the game.

"But it's my very best one." She picked a fruit out of the basket, cupping it in both her slender hands like a precious object.

"Well, I wouldn't want anything but your best," Redfern conceded. He gave her a penny, and she gave him an orange and a smile.

"And you only want one, sir?"

"I already have the best one, and that will do fine."

"And that is all you want? You don't want nothing

more than that?" She gave a lopsided smile. "There ain't much I can't get for you, sir, and not much I won't offer for a shilling."

Inwardly, Redfern winced. "Thank you for the offer, but no." He was feeling lovelorn, but was a long, long way from resorting to the orange girls for companionship.

She gave an elaborate curtsy worthy of a court presentation, and backed out the door to try her luck at the next box.

After she left, he sat back, peeling the orange and reading the program. The smell of the fruit was heavy and tart, filling the hot air of the box. The bill promised a full production of Shakespeare's *Comedy of Errors,* an entr'acte consisting of a ballet and several "plaintive songs sung most sweetly and with dramatic gesture" by Miss Dorcas Entwhistle, and a short ballad opera on the subject of "Black Jack Davies, Cunning and Infamous Gentleman of the Road."

It looks like a long night ahead. Why couldn't it be horse racing instead?

Redfern bit into the orange. It was just shy of rotten and not nearly as sweet as the fruit he had eaten in the tropics. Still, it slaked his thirst, so he ate it anyway. Growing restless, he picked up the playbill again and read the names of the actors in the Shakespeare play.

Thomas Hanson played the part of Antipholus of Syracuse. Barrett said he had seen Lord Bedford outside the Apollonian Rooms with Hanson, a fact Redfern had been quick to note. The actor had been out of London since that night, and this was the first opportunity Redfern had found to get a look at the man.

A general roar rose from the audience as the curtain went up. Orange peelings rained down from the gallery to the pit in a mild show of enthusiasm. Redfern leaned forward, his attention fixed on the stage.

Comedy of Errors was new to him and, despite his oppressed mood, he enjoyed the play. It was witty, involving mistaken identities and two sets of twins separated at birth. Thomas Hanson was young and handsome, with a thick mane of auburn hair. He played one of the noble twins with great comic aplomb. His double, one Mr. Andrew Coleman, looked like Hanson but did not act nearly so well.

Applause thundered at the appearance of the celebrated beauty, Laura Gianotta, who played Hanson's wife. Whenever she spoke, the audience cheered; when she raged, the crowd stomped their feet; and when Hanson kissed her hand, Redfern began to fear for the furniture. Had this been a packed night in one of the rowdier venues, there might have been another theater riot. Whether La Gianotta had talent remained an unknown— he never heard a line she said over the unruly crowd—but he had to concede she had an extremely pleasant figure.

At the end, he stood to applaud with everyone else, his gaze drifting for the hundredth time to Helen. He could not see her eyes at this distance, but the white oval of her face turned toward him and she straightened suddenly. Annoyed with himself for being discovered, Redfern looked away.

Just as Miss Dorcas Entwhistle entered, stage left, to sing her plaintive songs, a note arrived for the Earl of Waring. Distracted by her unexpected sighting of Nicholas, Helen barely noticed the interruption until Waring touched her arm.

"I have an invitation from my cousin to join him back-stage. Would you excuse me for a moment?"

"Your cousin?" Helen asked, puzzled. As happened so often lately, she was having trouble thinking clearly, and it seemed to be getting harder every day. Nothing made sense any longer. She felt sluggish and a trifle queasy, as if she had taken laudanum.

Waring shrugged one shoulder. "Yes. Thomas Hanson is my mother's sister's son. He is actually Viscount Farnwell, but ceased to use his title when he broke with his father." He smiled ruefully. "He is the family rebel. My uncle does not approve of the theater, and Thomas will not give it up."

"A heinous quoter of poetry in the family? I'm shocked, my lord, that your noble house has such dire secrets." Despite her malaise, remembering the vibrant, charismatic young actor stirred her imagination. "You do not jest? He really gave up a title and all that goes with it to act?"

"I'm not sure what he exactly sacrificed for his art. He seems to have plenty of money and writes chipper letters home to his mama. Nevertheless, he hasn't been welcome under his father's roof for over a year. He was even barred from partaking of the Christmas pudding."

"That is a great sacrifice for a young man."

"It would be. My uncle sets a fine table." The earl shrugged. "When the time comes, his charm will get him out of any difficulties. Would you like to meet him? He's quite harmless if you don't mind scraps of poetry hurling your way from time to time."

"I would be delighted. I shall duck whenever necessary." She turned to her brother, animated for the first time that evening. "James? Would you care to meet a tragic, puddingless, young actor?"

"What's that?" Barrett roused himself. He had begun to drop off at the beginning of act three.

Helen poked him, her voice warming with what now felt like rare enthusiasm. "Let us go meet Lord Waring's cousin. I want to meet an actor."

He yawned. "I don't think the back of a theater is any place for a young lady."

"James, what could possibly happen? You would be with me, and Lord Waring." She hated the pleading tone she put into her voice, but so little interested her now, she wanted to indulge this spark of curiosity.

It was true that actors had long been branded as immoral—to the point where, in some places, they could not be buried in a churchyard—but many a hostess was dying to attract celebrated thespians to her salons. With a chaperone or two, it would be a safe taste of forbidden excitement.

"Barrett, really, there is nothing alarming about Thomas," Waring put in.

Barrett blinked, obviously more interested in sleep. He slept long and often these days, when he wasn't tending to his parliamentary duties. "I've met him already, and I do not care to go."

"I will return her safe and sound." The earl gave a smooth smile. "It pleases me to please Helen."

"Very well. If you wish it, sister mine, then go. I will take a walk outside to stretch my legs." He closed his eyes, clearly intending to resume his nap instead.

Helen rewarded her brother with a smile he did not see. It was rare that a lady of her social station would ever explore the tiring-rooms of an acting troupe. What was a casual meeting to her brother amounted to a grand adventure for her.

Waring led the way backstage with confident familiarity. When they reached the doorway that led from the public to the private part of the theater, a huge doorman stopped them. Apparently admirers of La Gianotta were kept at bay for a time to allow the actress a period of rest—then she would consent to hold court. Only when the earl produced his cousin's letter were they allowed through the door. Their path then followed a narrower hallway up a flight of stairs and behind the stage.

"Mind your step here," said the earl. "They leave bits of scenery scattered about as they change the sets."

Looking from side to side, Helen saw another world: a frantic, hot, cramped universe of fabulously dressed dancers, musicians tuning their instruments, and theater hands running to and fro with wigs and scraps of costumes. A Harlequin smoking a Spanish cigarette bowed from where he lounged against the unpainted wall. Amused, she nodded back to him. This world behind the backdrop was illusion in the making. For a fleeting moment, Helen felt the excitement like a vibration against her skin. So much life, so much possibility. It would be hard for a young man like Thomas Hanson to give it all up for the stolid doldrums of the drawing room.

Deep inside, she felt a pang, as if part of her recognized a vitality that she was fast losing.

They were now in a wide hallway that served as an improvised reception area. A half dozen chambers opened onto the space, some of which seemed to be the tiring-rooms of the lead actors. At one end of the hall, a crowd of servants thronged the largest doorway, bearing letters, wrapped packages, and huge bouquets of flowers. Helen guessed that was the chamber of the dark beauty called La Gianotta, and the gifts tribute from the men she had conquered.

The earl glanced over at the procession and raised one eyebrow.

"She certainly has her admirers," Helen said with a twinge of awe. *What would it be like?* she wondered. It would be grand to have so many swains for a day or two, but would they soon get underfoot?

In her mind's eye, she suddenly saw Nicholas's upturned face gazing at her from his box across the theater. His sudden appearance had startled her, as if he were the ghost of her dreams, those visions of the future that had starved to nothing. Her head and heart were filled with the image for a long moment, until the earl snapped her thoughts back to the present.

"Indeed, La Gianotta rules a vast kingdom." Waring studied the scene, amusement in his eyes. "They are fools, every one of them. She would as soon ruin them as let them kiss the tips of her fingers."

"Do you know the lady?" Helen asked with frank curiosity.

"I know her by sight," said Waring with a shrug. "I have come back here now and again to view the spectacle."

Helen looked around. "There is not much of a spectacle." She wondered what it was her brother feared she might see. Bacchanalian debauchery seemed in short supply. Secretly, she felt let down.

"There will be in an hour or two, but I will have you well away by then. Are you disappointed?" With an impish look, Waring raised her hand to his lips. "Shall I imitate La Gianotta's faithful and ruin myself for the honor of kissing your hand?"

"My gloves will wash clean," said Helen. "It hardly seems worth your fortune and honor."

The earl met her gaze, the light, bright blue of his eyes almost startling. Despite the gloom cast by Nicholas's sudden appearance, she felt cheered. Waring's attention was comforting, like a warm, soft, insulating blanket. No unwelcome thoughts penetrated the shield of his presence. She was safe. When she listened to him, there was no turmoil in her heart.

He said nothing, but squeezed her hand and held it. Then, with a look of utter consternation, his attention traveled to something behind her. Still mesmerized by the earl's gaze, Helen turned.

A woman in Grecian-style dress was gliding toward them, her sandals silent on the carpet. She wore turquoise silk, her bare arms cuffed with bracelets of silver and pearls. Her hair, the same dark shade as polished walnut, was caught in a simple ivory comb. She was beautiful, graceful, and her hungry, dark brown eyes were fixed on the Earl of Waring.

This must be La Gianotta, Helen thought, her mind moving with glacial slowness. *She looks different up close. She's even lovelier.*

Helen glanced at the earl. He was regarding the beauty with a carefully schooled expression, as if he wanted to gape, but had just enough dignity to keep his composure. Despite the fog in her brain, Helen felt slighted by his interest in the woman.

Graceful as a naiad, the creature knelt at the earl's side, the gesture at once humble and provocative. The folds of her shimmering gown fell sinuously from the silver clasps at her shoulders, delicate, soft, and hiding nothing. She held up an orange, studded with cloves, in one long-fingered hand.

"My lord, will you partake of my fruit?" she said, her words just slightly accented with Italian.

A long pause followed, during which a flush crept up the earl's cheeks. "Laura, you are extravagant in all things. Can you not see I am with a young lady?" he replied, his tone just on the right side of civility.

Helen blinked, trying to absorb what was happening. Waring had used La Gianotta's first name, so he was obviously better acquainted with the woman than he had pretended. In fact, she behaved more like a mistress than a chance acquaintance. At that thought, Helen's annoyance grew. It occurred to her that she should insist they leave, but she was too curious to see what La Gianotta would do next. She might never meet anyone like her again.

"Madam Gianotta," she broke in, forgetting in her daze that she should be embarrassed by a half-dressed woman kneeling at the feet of her escort, "let me say how I thoroughly enjoyed your performance this evening."

The large brown eyes of the woman turned on Helen, measuring, curious. She continued to kneel, orange poised in the air, one eyebrow lifted. "I thank you, my lady." She tilted her head to the earl. "*Mi scusi,* do I interrupt?"

"Laura, behave yourself!" said the earl sharply.

The woman folded her hands on her knee, the orange dangling from her fingers. "My lord, for shame, you are so cold to me. I demand reparation. I will not go until you eat of my fruit." She looked at the earl from under her lashes, and then cut a glance to Helen. "Perhaps the lady would like to join the game?"

"Laura!"

"And what is your game?" Helen asked, her voice sounding distant in her own ears.

"It is simple," said the woman. "One lover takes a clove from the orange, like so." She stood, graceful as flowing water, and matched her actions to her words, plucking at the fruit with rouged nails. A drop of juice trickled down the orange, released from the hole where the clove had been forced through the rind. "Then, I bite it to sweeten the breath." She placed the clove on the tip of her pink tongue.

Helen watched in fascination as La Gianotta bit down. How did the woman manage to charge the act of chewing with such innuendo? Did she practice before a mirror?

La Gianotta's great, dark eyes fastened on the earl. "Then, I give the orange to the man I choose to kiss, and I kiss him."

Before he could move, she placed one hand on the back of the earl's head and brushed her lips to his. The gesture was swift, almost chaste, and lovely for its restraint. Afterward, the earl's eyes remained half-closed, as if he were still waiting for the touch of her full, lush mouth.

After a moment, he pulled away, clearing his throat. "What nonsense is this?" His protest did not sound convincing.

Laura looked at Helen, and winked. "Finally, I leave the stage while the audience yet begs for more. Observe, now the orange is his. He cannot be rid of it until he kisses a lady, and passes it on to her."

Waring's face was a mix of embarrassment and a desire he could not hide. Helen caught her breath, his need kindling something in her. Not love, not even lust. Just a detached fascination, like a rabbit before a snake.

Waring's eyes searched her face. "I'm sorry to subject you to this."

Helen knew she should be shocked. It was expected of ladies to be shocked by loose women proffering forbidden fruit. Yet, she felt nothing.

What is happening to me?

Chapter 9

Redfern saw Barrett slouch in his seat while Helen and Waring went down the hallway that led backstage. Barrett was obviously going nowhere so, with rising consternation, Redfern followed the others. Why was Waring taking Helen deep into the theater, where no young lady ought to go?

He evaded La Gianotta's doorkeepers simply by leaving the theater and coming back in through the tradesmen's entrance. It was busy enough no one stopped to question a gentleman picking his way through the flotsam scattered around the building's back door. From there it was an easy matter to reach the tiring-rooms.

With a flicker of satisfaction, he spotted Waring and Helen from the corner of his eye, but did not turn for a direct look. To confront Waring here would do no good; he needed to know what the earl was up to. He ducked into the nearest doorway, planning to watch from a discreet distance. A gnawing feeling in his gut reminded him he was as jealous as he was suspicious.

Redfern broke his surveillance long enough to glance around the room. Luck did not smile on him often, but for one moment she positively beamed. It was one of the tiring-rooms used by the male actors. He had wanted to learn more about Thomas Hanson, and this might be his chance.

Quickly he searched a small table that served as a desk. As he opened a writing case and looked at the bills and letters inside, he realized he had indeed found Hanson's room. Could he also find out what connected Hanson to Lord Bedford?

Redfern looked around. The room was bare of ornament, the furniture old. In the wavering glow of a single sconce, the white walls seemed alive with shadows. Hanson's costume trunk was open, spewing capes, doublets, and feathered hats over its lip and onto the floor in a riot of jewel-colored velvets. The paste sequins stitched to the garments shimmered in the light like living eyes.

A wooden crate filled with carpenter's tools sat in the corner. Redfern crossed to it and peered at the jumble of hammers and saws, shifting so his shadow did not obscure the shapes inside. He reached in, drawn by a rippling gleam of wire. His fingers closed around a coil of twisted brass, the same thickness as that used to garrote Bedford. It was not a conclusive discovery; such wire was used for a thousand purposes, but it was—interesting.

As Redfern straightened, something clicked into place in his memory. He went to the dressing table, his gaze alighting on a small leather traveling chest. Growing conscious of the passing moments, he quickly lifted the lid, angling the chest toward the sconce. Pots of paint, brushes, pencils, gums, and all the aids to an actor's disguise nestled in the velvet lining. A familiar smell of linseed oil struck Redfern's nose.

His scalp prickled with a rush of excitement. He had

found theater paint and squirrel-hair brushes. The smudge he had found on Bedford's clothes—white greasy paint, red bristle. Redfern took a deep breath. The evidence of guilt was mounting.

Bedford had definitely been in Hanson's company the night he died. The actor had left the marks of his trade behind. Redfern had found the wire and the face paint. But why would Hanson lure Bedford from the Apollonian Rooms and strangle him? Had he been hired? And, if he had been at the party as a guest, why would he be wearing makeup?

He lifted out the tray of the traveling chest that held the bottles and pots of paint, balancing it in one hand as he searched beneath. Below was a space crammed with papers, coins, and bits of cheap stage jewelry. A devil's head cast in brass caught his eye. *Accoutrements of the Hellfire League?* Redfern thought dryly. Probably a trinket for a costume. For all the emphasis the Master had put on the would-be sorcerers, he had seen no sign of anything but pedestrian evil.

On the top was a playing card, the three of diamonds, but a design had been drawn over the card. It was familiar, and Redfern wracked his memory. It was something he had seen recently.

He felt rather then heard a presence behind him. Dropping the tray back into place, he whirled around, his fingers automatically reaching for his knife. He barely stopped himself before he drew it.

Hanson leaned against the door frame, watching him with intense green eyes. The look was sharp with suspicion. "Why are you going through my things?"

The actor was a handsome man, with even, square features. Out of the stage lights, his hair was a dark auburn, his skin faintly freckled. He wore a bright green coat the color of spring grass, elegantly cut and clearly expensive. At the very least, the viscount turned actor had plenty of credit with his tailors.

Redfern nodded politely. "Pardon me. I seem to have strayed into the wrong chamber."

Hanson's expression was unimpressed, his gaze lingering on the chest of makeup that Redfern had barely reassembled. "Were you looking for someone?"

"I meant to meet the Earl of Waring. He said he would be backstage."

"Were you looking for my cousin, or the young woman he is with?" Hanson's wide mouth curled up at one corner. "I recall you from the other night at the Apollonian Rooms. I seem to remember you pulling a knife on Lord Waring. Discreetly done, by the way, and he probably deserved it."

Redfern flushed. "Waring is your cousin? Are you not Thomas Hanson, the actor?"

"I am he. Sometimes I am also the Viscount Farnwell."

Taken aback, Redfern did a quick genealogical calculation. He had not made the connection because Hanson was a relatively common name. What was a viscount doing here? Was Hanson in disgrace, vulnerable to the influence of a powerful man like Waring? Doubt filled Redfern. At least on the surface, nothing about the actor seemed desperate or down-at-heel.

Rather, he seemed annoyed. "Now that I have given you my name, who the blazes are you?"

"My name is Redfern."

"Ah, the mysterious Lord Redfern," said Hanson. "It's an honor to meet someone even more infamous than I am. I am but a rebellious scapegrace.

"And I?" Something was nagging at the back of Redfern's memory.

"Some think you kidnap innocents to sell to the slavers; others prefer the gentleman-thief theory. You are a man of mystery and provide too many options for their imagination."

"I am inclined to take your observation as an insult," Redfern replied, but his mind was still on the idea that was eluding his mental grasp like a fish in dark water.

"That is your prerogative, but I am merely reporting what others have said. I have no opinion about you myself, though I do take exception to finding strangers going through my dressing table. It lends credence to your characterization as a thief."

"I will trade you one impertinence for another." Bluntness was his best option. Hanson didn't seem a fool to be trapped by oblique questions. "If you are Lord Farnwell, your father is the Earl of Leyland."

Hanson looked confused. "The same. Is that relevant? It's too well-known a fact to qualify as impertinent."

"You must be acquainted with Lord Bedford. I believe his estate lies near your father's land."

The green eyes narrowed. "Why?"

"I wondered if you had heard your old neighbor had died."

Hanson crossed his arms over his chest in a classic posture of unease. "Yes, I had heard that. Sad. I liked the man."

Redfern risked pushing a little further. "Here is the gossip: You were seen outside the Apollonian Rooms together shortly before he was murdered."

Hanson's neck grew red, the color reaching to his ears.

"How very interesting. I had not heard that it was murder. We were both there, but I did not leave with him."

Redfern shrugged. "I am merely reporting what others have said."

Hanson lifted his eyebrows. "Isn't scandal glorious? It makes you a thief and me a killer. That is almost like having a common cause. Shall I offer you a drink?"

The actor lifted the lid of a leather box and, with steady hands, took out a decanter of brandy and two glasses. Redfern was impressed. The man's sangfroid was flawless.

Hanson poured and offered Redfern a glass. "What is your interest in Bedford?"

"He was a friend." At last Redfern's thought came clear, a memory retrieved. He licked his lips, a surge of unease oppressing his spirits. He took the glass, but did not lift it to his lips.

Hanson downed his drink in a single swallow. "Odd that he never mentioned you. You see, I knew him quite well."

"He was murdered. His body was thrown from a coach in Beacon Park. It was a funeral coach bearing the design of a black moth." He had finally remembered that was where he had seen the moth design scrawled on the playing card in Hanson's chest.

He waited for some reaction on the actor's face. The man had gone perfectly still, his hands resting on the decanter. A long moment passed before he spoke. "How very gothic."

Hanson turned, his eyes calculating. "What are you doing in my room, Lord Redfern? And don't tell me you were searching for Lord Waring. Unless you mean to murder my cousin, I doubt you were here to meet him. You aren't friends."

Redfern sipped the brandy, thinking fast. Hanson had given away nothing useful. He would not be easily trapped. "I was waiting out of the crush."

"There is hardly a crush yet tonight."

Redfern grasped at a straw. "I am here to see La Gianotta. I am a devoted admirer."

Hanson's eyes lifted heavenward in a look of complete disbelief. A moment later, his face went blank, and then he affected a look of sympathetic understanding. The fine control of his expression was remarkable, a true actor's skill. Had Redfern not seen the change, he would never have known the soft-eyed look of sympathy was utterly false. Clearly, Hanson knew he was lying, and was merely playing along.

A prickle went up Redfern's spine. If he was that accomplished a deceiver, nothing Hanson said or did could be trusted. It would have been less disconcerting if the actor had pulled a gun.

"In love with our diva? You unfortunate sod," Hanson said, a note of warning and of humor in his words. "If it will get you out of my room, I will introduce you to Laura."

A voice broke through the murk of Helen's thoughts.

"Laura Gianotta, what mischief are you making?"

"Tomasso!" cried the actress in extravagant delight, turning away from Waring to face the newcomer. "You will join our game!"

With a muted thrill, Helen saw it was the handsome young actor, Thomas Hanson, who was approaching. He was smiling broadly, his long, auburn hair lifting with the motion of his quick stride. Then she saw Nicholas, a stormy look on his face, close behind Thomas. Her pleasure turned to a vague, unsettled feeling. Why was *he* with Thomas Hanson?

"Laura, put that fruit away," Hanson went on. "Clearly you are bent on wreaking havoc and destruction. It's too early in the evening for that. Besides, we have guests."

Hanson kissed Laura on the brow, then on the lips. "It's my fault, you see," he said to no one in particular. "I found her in Bath and brought her to London, so she is here to torment us."

He sighed with great pathos. "Alas, I have fallen in love with my leading lady. Fortunately, we are in a comedy, so we are bound to end well."

La Gianotta smiled up at him. "You come just in time," she said archly. "Someone's virtue was about to be trampled, and it was not mine."

Waring shot her a red-faced look and Thomas laughed, the corners of his wide mouth curling like a cat's. "Well, cousin, I see you have been burdened with an orange."

"Thomas, you are a walking disgrace," said Waring. He eyed La Gianotta fearfully, as if she might thrust another fruit upon him.

Flashing a mischievous grin, Hanson put an arm around her waist. "Indeed, coz, and you are here to recite a litany of my faults while you nibble at forbidden sweets." He then looked across at Helen. "You brought a friend, I see."

Waring gave his cousin a dark look. "This is Miss Helen Barrett. Her brother is Mr. James Barrett, the Honorable Member for Widgley-on-Thornton."

Hanson looked taken aback and stood up straight,

releasing his hold on the actress. "I am honored." He gave
an elegant bow.

*How interesting that he is surprised I am respectable.
Whom did he expect to see in Waring's company?* Helen
wondered, but knew she wouldn't like the answer. True,
the earl had a life before he courted her, and that life
would include other women, but she was still put out of
sorts. Women like Laura Gianotta were not covered by
her governess's instruction.

As soon as it formed, her unease disintegrated. Her
mind was too placid to hold on to the emotion.

The earl was eyeing Nicholas. "Why is *that man* on
your heels?" Waring asked Hanson, his tone sharp.

Helen's gaze traveled to Nicholas, who had glowered,
mute, through the previous exchange. The sight of his
tall, dark presence was impossible to ignore. It made the
peaceful aura around her thoughts shiver, like ripples on
a pond.

"He asked to meet Laura. At least that's what he said
when I found him thieving from my room." Hanson gave
a sly and charming smile. "Is that not so, Lord Redfern?"

Her jaw falling a little, Helen stared. Thieving? The
word confirmed everything she had guessed about him.
But what would he want that belonged to Thomas Hanson? What was Nicholas up to now? Oh, but did it really
matter? The questions, like so many other unimportant
and troublesome details, fell away.

"I did ask for the honor of paying my respects,
madam." He bowed to La Gianotta, his words and manner gallant.

La Gianotta offered her hand for Nicholas to kiss.
Helen could not escape this new assault on her emotions.
This was nothing like the dull possessiveness she felt for

Waring. This was real jealousy. Helen clasped her hands, the nails digging deep into her skin. The cloud around her mind parted enough to let in the pain of betrayal.

As he bent over, Nicholas raised his eyes and his gaze caught Helen's, seeming to watch for a reaction. Her breath hitched, the tension closing her throat. At that moment she hated him for wounding her spirit, and hated La Gianotta for touching him. He saw her anger and glanced away.

The earl would never make her feel this way. Helen closed her eyes, feeling her skin go clammy under the silk of her dress. Nicholas was a heartless thief. Waring was kind. She turned to look at the earl, and his blue eyes calmed her.

The necklace felt hot and heavy around her throat.

A look of triumph lurked in the earl's expression. He snorted in weary disgust at the sight of Nicholas making obeisance to the actress. "I won't linger, Thomas, since you obviously have other entertainments. You asked to see me?"

"I wondered if you had news of my mother and sisters, that is all." The young man's voice was bright, but Helen's ear caught an undertone of sadness.

"If you are wondering that, you should go home and ask after their health in person," Waring replied evenly.

"Of course," Hanson replied, one corner of his wide mouth curling up. "That would involve nothing but complete surrender to my father's will."

And the conversation went on, edging as close to argument as two gentlemen in public could reasonably go.

It was Nicholas who moved closer to Helen, but she spoke first, wishing he would go away. "What brings you here?"

"I have a fondness for theater," he said in the voice of someone who does not expect to be believed. "I see you are wearing the earl's sapphires again. They do become you exceedingly well."

Helen looked at Nicholas, but she felt slow, as if she moved under water. "Thank you. Yes, they are beautiful."

"Helen, have you been drinking?" He looked shocked.

"No, of course not," she said, trying to notice if her speech was slurred. She was just tired. Perhaps she needed a doctor, a tonic. "I am merely fatigued."

He said nothing, but his dark eyes went so cold with anger that Helen felt herself shiver. She fingered her necklace.

"I suppose you think I should have held out for diamonds," she said, feeling a touch of bitterness. Even through this unaccountable fatigue, Nicholas had the power to annoy her.

His expression gave nothing away. "I merely hope you set as high a value on your happiness as I do. Diamonds would not be enough."

It was hard to tell what he meant by that. Uncomfortable, she turned her back on him. The Waring family debate still raged—stifled, subtextual, but undeniably present. Thankfully, Hanson's—or was that Waring's? or both the men's?—paramour had suffered it long enough.

"Come, family is a dull subject when there is a cloven fruit to be given away!" La Gianotta took Hanson's arm, all the while holding the earl's gaze in her own.

Waring shook himself, apparently just now realizing he still held the orange in his hand. "Your games are not for polite company." He gave Hanson a filthy glare. "I would not have come here had I thought . . ."

Helen gave a mutter of exasperation. It was just an orange, and she was weary of the awkward fencing between the earl and his cousin. She was tired of Nicholas, and very weary of La Gianotta. There were not many ways to end the conversation gracefully. She did not even pause to consider her reputation; she just wanted to go home. She felt ill and wanted to sleep.

And, after that kiss of La Gianotta's slender hand, she wanted to show Nicholas that she cared nothing for him.

"Here." Interrupting Lord Waring, she stepped forward and, holding a clove by the tips of her fingers, pulled it from the orange. "Open your mouth, my lord."

Startled, the earl looked at her in dismay, but that soon faded. With warmth dawning in his expression, the earl took the bud on his tongue. As his lips closed over the clove, his pale blue eyes cut a triumphant glance at Nicholas.

Helen stepped into the kiss, the taste of it hot and clove-sweet, her hand just resting on Lord Waring's shoulder. It was nothing like the kisses she had shared with Nicholas. This was tentative, a test to see if something could come of this unexpected moment.

"*Brava,*" said La Gianotta. "The pale beauty has spirit."

Helen heard a hushed intake of breath and knew it was Nicholas. But where she should have felt victory, all the pain of their parting came back, wrenching and raw. Ducking her head with sudden chagrin, Helen pulled back, panting for air.

Her head suddenly cleared by corrosive emotions, for a moment Helen was not even sure where she was. It was as if she had suddenly awakened from a deep sleep.

Then memory returned. Lord Waring was looking at her with a soft smile she did not want to see. She was left holding the orange. *Now what?* She felt her cheeks burning. She had to pass the wretched fruit on. *What have I done?* Under the influence of panic, her head was perfectly clear to perceive her embarrassing position.

She looked at Nicholas. His eyes were dark, filled with a storm of emotion that matched her own.

His lips twisted. "I have already done business with one orange-girl tonight. I have no need for another."

If she had hurt before, it had been mere beginner's play. Now, Helen gripped the orange so hard, juice ran from the holes where the cloves punctured the skin and splashed, sticky and sweet, onto the skirts of her gown.

"Lovely Miss Barrett." Breaking the painful moment, Thomas stepped forward and bowed. "You have a tidbit of delicious fruit I covet."

"Have a care!" the earl growled.

"Ah!" La Gianotta raised her finger. "These are the rules of the game—she must pass the orange along. You cannot object."

"I do not delight in your games, madam!" Waring retorted.

"I do not propose to dishonor the lady," Hanson said coldly.

"You have a conscience, then. How unexpected," said the earl with equal venom.

Hanson gave Lord Waring a long, narrow look. "Yes. I thought it high time that one of us acquire better instincts. Perhaps I shall start a fashion."

The earl snorted and looked away.

The bitter exchange made Helen's stomach knot. She looked around to see Nicholas standing in the entrance to the room, gazing back at her. Her scalp prickled with alarm. He was leaving and she wanted him to go—but dreaded never being able to explain herself. As if she ever could.

He was staring at her, his dark brows drawn together. *Oh, Lord, why did I kiss the earl before all these strangers? Before Nicholas?* A lurch of shame and regret fought off the spider's web that constantly trammeled her mind.

Helen turned away, only to see Hanson's wide green eyes full of speculation. This was all too unbearable. She quickly pulled a clove from the orange and bit it, feeling the color draining from her cheeks. Anxiety knotted her muscles. She could not bear to kiss Hanson in front of Nicholas. She had exposed herself enough already.

Yet nothing happened as she expected it. With a wistful smile, Hanson took her hand and bent over her fingers, the gesture chaste and courtly. "I am afraid I am too late to capture your heart, so let me simply salute your beauty."

Helen closed her eyes in gratitude. A reprieve. She felt her muscles uncoil, blood returning to her veins. "Thank you, Thomas Hanson. You do me great honor."

He smiled his catlike grin. "The honor is mine."

Feeling shaky, Helen passed the orange to him. "There you are, sir, fruit for tonight's labors."

He released her hand and lifted the sphere, sniffing the spicy scent. "I think I had best beware. I have an unsettling sense the comedy of errors continues."

"Oh, I hope not. There will be a tragedy if it does not end soon."

"Then, behold, the cause of the trouble is gone." Hanson made an elaborate gesture, and the orange disappeared. "You see, I perform magic to rescue fair maids in distress. Such is the prerogative of the theater—I can take a sorrowing heart and make it laugh. I can draw down the darkness and then send it back from whence it came."

Helen did her best to smile at his attempt to cheer her. "You are a sorcerer."

"I am a thespian and a poet." He kissed her hand once more. "My wages are far more reasonable, and sorcery only lands one in complicated problems."

Hanson's smile held her for a moment but, as if drawn by a stronger will, Helen's attention reverted to the spot where Nicholas stood.

He was gone.

Her heart sank, but she breathed a sigh of relief.

Chapter 10

The next morning at nine o'clock Redfern received a summons from the Master. Only such a command performance would have roused Redfern, cross and thick-headed after barely three hours' sleep. As the maid flung back the curtains in his bedroom, the heat and brightness of the sun oppressed him like a lead weight.

The Master's envoy directed him to an apartment above a bakeshop on Feather Lane, a quiet nook in a respectable neighborhood near Berkeley Square. As Redfern mounted the stairs to the rendezvous, the smell of fresh currant buns made his mouth water.

He knocked on the door to the upstairs parlor. A well-built man in his late twenties opened it.

"Good morning, Wilson," Redfern said, passing him his hat and gloves.

"Come in, my lord," Wilson replied. His accent still had a trace of the slums in it. "Sir Alaric's waiting for you."

Redfern nodded, conscious he was avoiding Wilson's cold blue eyes. The man looked like an overgrown choir-boy with a murderous soul, and Redfern knew he had seen to plenty of the Master's most deadly chores. Wilson's presence bothered Redfern. It was like having a dangerous dog about the place.

Wilson ushered Redfern into a modest morning room decorated with frilly, feminine taste—obviously the landlady's. These rooms had probably been intended to house widows and spinster aunts, thought Redfern, not to serve as a meeting place for spies. Sir Alaric Fitzwilliam sat to one side of the window, his back to the light that filtered softly through filmy white curtains. His greyhound, Lady, was curled up in a patch of sunlight at his feet.

"Have you breakfasted?" Sir Alaric asked by way of greeting. "There is coffee here, and I see our hostess has sent up some delightful-looking apricot preserves." He sounded amused.

Indeed, there was a round table at the side of the room spread with a dainty white breakfast service. Fine china, jam, and an early-morning summons to discuss murder did not harmonize in Redfern's imagination. "Coffee would be welcome."

The Master made a gesture, and Wilson hastened to pour the rich-smelling brew. Redfern sat opposite Sir Alaric, directly facing the clear morning light. He knew the chairs had been positioned with care—the Master could see Redfern's every expression, but the Master himself was in shadow. To men like Sir Alaric, every conversation was in part interrogation.

Obedient, or at least resigned, Redfern sipped his coffee and made his report on events up to and including the previous night at the theater, omitting only the parts concerning Helen and that ridiculous orange. Some things did not bear repeating.

When he was done, the Master sat back in his chair.

"Let me summarize: You are telling me Hanson was seen outside the Apollonian Rooms with Lord Bedford the night of his murder, that Hanson is in possession of stage makeup similar to that found on Bedford's clothing, and that a coil of the same or similar wire used to garrote Bedford is in a box in Hanson's dressing room?"

"Yes," replied Redfern.

Sir Alaric tilted his head. "Please tell me why Hanson is not in a prison cell as we speak."

Redfern took another swallow of coffee, quickly organizing his thoughts. "What possible motive would Hanson have, unless he was coerced or paid off to commit murder? In that case, we have found a hired killer but not the criminal mind pulling the strings. We are still missing something important, and would do better to follow Hanson a while to see whom he visits."

"On the other hand, could we not *extract* this kind of information out of a prisoner more quickly? That is Wilson's specialty, after all." Sir Alaric chewed, his appetite apparently unhindered by the prospect of torture.

With an involuntary glance at Wilson, Redfern set his cup to one side. "My other reason for not apprehending Hanson is that it was impossible to get him alone. I waited outside the theater until nearly dawn, thinking to catch him as he walked home and question him further, but he left in a large company of his fellow actors to carouse at the Boar and Stars. It was too public a place to approach him."

"I see."

"I will take reinforcements and try again tonight. He is the lead actor in a play; he will not be hard to find. He has to go back to the theater."

Wiping his fingers on a napkin, Sir Alaric nodded. "Never mind, I will send Wilson for him."

Redfern frowned. "By rights, Hanson is mine." Watching the breeze dance in the curtains, he remembered Bedford's body on the dark, wet grass of the park. He could deliver justice just as brutally as Wilson, if the occasion demanded.

The Master coughed, calling back his attention. "By rights, yes, Hanson is yours. However, for now he is no longer your concern. I have other work for you."

"What is that?" Irked, Redfern tried to appear receptive.

Sir Alaric crossed his legs. "I, too, have been looking into this affair."

He signaled to Wilson, who brought a portfolio from the next room. With a lift of his eyebrow, Sir Alaric handed it to Redfern. "Your pursuit of Barrett, as you say, is also a pursuit of the Earl of Waring. Once again, you've proven you have a good nose for a rascal. If nothing else, Waring is a walking homily on the ugliness of ambition."

Redfern opened the portfolio. Within it was a sheaf of paper, mostly copies of correspondence. He took a moment to look the pages over. "There is plenty of proof here of bribes and purchasing votes in the House, but that is—and I despise the fact that I can say it—somewhat commonplace villainy. What makes him more of a traitor than a half dozen other men prepared to buy and sell influence?"

Sir Alaric shrugged, his expression sardonic. "I'm sure you will be shocked to learn Waring seems to be attracted to large sums of money. Foreign governments are frequent correspondents. Given the connection you have made between Barrett and the War Office, I think Waring may well be our Irish traitor. You will note many of the transactions outlined in those letters concern military matters, some of them with the French."

Redfern put the papers back in the portfolio. "Besides my interest in his protégé, what made you look into Waring?"

"I have long suspected him of a connection to the Hellfire League. While you followed your suspicions, I followed mine. Both led to the same man." The Master set down his empty plate. "Describe to me again the coach that carried Bedford's body."

Redfern did so. "As I mentioned before, the device on the door was the same design I saw on the playing card in Hanson's possession."

"Interesting, especially since you say Hanson is at odds with his cousin. Nothing here is simple." Sir Alaric toyed with one of his rings. "Did you see the coachman?"

Redfern pondered. "Not really, he was cloaked."

The Master gave a smile that was more like a grimace. "I have heard stories about the coach, but they are more fireside tales than useful information. Legend states it is like a banshee, a warning ghost, to the families of the Circle. I have never heard of it transporting a body."

"Was Lord Bedford a member of the Circle?" Redfern asked.

"No," replied the Master. "Not at all."

Redfern wondered how the Master could be so certain, and then decided it was a fruitless question. What Sir Alaric wanted him to know, he would tell. "Perhaps the coach was merely a sham meant to frighten us."

A flicker of annoyance crossed the Master's face. "Whether it is real or an apparition does not matter. The murder itself means Bedford was getting close to the truth."

Wilson refilled their coffee cups.

"The black moth is the mark of the Hellfire League," Sir Alaric continued. "If Hanson had a sketch of it in his possession, he is somehow involved. As you say, he knew Lord Bedford and is the Earl of Waring's cousin. Added to that, the papers in that folder confirm Waring's willingness to do business with foreign powers—and, through Barrett, Waring has access to military information. I begin to see pieces of this puzzle though I still cannot see the whole."

Redfern digested this. "What must I do?"

"For now, I will stay with Hanson and Bedford's murder. I need you to follow Waring. While you were tracking our celebrated young actor, the earl left this morning for his country estate."

Surprised, Redfern set the folder of papers aside. "I knew he was going, but so soon? It is weeks too early for shooting grouse."

"But not too early for ennui. Every year around this time, Waring retreats to the country for a week or so, declaring himself bored into a stupor by the demands of London. As expected, his fashionably weary sycophants toddle along like ducklings after their mother. The Barretts are preparing to leave. I need you to go, too."

Redfern barely stopped his jaw from dropping open. "I'm hardly his intimate. He would never let me in the door."

Sir Alaric gave a dry chuckle, showing long, white teeth. "I'm counting on the fact that your presence will make him agitated. That's when men like him make mistakes. I want him distracted."

"But . . ."

"If he is going to meet with the Irish, the French, or the devil, it may well be during this time he is safely tucked up in his own territory. The very first of the letters Lord Bedford intercepted referred to a gathering at the *usual place* at the *time of the Lion*. It could well have been speaking of Waring's annual retreat to Arden Hall in the summer."

The thought of close confinement with Waring set Redfern's teeth on edge. "And what if my presence makes him put off the meeting?"

"My guess is timelines are too tight for that. Invasions are run on schedule or not at all. He will keep his appointments because they represent French gold."

Redfern did not like this plan at all. "I see, but how will I get an invitation? Our last conversation nearly ended in a brawl."

Sir Alaric waved a hand, brushing away the objection. "I'm sending you with my late wife's half brother, Lord Fairmeadow. Waring has already invited him because he holds considerable influence over a pocket borough Waring is desirous of controlling. The earl dare not offend him."

"He will get me inside Waring's house?"

"Yes, and more than that—he will help you. Fairmeadow gives the appearance of being a foaming idiot, but do not underestimate him. The fact that men like Waring dismiss him as a fop is his chief weapon. I've told him not to let Waring bully you."

"*He* is to protect *me*?" Redfern asked, incredulous. "Will Lord Fairmeadow knock Waring down if he insults my ancestry?"

"Fairmeadow may not fit the role of knight defender,"

Sir Alaric smiled, "but if I ask it, he will protect you with his last breath, or at least down to his last clean cravat."

Picking up his coffee cup, Redfern sighed irritably. "Very well, Lord Fairmeadow shall be my Knight Champion."

The Master signaled for more buttered toast. "Excellent. There is one other matter. You mentioned that Barrett is not behaving like himself. Tell me more."

"Yes. Of late he has turned against old friends. Not just me, but others as well. He neglects his wife and child. Strangest of all, he seems—vacant. I wondered if it was the weight of guilt, or even the effects of illness."

The Master narrowed his eyes. "Can you tell if he sleeps a great deal?"

"He fell asleep at the theater last night." Redfern took a deep breath. "I am reluctant to give the thought breath, but I believe whatever ails Barrett is afflicting his sister as well. She appears drunk or drugged, and only revives under the influence of strong emotion. Anger, actually." Redfern felt himself flush.

"Has Waring given either of the Barretts any gifts of late?"

"I do not know if he has given anything to James Barrett. However, the earl presented Miss Barrett with a necklace of pink sapphires at the Apollonian Rooms the other night. She has worn it every time I have seen her since that night."

"Damnation," Sir Alaric said under his breath.

Redfern tensed. He had never heard such anxiety in the Master's voice before.

The older man rested his chin on his hand. "I'm going to give you a piece of advice I may regret."

Redfern frowned. "And what is that?"

The Master reached down and stroked the head of his greyhound. "I strongly suspect Miss Barrett is an innocent in a coliseum filled with savage beasts. I give you permission—no, I order you to rescue your young lady."

Redfern felt a thrill of alarm. "Rescue her from what? And why? I thought you did not approve of her."

"Don't be an idiot, Redfern. I may not be a romantic, but I dislike unnecessary cruelty. I regret to say, I would not credit the Earl of Waring with such restraint. Get the necklace away from her—it may well be the object creating her malaise."

"The necklace?" Redfern heard his voice rising with incredulity.

"If I am right, and he is a member of the League, Waring may be using it to bend her will to his own. Dark forces have often employed pretty playthings."

"A magical necklace?" Redfern repeated, his mind grappling with what Sir Alaric was saying.

The Master sighed impatiently. "Think of it this way: If you take the trinket and if there is no result, you can always return it to the lady."

"Why would Waring resort to magic to court a woman? Surely his lands and title are recommendation enough to find him a wife?"

"If Waring courts Miss Barrett with magic, there is something he wants from her besides her gentle favors, and he will not hesitate to take it. Perhaps it is her dowry, perhaps something else."

"You would like me to find out what that is."

Sir Alaric gave a smooth smile. "You know me too well to think I would mention her name for nothing. Save her, but get some solid work done while you're about it. I want to know everything that Waring desires."

When Redfern returned home, there was a letter from his young sister, Lady Panthea, waiting on the hall table. He broke the seal eagerly and did not wait to reach his study before unfolding the pages and starting to read.

"Dearest Nicholas," Panthea began, and he could hear her light voice in his mind. *"I am going to begin these pages by scolding you for not coming to see us last week as you promised you would. The Saville family was short by one at table, and that was you, dear brother. And after you have been away so long!"*

Redfern grimaced. He had meant to go for a day or two, but had been following Waring instead. There was always something that kept him from seeing his family, just as it had kept him from being with Helen.

The shadow of Michael. There was not one empty seat at the family table, but two.

"I know complaining of your neglect has no effect, but form must be observed. My displeasure stated, I will move on to torture you with details of everything you missed. Lord Richard's dance was a grand event and at least a dozen couples stood up for every set . . ."

Redfern sat down in his chair by the unlit study fireplace.

"I have the most intoxicating news," Panthea rambled on. *"I danced over and over again with Sir Richard's son, Andrew."*

Redfern frowned. *What sort of boy is this Andrew? I will have to think of her future.*

Their father, the Earl of Whitford, had little money. Redfern, on the other hand, had been well rewarded for his work for the Master. He was not fabulously wealthy, but lived as well as any rational man could want. He would be dowering his sister and paying for his younger brother's commission in the cavalry. He made sure his family lived in comfort. Of course, that was all through the grace of Sir Alaric Fitzwilliam, who could ruin them once again with a lift of his finger.

"I think I would like to marry Andrew," Panthea wrote. *"I may change my mind, though. I am but seventeen."*

Redfern set the letter down again, unsettled. When had Panthea turned into a young woman? He had missed far too much.

The letter left him distracted, but there was nothing to be gained by brooding. He gave his valet orders to pack his trunks and send them on to Arden Hall, Waring's country residence. Redfern would travel with Fairmeadow in the morning.

In the late afternoon, he went out for a walk, charging through the streets in an effort to burn off excess energy. When he arrived home, Wilson was sitting in Redfern's best chair and drinking his best port. The man's small blue eyes looked Redfern up and down when the latter walked into the room.

"I thought you would be at the Ash Lane," said Redfern, pouring himself a glass of the heavy red wine. He turned to face his unwanted guest, masking his displeasure. The man was little more than Sir Alaric's servant, and yet he had made himself completely at home.

"I was." Wilson slouched in the chair, his beefy hand engulfing Redfern's delicate Venetian wineglass.

Redfern forced himself to be polite. The man would make an inconvenient enemy. "Did you find Hanson?"

Wilson reached into his jacket and pulled out a

cheaply printed notice. With a curl of his lip, he tossed it onto the carpet at Redfern's feet. "Look for yourself."

Redfern bent to pick up the paper, fighting back the urge to thrash the insolent sneer off Wilson's face. He turned the notice right-side-up to read it and immediately forgot everything else.

It stated the *Comedy of Errors* had been cancelled until further notice. Instead, a traveling company from Dublin would be performing a comedy. The page was ragged at the edges. Wilson had probably torn it off the theater door.

"What happened?" Redfern asked. "Where is Hanson?"

"Our pigeon flew the coop early this morning and no one knows where he's gone. Hanson's disappearance has shut down the play. I'd say that answers any doubts about the sod's guilt. Should've taken him last night."

Redfern was forced to agree.

"Leave it with me," said Wilson without much cheer. "I'll see to him, one way or t'other."

Redfern was still fuming as he climbed into Lord Fairmeadow's carriage the next morning. His traveling companion did nothing to improve his mood.

Fairmeadow was probably around forty, but it was hard to tell. His face was unlined and his soft, oak-brown hair showed no gray. Evidently a devotee of fashion, he wore a dark blue coat of the latest style, cut precisely to the lines of his small, slim frame. Beneath, his waistcoat was buttercup yellow.

As Redfern settled into his seat, Fairmeadow regarded him sleepily. The little man sniffed a nosegay of flowers. "The odor of violets keeps the vapors of long carriage rides from the blood," he announced. "I have been thoroughly briefed on your mission. I will help however I can. I am your native guide in Lord Waring's darkling realm."

The scent of the posy was overpowering in the hot, enclosed space. Redfern fought the instinct to gag.

"Do you know Lord Waring well?" he asked, wondering if Fairmeadow really knew anything of use or if he was as vapid as he looked.

"He belongs to White's," Fairmeadow replied languidly, as if that answered all. "And wherever he goes, he searches out the weaknesses of other men."

As that described most politicians, the statement answered nothing. Redfern sighed inwardly and groped for another conversational gambit more suited to a fop with a violet nosegay.

"What is the gossip about Waring and La Gianotta?"

"The actress?"

"Yes. What do you know of her?"

Fairmeadow snorted. "Like Lillith, she is beautiful and terrifying. Nevertheless, if she is a true Italian, then I'm a pineapple. She puts on a good accent, but not good enough for my ear."

Now here was something interesting. "If she is not really Laura Gianotta, then who is she?"

"She has buried her past very deep. She has been Waring's mistress for years, you know."

"Hmm. When I saw her last, she seemed to be bent on embarrassing the earl."

"Waring is courting Miss Barrett. That means Gianotta's value is waning. No doubt she feels angry and vulnerable."

Mention of Helen made Redfern tense. "The actor, Thomas Hanson, is in love with the so-called Italian."

Fairmeadow twizzled the flowers between his fingers. "Either she is lying to him, or he is lying to you."

"Or Laura Gianotta is playing Hanson and Waring against one another."

"Ha! That's true enough. The two men share a mutual hatred. Nothing like a jealous woman to add interest. There is no one crueler or more inventive, and La Gianotta is reputed to be the most wicked of them all."

Plagued by his own jealousy, Redfern left the topic at that. Fairmeadow rested his head against the squabs of the seats and fanned himself gently with the morning paper. It was folded back to the society page.

Redfern reflected again on the fact that Fairmeadow was appointed to protect him from Waring. Unconsciously, Redfern felt along his cuffs to reassure himself that both knives were in their wrist sheaths.

Chapter 11

Helen loved Arden Hall from the moment she saw it. It was new, built in the Palladian style only fifty years earlier. It sat at the end of a long and winding drive, hidden from the road. When the carriage emerged from the stands of oak trees surrounding the grounds, she caught her breath as the building came into view. Poised like a jewel on the velvet lawns, the house shone white and perfect, tall columns supporting the elegantly proportioned pediment above the entry. Peacocks sunned themselves around a fountain in the middle of the lawn. It might have been an engraving, it was so perfect.

I could be mistress of this, she thought. *I could be standing on those marble steps, greeting my guests.* Her brother's desire that she marry the Earl of Waring made perfect sense.

As she alighted from the carriage, servants hurried out to unload bags. Waring emerged from the house, looking casual and pleased. He wore no coat, the full sleeves of his shirt rippling in the afternoon breeze. He was a fine physical specimen.

"I trust your journey was uneventful," he said, his

shoes crunching on the white gravel of the path. "It is ideal weather for travel, sunny but not too hot."

"It was very pleasant," Helen agreed, taking his arm.

Barrett climbed down the steps behind her and lit up the cheroot Helen had forbidden him to enjoy inside the vehicle. "It was deuced dull." He exhaled a stream of smoke and leaned wearily against the outside of the carriage. "I slept the entire time."

"You are rested, then." Waring said absently and smiled down at Helen. His face had tanned in the few days since he left London, emphasizing the clear blue of his eyes. "Some of the other guests have already arrived. I will have Mrs. Johnson, the housekeeper, show you to your rooms. Once you have refreshed yourselves and dressed, please join us in the yellow parlor. We dine early here, but that still gives you some time to restore yourselves."

The entry seemed dark after the bright sun, but once her eyes adjusted, Helen could admire the high, frescoed ceiling. Twin staircases curved to the upper floors. Mrs. Johnson led Helen and her maid, Violet, up the south stairs and down a portrait-hung corridor. Eventually, they reached a large room overlooking the back lawn.

"I trust this is suitable, madam," Mrs. Johnson said, her eyes lowered. She was an older woman dressed in a style at least twenty years out of date.

"Yes, thank you," replied Helen. "It's lovely."

"It was Lady Waring's room when she was alive," the housekeeper added, a slight weight to the words catching Helen's ear. Did she mean the future mistress was staying in the former mistress's quarters?

"I am honored, then," she said. "It seems I will enjoy one of the best rooms in the house."

With a curtsy, Mrs. Johnson left. Helen looked around the chamber. Violet was already unpacking and putting Helen's dresses into the armoire.

The earl's late wife slept here, Helen thought, glancing at the bed. The wood was rich mahogany, the bedding covered with a whitework counterpane. The dark and light contrast made the bed look cool and clean, and she ached to lie down after the long, jolting carriage ride. Nevertheless, a superstitious feeling crept over her. She did not like to think of sleeping in Lady Waring's bed. Some small, traitorous part of her resisted taking what felt like a symbolic step.

Instead, she sat in the window and watched the other guests play at bowls on the back lawn. Only when Helen's eyes grew too heavy to stay open could Violet persuade her mistress to lie down.

Downstairs, Barrett was in fine form, probably owing to a liberal application of Waring's brandy. When Helen joined him in the parlor, his fleshy face was pink and his voice pitched just above the general conversation. *At least I am spared the task of soothing his temper,* she thought. Her brother had been cross and hard to live with lately.

Perhaps it was because, like her, he seemed to be perpetually exhausted. For the moment, all she wanted to do was observe the gathering. She spotted a seat at the other end of the room, just before the heavy gold draperies that gave the yellow parlor its name. Unobserved, she crossed the room and sat, taking stock of the room and its occupants.

"Do you have a brilliant inspiration as to how to dispose of our—um—extraneous visitors? Given the nature of our labors . . ." The speaker standing to Helen's right let his words trail off, the following silence ripe with meaning.

Helen could not help but listen for what came next.

"There will be no unwelcome revelations. I have planned too well for that," Waring replied to the speaker. He stood with his back angled to Helen. He was facing the wrong way to see her, but she could hear his words clearly.

"How many outside guests are there to be, then? Who is still to come?" asked the first man, whom Helen now identified as Lord Stephen Layton, lately returned from the wars on the Continent.

He had attended a few dinner parties at the Barretts' home with a view to entering politics. With a long, handsome face spoiled by a saber slash, Layton was an elegant adventurer with an eye for heiresses. He was the sort of drawing-room predator that made Helen's skin crawl.

"There's still Lord Fairmeadow and his guest. I'm not sure whom he's bringing, but they should be here this afternoon."

"Well, you know Fairmeadow. It probably takes him a fortnight to decide which waistcoats to pack. Whatever possessed you to invite him?" Layton drawled. "His family never held with the League. Will he be a problem?"

"That ninny? I think not. I invited him because we have a mutual interest in the seat at Longbottom. I am hoping Fairmeadow will allow me to suggest a candidate of my choosing."

Layton curled his lip. "Will he remember the candidate's name long enough to fix the vote?"

"I hope to make it worth his while. I intend to devote at least part of this week to persuading him." Waring took a sip from his wineglass. He was dressed formally now, his shoulders shown to advantage by a dark green jacket.

"And you can be so persuasive. I never thought you a man for working holidays," Layton laughed. "I would be loath to talk boroughs when the shooting season is just about on us."

"I'm always at work. Politics is not an occupation; it is a calling."

"Of course," Layton replied in a disbelieving tone.

"On the other hand," Waring said confidentially, "it's a business like any other. If I speculate well . . ."

"I think you are a clever man of business."

"I have my moments of genius."

Helen lost interest in the discussion. She did not know specifically to what the men referred, and could not concentrate anyhow. She turned to look out the window at the peacocks. They sat on the lawn and perched on the edge of the fountain, brilliant, beautiful, and lazy. She longed to be with them. She could almost feel the prickle of the soft grass on her bare feet. With a sigh, she turned back to the room and stood, smoothing her dress. It was time to be the witty and charming guest. As she gathered her thoughts, she remembered the atmosphere of the Ash Lane Theater. Why had she longed to be an actress that night? She performed daily.

If the evening's activities were a play, the performance was rich with dialogue but had a thin plot. Helen was mildly bored and yearned for a conclusion. Docile, she accepted Layton's arm and entered Waring's elegant dining room at the appointed hour. The walls were painted dark rose with white and gold trim, each panel set with a decorative painting of some mythological scene. Here a satyr, there a nymph—scenes of pastoral dalliance frolicked in the shadows where the candlelight could not reach. The high ceiling was painted like a vault of stars, Luna and her chariot riding around the south end of the room.

All the guests fit around one long table, with two empty seats for Fairmeadow and his traveling companion, who now had arrived and would join the party momentarily. Helen counted the diners. There were twenty visitors, all of them from titled families, except for the Barretts. Waring sat at the head of the table, his guests carefully arranged to mesh interests and make new acquaintances. He had seated the ranking ladies on either side of him, paying them the compliment of his special attention. Finding herself farther down the table between Layton and an empty chair, Helen made polite small talk but spent more time observing the others. The women at the table, two countesses and a marchioness, glittered with jewels, each *ensemble* worth at least a village. A phalanx of footmen lined the walls, poised to remove, refill, or serve as required.

Helen found it relaxing to look on, daydreaming. She could not help picturing herself in the place of the marchioness, presiding as the reigning female of the house. Woolgathering was easier than finding the energy to talk or eat.

For a country party, Waring had spared no trouble. Candlelight glinted on the fine glassware. Footed, silver dishes spilled fruit, flowers, and sweetmeats down the length of the table, the colors shimmering like jewels against the white damask linens. To Helen's delight, a string trio played softly in the background. The atmosphere was opulent, almost overwhelming the senses.

The first few courses had come and gone when a footman opened the door to admit the latecomers. On Helen's left, Lord Stephen Layton was saying something about angling—there had been a tenuous connection between the topic and the fish course—when she glanced toward the door to see Lord Fairmeadow make his fluttering entrance.

"Ah, you're here at last!" Waring stood to greet his guest. "I'm so pleased to see you."

Helen blinked as the light glittered on Fairmeadow's cerise waistcoat. The embroidery was picked out in tiny jewels, making a scatter of sparkles every time he moved.

"Come, have a seat by Lady Gray. Have you met?" Waring directed Fairmeadow by the elbow to the chair, where a footman was already pouring wine.

"And your guest?" Waring turned, and stopped dead, like an automaton suddenly robbed of power.

Squinting, Helen tried to make out the face of the other newcomer. The light was too dim by the door to see anything but the outline of a tall man. Then he took a step forward into the light, and Helen's lips parted in slow, unhappy surprise. What was Nicholas doing here?

Devastating in severely cut evening dress, he nodded to Waring, all geniality. "My lord, I was honored to accept Fairmeadow's invitation to keep him company on the journey. Your reputation as a host is well-known."

"Come, sit down so we all can eat," complained Fairmeadow. "I'm famished." He fanned himself with his napkin. "I will fade away unless I'm fed."

"Pray, do sit down, Viscount," Waring said, his voice entirely neutral. He dropped Redfern's gaze and resumed his seat, looking down at his plate for a moment. The other guests exchanged curious glances, but salvers of roast duck arrived to distract from the awkward moment.

"The roads *must* be looked at," Fairmeadow declared.

"My portmanteaux were shaken beyond repair. One could not tell my valet had packed them; it looked like an army of pixies had rummaged through my linens. Valois will have to wash and press everything." He picked up his knife and fork. "A little more sauce there, my man," he said to the footman who had hastened to assist Fairmeadow to fill his plate. "No, not on the peas, the duck, you oaf, the duck."

Helen felt a stir of air next to her and looked to her right. Nicholas was sitting down in the empty seat.

"Miss Barrett," he said formally.

"Lord Redfern," she returned stiffly, glancing down the table at Waring. The earl was looking her way, clearly displeased with the seating arrangements. Yet, he could hardly shuffle a roomful of diners already well into their meals.

Helen and Nicholas sat awkwardly for a moment. Transfixed, unable to think, Helen watched his hands as he picked up a roll and broke it, the crumbs of the rich bread scattering across his plate. His fingers were long, the palms of his hands broad and strong. She had seen him catch and gentle a stallion with those hands, but then again she had seen him holding a dagger to Lord Waring's ribs. Those hands were capable of much.

Traitorous feelings of warmth stirred beneath the mists that shrouded her mind. She pushed them away. She would be just polite enough to avoid bad manners.

"I did not know you were acquainted with Lord Fairmeadow," Helen said, just to say something.

Nicholas buttered a piece of the roll. "We are acquainted." His voice, his eyes were guarded.

Another silence ensued. Helen considered making another conversational sally, but then decided against it. It was too painful an effort. Other guests, however, were happy to fill the void.

"I am curious to hear of your travels, Lord Redfern," said Layton, talking around Helen by leaning back in his chair like a schoolboy. "You have been gone some time."

"I was in the Americas," Nicholas replied. "I have investments there."

"Rumor would have you selling beggar girls to the pashas of the Orient," said Lady Gray, the feathers in her turban nodding in rather pasha-like fashion.

"I think not," said Nicholas with an icy smile. "I have been informed such despots accept nothing less than a pure blood aristocrat either in trade or gift." He shrugged, softening his tone. "And I was sailing in the wrong direction for Eastern harems."

"You trifle with us, Lord Redfern," Lady Gray returned archly. "There must be some basis to these scandalous tales about you."

Nicholas stiffened, not quite hiding his annoyance. "I am a man of business, nothing more. My ledgers are at your disposal if you require proof of how dull my journey really was."

Helen bit her lip, memory sluggishly stirring. There had to be more than mere business in his dealings with Lord Bedford. Nicholas's lie was so expertly done it robbed her of breath. Yet she hung on his words, wondering if he would let slip a clue as to what kept him from her side for so many years.

"You don't worry, putting your money with those rebels?" Layton asked.

"Rebels?" Nicholas speared a slice of duck. "I don't understand your meaning."

Helen noticed she had been ignoring her food and

pushed a bit of meat around her plate to look like she was eating. The fowl was very good, flavored with port and raisins, but she had no appetite.

"The Americans," Layton responded.

Nicholas shrugged. "I thought perhaps you meant the Irish."

The Marchioness of Avonsea put down her fork as though the duck had suddenly turned cold. She was an elderly woman dressed in too many ruffles and a ring set with an enormous diamond. "The Irish wars are not suitable dinner conversation."

Nicholas leaned forward a little, accommodating the marchioness's faulty hearing. "You're quite right, my lady. We should choose a different topic for the dinner table. Rebellions and business deals are hardly conducive to good digestion."

"Hear, hear," put in Fairmeadow, his tone one of forced cheerfulness.

"And I assure you once more my journeys are all in pursuit of cotton and tobacco."

The marchioness aimed for a pea with her fork, but sent it scooting across her plate. "It is not suitable for a peer to dabble in trade. It is a dirty business. Not the thing at all for a gentleman. Your father should have brought up his sons with more sense than that."

Helen turned to Nicholas, who was still frozen, the knife-edged quiet of a cat waiting to pounce. His eyes fixed on the marchioness, he was clearly annoyed but keeping himself in check.

"Will you not defend yourself?" she asked in a biting undertone. She heard the slur in her words. Did she sound as addled as her brother did of late?

It occurred to Helen that her brother had not even

greeted his school friend. Well, Nicholas was no longer one of their circle, especially not since they had the patronage of the Earl of Waring. A feeling of confidence settled on her, as if she could hear Waring's voice encouraging the thought.

Nicholas turned to answer her. "How should I defend myself? Deny that I have any mercantile interests? Storm from the room? Call the marchioness out for a duel?" His face was completely bland, as if she had asked about the weather.

She shrugged. "I don't know what to think, and you do nothing to help your cause. It was folly for you to come here."

She reached for her wine, but drew her hand back. She had only taken a swallow so far, but it seemed to be more than she could tolerate. The conversation in the room was lively, and she had to lean close to him to be heard without shouting.

"Perhaps you are right. Yet I may still win these gossips over with my wit and bounteous charm." His tone was ironic, his eyes as unreadable as a frozen lake.

She knew the complex depths beneath that layer of ice. The urge to explore them had undone her more than once. She felt her own detachment eroding.

"Truly, is it just gossip? What do you do abroad, Nicholas? Do you sell girls to slavers?" Their faces were close together, so close she could feel his breath on her cheek. Helen felt a fine tremor in her limbs, the memory of long-ago heat.

"I really, truly, have investments there," he answered. His lower lip curled into a slight smile, as if he had a secret he would not share.

At least, she thought she saw a smile. Perhaps it was

actually an unhappy expression—her eyes were dazzled by the candles and wanted to drift closed. She couldn't see clearly anymore. "Is trade your only concern? There must have been more that kept you away from me than cargos and percentages."

Nicholas's expression became completely bland, but then looked considering. "Yes, there was. My business is varied."

Helen felt the words like a blow. Of course, he had been keeping secrets. "Are you ever going to share your secrets?"

He looked as if he would answer, but then his gaze slid away. "No."

"Why not?"

He looked calm again, the mask back in place. "Many of my business dealings are sensitive. There are people I might harm by sharing their confidences."

Helen struggled, her hazy mind groping to gather the full meaning of his words. The one thing she was sure of was that she was angry. "Do you know what I think you do?"

He smiled faintly. "What is that?"

I feel as if I am in my cups, Helen thought groggily.

"You're a thief." She picked up a sweetmeat and considered it, then bit down daintily. "I know the rumor has circulated for years. I always dis—er—disbelieved it because I loved you."

I'm rambling, she thought with shame, but could not control her words or her tongue.

"I—I wanted you to be filled with honor and fine sentiments. Now that I realize how little you cared for me, I don't need to make excuses for you any longer. I believe you're a criminal."

Nicholas stared, his dark eyes huge with hurt. The expression sent blazing triumph into her veins, heady as brandy. Even through her leaden fatigue, she had got him as surely as a champion fighter knocks down his opponent.

Nicholas took in a breath and let it out. It was not a sigh, but rather as though he was bracing against pain. Helen's sense of triumph went flat.

"Well." He looked around the room. All the heads at the table were bent to other conversations. "I do so enjoy our friendly exchanges."

Helen said nothing, but ate another sweetmeat. The fog was claiming her brain again, making her limbs heavy, dead weight.

"You really take me for a thief or a confidence man."

"Yes, I do." Her triumph and regret were both fading, leaving behind a vague confusion.

He pushed back his chair. "If that is what you choose to believe, I cannot prevent it. Do as you will."

With that, he left the table and walked out of the room without a word.

"What a rude young man," said the marchioness. "Young people have no manners."

Helen ate another sweet, the excess of honey and nut-meats making her feel queasy. She realized she couldn't remember what she and Nicholas had been talking about.

"You should save some room," advised Layton. "I understand there are more courses to come."

"I have a strong constitution," Helen said dully. "I somehow manage to swallow whatever is set before me."

Chapter 12

Helen had never spoken to Redfern that way before, and he was stunned.

It was the morning after he had arrived at Arden Hall. Alone in the library, Redfern was able to think in peace. He looked out of the tall, arched windows, his hands folded behind his back. On the sunlit lawn below, Helen was walking with Waring, her hand on his arm. The sight made Redfern seethe.

She had called him a criminal. By some pernicious alchemy, her coolness had turned to outright hostility.

Redfern turned his back on the window, pacing across the room. *I will not accept this!*

Below the sharp edge of anger, he ached. Helen's words had knifed him to the quick. So much had changed between them.

It did not seem so long ago that they had spun out long summer afternoons in the Barretts' music room, lost in a fantasy of love and privilege. Their future had been golden, their happiness assured.

One time in particular, they had perched side by side on the stool before the harpsichord, not quite touching, ever so correct, until she had leaned across him to turn the page of the score.

There had been much seduction in young Helen's demure manners. He remembered the fabric of the dress she wore sounded like the rustling of wings when she moved. The scent of flowering herbs floated, flesh-warm, from the embroidered secrets of her toilette. Coy, she pressed her breast against his arm as she reached for the page, and he never knew for certain if she had meant to invite what followed.

At that moment, a thrush had trilled outside, wild with pure, God-given joy. The sound had rung in his body like the clarion call of battle. He had pulled Helen into his arms before he knew his own intentions, and he had kissed her for the first time. Warm and soft, she filled and honed his need all at once.

The harpsichord had made a discordant protest when his elbow hit the keys.

Her lips had made him think of a forest spring, cool, untouched, and ripe with new life. Then and there, he had decided she would be his. It had been that simple, as if they had needed only to turn that page to decide their fates.

Lost in recollection, Redfern hung his head. He was not naturally sentimental, but a few memories were sacred. That moment was one of them. The possibility of losing her brought it back, sharp and bittersweet.

Redfern stopped pacing and returned to his position by the window. A messenger boy ran across the lawn, scattering the peacocks. He handed Waring a letter, then scampered away, sending the birds into ungainly dishevelment once more. From what Redfern could tell at a distance, Helen seemed to notice little of what went on around her.

What in hell's name has Waring done to her? Redfern's anger rose like a fell tide. He would bring the earl down, down into a pit even the Master's fabled Hellfire League could not conjure!

Think! Where would he begin to unravel Waring's web? He turned away, roaming the room again.

He recalled the Master's warning about the jewels. It was an obvious place to start, though he was not convinced the necklace was the cause of Helen's malaise. Nevertheless, he could not afford to discount any possible cures.

Helen had been wearing the necklace the night before, but the dinner table was no place to risk being caught thieving a small fortune in sapphires. Today might present better opportunities.

Redfern stopped pacing to examine a display of shadow boxes on the library wall. The collection was grotesque enough to break through his fevered concentration. Ornate, gold-painted frames surrounded groupings of mounted beetles, small lizards, and spiders. Some of the specimens Redfern recognized from his travels overseas, including caterpillars that shot toxins through their poisoned spines. The only commonality he could detect was that the creatures were all poisonous.

In the center of a clutch of flying things was a small, black moth.

Interesting, thought Redfern. The presence of the moth was too slight to qualify as a clue, but it was more than a coincidence.

A moth and a necklace, he thought dryly. Not much

evidence of a sorcerous conspiracy, but that was all he had to work with.

They would have to do.

As Helen and Waring rounded a corner in the path, the peacocks came into view. A half dozen rested on the grass, their tails dragging behind them like Indian shawls. One had his plumage up, the sweep of brilliant color in ostentatious display.

"Good heavens," Waring said. "I thought Lord Fairmeadow was in the drawing room."

Helen gave a dutiful chuckle at the quip. A houseboy came pelting across the lawn, pink-cheeked with exertion.

"Please, my lord," he said, panting out the words as he skidded to a stop, "a gentleman brought this letter for you and said to deliver it without delay." He held up a sealed letter, the paper slightly crumpled from its exuberant method of delivery.

Waring took the missive, briefly examining the address. "Thank you, Perkins," he said without looking at the servant.

The earl put the unopened letter in his coat, a smile of satisfaction on his lips.

"What is it, my lord?" Helen asked.

"Nothing. An invitation, most likely." Waring tilted his face up to the sun. "What do you know of genealogy?"

"A little."

"Of your own, I mean."

"Still less. We are not from an old and worthy bloodline like you are, my lord."

"I beg to differ." Waring swung his walking stick, decapitating an innocent carnation. "I uncovered an interesting detail in one of my books. Did you know that in 1732, the Earl of Leyland produced a son by Emma Barrett, the daughter of the blacksmith at Howe? She named the boy Peter."

Helen furrowed her brow. "Peter Barrett, son of the village blacksmith in Howe?"

"The same. He grew up to be your grandfather, and he was the earl's illegitimate son."

This was new information to Helen. "No wonder the Earl of Leyland paid to have him educated. I heard that part from my father."

"Educated and put to work in a prosperous trading company. He made quite a successful career there."

And so began the Barretts' climb up the social ranks, thought Helen.

The earl looked pleased. "Which makes you and James distant cousins to me."

"And Thomas Hanson," she said without thinking.

He looked less pleased. "Yes."

They walked a few more paces. "You may wonder why I have been enquiring into your forefathers," he said.

Helen's fogged mind had not, but she nodded nonetheless. It was best to appear attentive.

Waring twirled his cane. "Let us just say for now that you may have inherited some family qualities that would make you a desirable match in some circles."

What did that mean? Inwardly, Helen grimaced. It was bad enough to be hunted for her money. She had assumed, as the daughter of a commoner, to be exempt from the burden of pedigrees and blood alliances as well.

Her reply was neutral. "The only fortunate quality my family has is a gift for commerce."

The earl smiled slowly. "The power to attract money,

my love, is nothing to disdain. That is one piece of magic I lack, and that the Warings could definitely use."

Barrett had wandered into the library, inadvertently joining Redfern.

"I do not know what you intend by coming here," James grumbled, cross as a sleepy bear. "You were certainly not invited."

Barrett slouched in his armchair, the sunlight streaming into Waring's library only accentuating his pallor.

"I was invited by Fairmeadow."

There was a long pause. Barrett seemed to be drifting, blank, like someone who had taken opium.

"I don't like you being around Helen," Barrett finally said, the words sounding flat and automatic, like something rehearsed.

"So you have informed me." Redfern looked at the man's damp, pasty complexion. Was this the effect of magic or was Barrett being poisoned?

"Then stay far away from my sister."

"Do not concern your empty heads with me." Helen stepped into the room, Waring on her heels. "You may scrap amongst yourselves, and I shall pay no attention whatsoever."

Barrett looked up and Redfern turned around, both men flustered by her sudden appearance. With a nervous gesture, she reached up to finger her sapphire necklace.

Redfern watched her as she came toward them. He could see her much more clearly than he had in the semi-darkness of last night's dinner. Like her brother, she looked unwell, with circles of fatigue under her eyes. She spoke with the careful enunciation of a drunk.

Redfern was appalled. *I will attempt anything if it will help her. Stealing a necklace will be a mere nothing.*

Redfern's gaze devoured Helen, every instinct drawing him across the floor toward her tall, lithe form. The need to hold her burned along the length of his body.

"It would only make sense for my former fiancé to absent himself if he disturbed my peace of mind. Let me assure you, my peace of mind is absolutely intact." With a bland smile, she slowly crossed the room to the bookcases that filled two walls from floor to ceiling.

She put her back to him, showing the graceful arc of her neck and shoulders. He came up beside her, resting one hand on the edge of the bookshelf to still the urge to stroke her skin. Rubbed raw by all the sadness and anger between them, he struggled to preserve some scrap of propriety, to keep from burying his face in her hair and begging forgiveness for ever having left her side.

Redfern's teeth clenched until his jaw ached. He had to save her before he could do anything else. His hand lifted to unhook the clasp holding the necklace of sapphires in place; then he lowered it again as she moved to slide a volume from the shelf.

He glanced over his shoulder. From his place by the door, Waring was watching him, eyes intent.

Damnation. It was going to be difficult to get Helen alone and get the necklace off her in the close confines of a country house party.

Waring took Redfern's look as his cue to join the conversation. "Good morning. Did you sleep well?"

"Very well, thank you," Redfern said with civility, but lied. He had been put above the kitchens. From the sounds and smells, he was able to anticipate breakfast for hours before the event.

"I am happy to hear it," Waring replied with reptilian charm. "Barrett, would you be so good as to see if Lord Stephen has arisen?" said Waring. "I was hoping for a conversation with the three of us this morning. A few pieces of business from town, I'm afraid."

Redfern watched with grim fascination as Barrett rose and left the room. The man moved like an animated corpse, slack-limbed and lumbering. He had been a fine athlete in his day.

"After that, may I enjoy the privilege of showing you both around the estate?" the earl asked, his eyes crinkling in a practiced smile.

"Of course," Helen said with neither pleasure nor reluctance. She might as well have been made of springs and wires.

Redfern ground his teeth. The Master would not understand if he simply shot the earl, grabbed Helen, and ran. Still, he would hold that plan in reserve. He was not going to let another night pass without freeing Helen from Waring's clutches.

The only way through the morass was forward. Unfortunately, as he had earlier observed, one of his two clues was merely an insect under glass.

Redfern adopted his most agreeable tone. Not to be too obvious, he pointed to a collection of spiders rather than directly at the moth. "As an aperitif for this afternoon's tour, Waring, can you tell us about these? I have an abiding interest in natural history."

Waring nodded, all graciousness. "With pleasure. I cannot claim to have collected these myself, but I have contributed to several scientific expeditions."

Helen looked on with dull obedience. "I like the

butterfly," she said. "The color is ugly, but at least its form is pleasant to look at."

"It is nothing but a moth," Waring said with a dismissive air. "It is only poisonous if eaten. Small amounts ground into wine are said to produce horrific hallucinations. Some tribesmen use the poison in ceremonies, believing the resulting trance is actually a journey to the spirit world."

"I believe I have seen this creature," Redfern said carelessly, but with an eye to Waring's reaction.

Waring's features remained still. "This moth flourishes only in Africa, Lord Redfern."

"Then it must be some other creature that resembles it that I saw nearby."

"I would be careful with your entomological researches, Viscount," said Waring. "Choose carefully where you hunt your specimens. There are occasionally snakes in the grass, and one must be careful not to tread on them."

"Then I shall wear very heavy boots, my lord," returned Redfern with a diplomatic smile.

As Waring had promised, the day's itinerary for the guests of Arden Hall was a tour of the estate. This included a scenic hilltop lunch alfresco. If the weather was fine, they would return via the ruins of the Abbey of St. Agnes, a gothic splendor suitable for sketching. It was an ideal plan, and discussion soon fell to who would ride with whom in what vehicle.

Redfern concurred that the trip sounded splendid, inwardly adding it fit his schemes to perfection. Pleading indigestion, he retired to his room until the others left. With luck, he would be left in peace for most of the day.

When the convoy of horses and vehicles had left to view the estate, Redfern began a tour of his own. As a boy, he had mastered the art of slipping past servants unobserved, and he called on those skills now. Arden Hall was newly built, without the additions and excrescences that sprung up around old homes. It was easy to find his way through the wide, well-lit hallways that ran with mathematical precision around the central staircases. In no time, he found Waring's private rooms.

The earl had a dressing room, a bedchamber, and a small study laid out much like Redfern's own London abode. The bedchamber and dressing room revealed little but Waring's taste in tailors. The study promised more. A desk and short cabinet sat against the far wall, the scatter of papers and writing implements on the blotter showing this was where Waring worked. Listening for the footfall of chambermaid or valet, Redfern crept across the carpet. He tried the drawers of the desk, the doors of the cabinet. Locked. A tingle of excitement ran through Redfern's fingers. Secrets easy to plunder were no secrets at all. Here was a challenge.

When he was eight, one of the young footmen had showed him how to pick locks—one of those childhood foibles that unexpectedly serve in later life. Redfern knelt on the floor to peer closely at the brass workings on the desk and nearly laughed out loud. It was nothing but a simple tongue-and-groove mechanism, the first kind he had learned to open. Drawing a flat leather case from his waistcoat, he listened once more for movement outside the door. There was nothing, just the sound of hedge clippers from the garden beyond the window. He slid a tool into the lock and had the drawer open almost at once.

The typical desk jumble emerged as Redfern slid the

drawer toward himself. A stack of papers too high for the drawer was jammed under the upper lip of the opening. Sliding a paper knife over the top letter, he freed the wad of correspondence and pulled the stack into his lap. With the speed of long practice, he scanned the pages. On top were bills, including those from vintners, butchers, and a chandler. It appeared the current house party was costing the earl a pretty penny. There were a number of gaming slips—Fairmeadow had mentioned that Waring gambled. Beneath those were letters of recent date, probably awaiting a reply. There was nothing of note.

Redfern poked in the drawer, finding pencil stubs, a rubber ball, and a chipped lead soldier Waring was definitely too old to play with. He was about to stuff the letters back in place when his fingers met something soft. He closed his hand on what felt like silk and drew out the object. It was a woman's scarf, painted in hues of cerise and emerald and fringed in black. Redolent with the scent of frangipani, it draped, warm and soft, against his skin—as sensuous as an inanimate object could be. Redfern frowned, searching along the edge of the scarf until he found the monogram. Eventually, it emerged from the folds of silk, picked out in gold thread: L.G. Laura Gianotta, Waring's mistress. It was a keepsake, a token, a reminder of their passion.

Disgusted, Redfern replaced the scarf and letters and pushed the drawer closed. He would not have cared, except for Helen. A wealthy man would often have a mistress and a wife, but he could not imagine wanting anyone besides Helen—she was worth a thousand sirens of the demimonde.

Redfern turned his attention to the cabinet beside the desk, studying the lock on the doors. This one would take more time. He selected a tool from his leather case and set to work.

The Master had said Waring wanted Helen for more than her personal attractions. At the thought of her soft beauty, Redfern pressed his lips together, struggling to keep his imagination on the task at hand. What could be more enticing than Helen herself?

The doors pushed forward as the lock released, the weight of the cabinet contents forcing them open. Redfern caught the papers with one hand, stopping an avalanche. He steadied the stack and removed the top inch of documents, his stomach sinking at the amount of information to sort through.

Expecting a wilderness of political briefs and business correspondence, Redfern was surprised to find the documents all related to the building of Arden Hall some fifty years before. Much of it was written by Waring's father and grandfather, the architect, the company of stonemasons, the landscape experts who had installed the fountain and designed the magnificent drive that wound from the road to the house. Their ideas were ambitious, the execution labor-intensive. And expensive. The plans had everything, including tunnels that connected the cellars of the house and several of the outbuildings. *What would they need those for?* wondered Redfern.

The most recent documents showed Waring still made payments on the debt, and most of the principal expense was still outstanding. In short, Waring was broke. Arden Hall had ruined the family with the same profligacy as Redfern's brother had beggared the Savilles. If Waring had a gaming habit, that could only add to his woes.

No wonder he has turned his political career into a source of funding, thought Redfern. Both Redfern and

Waring, nobles without an honest trade, had done what they could to earn a living. Redfern hired out his sword, and Waring turned political highwayman. It was ironic that they became enemies—they had so much in common.

Including Helen, he thought.

The Master had wanted to know why Waring would court a woman with no title and merchant-class family connections. The answer was simple: Helen was a banker's daughter with a lavish dowry, large enough to pay off a sizeable portion of Waring's debts. It was a matter of economic survival.

Grimacing to himself, Redfern stuffed the papers back in the cabinet and gathered up his tools. His search had not revealed anything more about the Hellfire League, but he had answered the question of motive. The earl would do anything for a big enough purse—from summoning the devil to committing treason to marrying beneath his class.

Redfern rose from his crouched position, feeling the blood rush back to his toes. Somehow he had to make Helen understand Waring only wanted her for her money. Any other woman might reply that her dowry was a fair trade for the title of countess, but he knew Helen better than that.

After all, Redfern was the heir to an earldom. If Helen's heart could be won with a title alone, she would never have sent him away. She demanded more. She was proud.

And he had failed her utterly. It wouldn't happen again.

Redfern continued his search of the house. Neither Barrett's chamber nor Helen's revealed anything unusual.

Their dressing tables were innocent of any drugs that would explain their strange, debilitated state.

It never hurts to rule out the obvious, thought Redfern. He had found little to support the Master's theories about the Hellfire League. Still, Sir Alaric Fitzwilliam could hardly be characterized as a credulous fool. So, Redfern kept searching, just to be thorough.

There was a locked door in the back of a cold-storage room filled with bins of turnips and potatoes. The door was crusted with dirt and likely only to be noticed by curious children and spies. It had a large, enticing padlock.

Behind the door was a steep stairway with no handrail. Making sure he kept the lock in his coat pocket—he had no desire to get shut in—Redfern lit a candle and descended the stairs.

This had to be one of the tunnels he had seen on Waring's house plans. The brickwork looked new and sturdy. The tunnel was high enough that he could stand upright and wide enough that three men could stand abreast. It had the earthy smell of underground places, but he could still feel a draft that indicated good ventilation. He tried to remember where this particular tunnel ran. A few went to outbuildings and others joined the main branches into an elaborate network. The Warings seemed to have a dose of badger in their family tree.

Redfern walked for a few dozen paces, puzzling over the existence of the underground labyrinth. He stretched out his hand, extending the candle into the gloom ahead. A few yards away, the bricks on the floor gave way to paving stones. Every third stone was inlaid with a design of a darker color—the sign of the black moth.

Wary, Redfern drew one of his knives, holding it lightly in his right hand and taking the candle with his left. He followed the moths another dozen yards. The tunnel widened still more, opening into a huge, vaulted chamber. The vaults rested on nine hexagonal pillars faced with bloodred marble. Enormous lamps on long chains hung from the ceiling, elaborate dragons etched into the brass and silver housings. Each would have been worth a ransom. The floor was covered with a black-and-white mosaic of sinuous design that reminded Redfern of a nest of adders. The room was otherwise empty.

This was the lair of the Hellfire League. Redfern stifled a shout of triumph. He had smoked them out!

An underground society that is literally underground, he thought, his mind racing with newfound energy. If membership in the Hellfire League was based on an inherited birthright, then it made sense the Warings built for generations of League members to come. The fact that this was their property seemed to indicate the Warings ranked high in the sorcerous society. By definition, this meant the earl was a powerful foe.

Snake in the grass, indeed, thought Redfern. *More like a crocodile for size and pure malice.* His sense of triumph abating, the stillness of the room wore on his nerves. Somewhere water dripped, echoing eerily in the dark tunnels.

So the Hellfire League did exist. If the Master was right about that, was he also right about their intent to use dark magic? Now that he had seen the tunnels and seen the influence Waring had over the Barretts, it did not seem so far-fetched.

Though he did not move, the candle flame fluttered. There was movement of air where there was—nothing. Redfern clamped down hard on his imagination and looked behind him. The entrance to the tunnel by which he came was gone. Nothing but solid bricks. Redfern froze.

Air seemed to swirl around the chamber, a faint, confidential exhalation that smelled of the deep, cold earth and fallen leaves. He gripped his knife, the hair rising along his neck.

"What the devil?" he said aloud, the sound of his voice odd and echoing.

Something—the feeling of eyes on the back of his neck—made him spin around. He felt like prey, and that sensation made him angry.

A figure stood at the far side of the room, just close enough to the light to be seen. He wore a caped coat and in one hand held a coachman's whip.

The memory of Bedford's body falling from the funeral coach assaulted Redfern. "Who are you?" he demanded, getting his balance to throw the knife at any instant.

"Go," said the figure. "Get out of here while you can. If you stay too long, the house will not let you leave."

Redfern took a step back, too many questions arising at once. He glanced back at the tunnel. The entrance was where it should have been. Startled, he looked back at the coachman. There was a shadow, but no man.

Damnation! Hand slippery on the hilt of his knife, Redfern retreated backward toward the tunnel, never taking his eyes from the place where the figure had been.

Perhaps I have eaten of the black moth, he thought. *I am hallucinating.*

He hovered for a moment in the mouth of the tunnel, taking one last, grim look at the vaulted chamber. The darkness there seemed solid, far thicker than it had any right to be. Redfern swallowed, his mouth tasting coppery with fear.

The coachman's voice was Michael's, and my brother is five years dead.

Chapter 13

Redfern left Arden Hall for the long shadows of the late afternoon, glad to be outside and breathing air unfettered by bricks and tunnels. He ducked into the gardens, wanting to be alone with his shattered thoughts.

Michael!

He had argued with Michael mere hours before his brother had turned a gun to his head. Hot words were spoken on both sides, but Redfern remembered most his own recriminations. They were true: Michael had ruined himself and crushed the chances of his siblings. Still, a breath of compassion from Redfern might have stayed his brother's self-destruction. It was a failure for which Redfern would never forgive himself.

He had all but put the pistol in Michael's hand. If he deserved anything, he deserved his brother's wrath.

So, why would Michael want to keep him from harm? No, some devilry was playing with his mind, stirring up the silt of old guilt.

Driven by agitation, Redfern walked on, his long legs covering ground at a frantic pace. It was a long time before he noticed his surroundings.

The sun still clung to rims and edges of the sloping lawns, syrupy pools of gold running to deep blue-green where the trees shaded the grass. At the side of the garden, a maze was laid out beside a stand of plane trees. The cooling earth smelled good, faintly spicy with wild herbs and the scent of the fertile land itself—so different from the chill chambers deep beneath the hall.

He paused at the maze's entrance, wondering if he should pass around it. It would be too ironic, too literal if he got lost in its turnings, his inner confusion made manifest. He began to turn away when he saw movement. Looking around the corner of the boxwood hedge, he saw Fairmeadow sitting on a stone bench, feeding bread to one of the peacocks. The bird's brilliant turquoise feathers were an almost-perfect match to Fairmeadow's waistcoat. Despite himself, Redfern was amused.

"Come, join me," Fairmeadow said without turning his head.

Redfern wondered how he had been detected, and then saw a reflecting pond a few feet beyond the bench. The water was perfectly still, no wind reaching the sheltered world at the mouth of the maze. The peacock looked up as he approached, sidestepping a few feet before the lure of the bread drew him back.

"This bold lad reminds me of so many young bloods I meet at the clubs," Fairmeadow said with a bored drawl. "Except I think he has better conversation."

"And Nature pays his tailor's bills." Redfern sat on the other end of the bench. "A new coat for free every Season."

The little man turned his head. " 'Sdeath, you look as grim as Old Nick himself, or should I say the very devil. I should not confuse the issue, as I think Nicholas is your

Christian name. You take my meaning, I'm sure. You're grim, man, fierce as a pirate lord."

Redfern frowned, and, as if to illustrate Fairmeadow's point, the peacock sidled uneasily away.

"What troubles you?" Fairmeadow persisted, interest plain in his voice. He dusted crumbs off his hands, the bird having finished its meal.

While the inquiry was no doubt meant in kindness, Redfern hesitated to make Fairmeadow his confidante. All he needed was to become the *on dit* of London as the man who saw his brother's ghost. His reputation was dark enough as it was.

Redfern shook his head and chose to be vague. "Ask rather what is not going amiss. My answer will be briefer."

"I was sent here to support you. My time is your time." Fairmeadow flicked a crumb from his sleeve.

"I would not know where to begin." Redfern put his face in his hands, glad of the warm sun. He felt as if the shadows from beneath Arden Hall still clung to him like tar.

"What have you found?" asked Fairmeadow, his tone suddenly serious.

Redfern looked at him. All frivolity had left the man's demeanor. Still, Redfern hesitated before answering.

"You said you would be my guide to Waring's darkling realm. I need your guidance now. I have found the League's meeting place."

He told Fairmeadow about the tunnels and chamber beneath the hall. The little man listened, his gaze never wavering from Redfern's face, even when he described the coachman.

"The coach is a harbinger of death for members of the

Circle," said Fairmeadow. "You are not of the Circle and, even more unusual, the coachman seemed to be warning you off instead of predicting your end. This is a most peculiar sighting."

"The specter's voice sounded like that of my dead brother. Is there a reason it would mimic him?"

Fairmeadow raised carefully plucked eyebrows. "I do not know. Those passed beyond will sometimes warn the living out of unfulfilled obligation, or to warn others away from their fate. I think you would know better than I what that might have to do with your brother."

Redfern studied the grass at his feet, wondering again why Michael would return from the grave. It made so little sense, he wondered if he had imagined the encounter.

Fairmeadow raised a finger, reminding Redfern of an old mathematics tutor. "What is more pertinent is the coachman's warning about the house. Some members of the League are known to have mastered techniques that cloud the mind, either bending the will of others or altering their perception altogether. They can set traps to bewilder intruders."

"Do you think it is the earl who leads the League?"

"Yes. You have noticed the effect of Lord Waring's will upon the Barretts?"

Despite the warm sun, Redfern's skin grew clammy with apprehension. "I have, but hearing you confirm my suspicions renders them all the more horrific."

"I saw it this morning." Fairmeadow pursed his lips. "God in Heaven, you must get them away from Waring, especially Miss Barrett. You have some sway with the young lady, do you not?"

"I did once."

"Once? But no more?" Fairmeadow's voice held an arch note.

Redfern scowled at the ground.

The other man turned his palms upward, smiling significantly. "Ah, your affair of the heart has gone awry, then! Is this the secret to your constant brooding?"

Picking up a twig, Fairmeadow began cleaning under his nails. "The advice I was given in a similar case was simply to charge ahead with a warrior's cry on my lips and a healthy purse in my pocket. The rest is details. And frankly, with the Hellfire League ranged against you, there are no other options. It's the charge of the Forlorn Hope, or nothing."

Redfern disliked the comparison of his plight with a suicidal military maneuver. "I don't wish to discuss it."

Fairmeadow laughed, but his tone was merry rather than derisive. "I have yet to meet a man of the world who would. Amputate a limb, but don't ask me to describe how I feel. Oh, no, not that."

Redfern shrugged. "As you say, I choose not to confer on private matters."

Fairmeadow looked at him sadly. "Then I will say merely that love—in any of its forms—is too precious to squander on pride or hesitation. If there is any hope of happiness, damn the odds and grab it with both hands."

There was something poignant in the man's tone, as if he spoke of more than just Redfern's romantic turmoil. Narrowing his eyes, Redfern studied the man. "And if she no longer loves me?"

Fairmeadow threw away the twig and straightened the cuffs of his jacket. "If you continue to see nothing but complexities, I am not surprised she has abandoned you. A lady has only so much patience."

Redfern swore truculently. At once, the fop had struck the mark. Was his failure so plain to see? Struggling with his temper, Redfern gripped the edge of the bench.

Fairmeadow plucked a leaf from the ground and twirled it by its stem. "Ah. But take heart—you are in the business of defeating complexities, are you not? My brother-in-law would not have hired you if that were not the case."

Redfern blinked. What if he defeated the League and Sir Alaric set him free? It was a beginning, but that still did not guarantee him Helen's love. Circumstance was only part of the problem. The real problem was Redfern himself. He had neglected Helen long enough, given so little of himself, she believed the worst of him—magic or no magic. That was a humbling realization.

Anger and embarrassment made him flush hot. Redfern paced to the entrance of the maze, stung by sudden insight.

He had often worried that, if he could not extend a compassionate hand to his distraught brother, what sort of a husband could he hope to be? He had tried to force the doubts away, but the specter of his failure kept him abroad, safe from disappointing himself or his love. The sense of duty that drove him into the Master's service was real—he needed to save his family—but it was also convenient.

I am such an incredible fool. Even in a thousand lifetimes, his love for Helen would never fade. It had survived all his misgivings. The tragedy was that now, when he finally understood his error in leaving her, she was slipping away.

"Your silence speaks of mountainous doubts," observed Fairmeadow with a sad little shake of his head. "It appears your mission is doomed before it begins."

"Bollocks." Redfern turned on his heel and strode toward the house. "As you say, I'm accustomed to defeating long odds."

He heard Fairmeadow laugh and call after him. "You should inscribe that on your calling card!"

Redfern waved his hand, feeling a sudden wash of energy, as if his inner tide had turned. Regardless of the Hellfire League, the Master, the Saville family honor, and his own deplorable past performance, Redfern had to win Helen back, and he had to do it before she succumbed to Waring's sorcerous blandishments.

He had to take that blasted necklace. Immediately.

As Redfern reentered Arden Hall, the light was fading to a violet dusk. Footmen were lighting candles as he bounded up the stairs, taking the steps two at a time. As he reached the doorway, wondering where he might find Helen, the bell rang for dinner.

He skidded to a stop before her door, but it was closed and locked, a sure sign Helen's maid was dressing her mistress.

Damnation! Hours of regulated protocol stretched before him, a desert of etiquette-laden boredom and delay.

For Redfern, the food that night was a veritable carpenter's shop: The bread was sawdust, the sauce varnish, and the choice cuts of meat had no more savor than a chamois. The only point of importance was the corner of the table where Helen sat at Waring's side. As informality took over the country gathering, she had moved up the table to sit beside him. The positioning was significant, a prelude to marriage negotiations.

Redfern sizzled with ill humor. Whatever his claims to unearthly power, Waring was a fortune hunter, and Helen nothing more to him than prized bounty. Every glance that passed between them, every confidence Waring bent to whisper in her ear taunted Redfern. He longed to lunge across the table, fork poised for murder.

As dessert was placed on the table, the earl insisted on serving Helen himself, spooning wiggling mounds of zabaglione onto the delicate spears of sponge cake arranged on her plate.

Redfern could hear the obscene plop of the whipped cream from where he sat across the table. Waring scooped up some of Helen's dessert on his own spoon, slipping it between his lips with a look of devastated delight. Inwardly, Redfern gagged. When the bowl of dessert came his way, he waved it past in disgust.

He began counting the times Waring found an opportunity to brush the lace of his cuffs across Helen's hand, and how many remarks were for her ears alone. He seemed to bend over her as often as possible, his face mere inches from hers. Helen smiled back brilliantly, once putting her hand on Waring's as he fed her a tidbit from his own fork. Beneath the table, Redfern mashed his napkin to a crumpled rag.

By the time dinner finally limped to a conclusion, he had a plan. If he was going to mend their love, it had to be done with the intuition of a master musician and all the cunning of a spy.

He knew Helen's habits of old—he had stayed in the Barretts' house often enough—and prayed the influence of the necklace would not interfere with her nighttime routine. He took up his position in the shadows of the library. An old tufted leather chair was half-hidden by the corner of a bookcase, the darkest angle in a room without fire or candles. As the clock struck eleven, the library door swung open.

Helen walked to the center of the room, her slippered feet silent on the Aubusson carpet. She wore a gown of pale green, the bodice smocked into a lattice of fine gold braid. The bright moon shone through the windows, glancing off the glass doors of the bookcases. For a moment, Helen was still, her arms and hair luminous in the indirect glow.

"Bother," she said under her breath. "I should have brought a candle."

Redfern rose, the rustle of his clothes loud in the darkness. She caught her breath, turning toward him.

She was so beautiful, he lost all command of thought.

"What are you doing here?" she demanded.

"Sitting. It is a most relaxing occupation."

"Well, I won't keep you from your repose." She looked at the book in her hand, the same one she had taken from the library that morning. "I just came to return this."

She turned to the shelf, her back to him. With all the dexterity of a London pickpocket, Redfern unhooked the clasp of the necklace, whisking it from around her throat before she felt a thing. Years in the Master's service had taught him a thing or two.

Redfern clasped his hands behind his back, the sapphires safely in his pocket. "But it is nearly impossible to see. How can you know where to put it?"

She turned, a furrow in her brow. She rubbed her forehead pensively. "I can't. I shall leave it on the table."

"Did you not enjoy the story?" He tried to take it from her, but her fingers held tight to the calfskin binding.

"I should like a different book. I picked it up in error."

Her fingers slipped and Redfern wrested it away. He thought he caught a flash of annoyance. *Good,* he thought. *If she is thoroughly angry, maybe this malaise she is in will crumble, and I shall see the old Helen.*

She flinched as he opened the cover and tilted the page to catch the moonlight. He saw at once the work explained in detail the pursuit of anguish. A manual of torture? Flipping through the pages, he saw engravings of cunning machines. He stopped at a particularly graphic picture involving a spider's nest of straps and chains.

"I should prefer something else for my bedtime reading," Helen said, discomfort shading the words. "Put it away. I think that image shall give me nightmares."

"Oh, I don't know." Redfern rotated the book so the picture was upside down. "He looks rather more comfortable this way, more like a baby in leading strings."

"Nicholas!" Helen snapped, her tone one of exasperation. "You turn the most terrible things into a jest."

"I would pull their teeth." Redfern snapped the book shut and set it aside. His stomach was icy with nerves, hoping and dreading what Helen would do next. She did not seem to notice the necklace was gone, but her speech and manner were already more clear and lively.

"Please, find me something cheerful to drive the thought of that thing from my mind." Her eyes caught the gleam of the pale light. "Perhaps some poetry."

The moment had unfolded beyond Redfern's fondest hopes. The quiet of the room was perfection. Redfern rested his hand on Helen's arm, turning her to the shelf.

Come live with me, and be my love,
And we will some new pleasures prove

Of golden sands, and crystal brooks,
With silken lines and silver hooks.

He had recited John Donne's lines to her a dozen times in the days of their courtship, spooling out the words to catch her in their net, luring her close with their music.

There will the river whisp'ring run
Warm'd by thy eyes, more than the sun . . .

"Stop," Helen protested, putting her fingers over his lips. "You know better than to give voice to those verses."

Her fingers smelled of the almond paste women used to soften their hands. He folded his hand around hers and kissed her palm, drawing her into the circle of his arms. "Helen," he coaxed, every soft feeling vibrating in those syllables.

"No more!" she breathed. "It is not fair to lie and smile and say you are mine forever when you will push me aside at the next opportunity to carry out your dark business!"

He could feel her spirit returning. The spell of the necklace was broken. If the first thing she felt was wrath at his shortcomings, so be it. Still . . .

"That is unfair. I am here, am I not?"

"Do you want fairness?" She pushed away from his arms. "Paint this picture in your mind, Nicholas. Remember the day you first left for the Americas. We were barely engaged, and I held you in the highest regard. I worshipped you. You were the tall, strong, handsome stranger who strode through my girlish fantasies since my brother first brought you home from school. You were the prince in my fairy stories, the dashing highwayman, and the pirate lord bundled up into one man. And you had really come in the flesh. You had asked me to be your bride. I grew faint at the mention of your name."

Redfern felt the blood draining from his face. At once, he was astonished, nostalgic, and staggered with remorse. He reached out, his hand just grazing the sleeve of her dress. He could feel her heat through the fabric, palpable even to the lightest brush of his fingers' ends.

With a flash in her eyes, Helen swatted his hand aside. "And then one day you walked in and said you were going. Just like that!" She clapped her hands together under his nose, making him jerk. "A blast of lightning for poor Helen. You kissed my brow and were gone in a flurry of vague promises. Yes, you would be back. No, you did not know when. You would write when you could. La, la, la, la—so you went on like a monotonous song. Never once would you look me in the eyes. You think I cannot tell a liar? You lied then, Lord Redfern, about where you were going and what you would do there. And then I lied furiously to myself for five more years to hide your betrayal from my heart!"

She glared. "That did *not* make me happy."

For a long moment, Redfern's mouth seemed filled with ashes. Dry, mute, speechless.

"I'm sorry," he said at last, his voice barely a croak. He might have defended himself, but the moment had gone beyond blame. Helen's will was free and she was simply giving him her truth.

He deserved it. Redfern closed his eyes, shutting out her stormy face. He wobbled on the brink of a precipice of a decision, summoning up the courage to fall. "Helen, if I take one step further, I must trust you with the truth, or at least as much of it as is safe for you to know."

Opening his eyes, he looked at the soft oval of her visage. Her gray eyes were smoky pools in the half light.

"Trust me," she said in a whisper.

"When Michael died, I thought the only way to save my family's good name was to hire out my sword. He left an incredible mess in his wake. The family was ruined."

"You could have married me. I have a large dowry." Her voice was cool, pain packed with ice.

"If only it had been so simple. Michael left problems money alone would not fix. I needed political and social influence that would shut mouths and hide scandal. If you had married me then, you would have wed a ruined man. I had to spare you that, and I had to protect the family name."

"You worry about your reputation, and yet you carry on as you do, giving rise to rumors that you are a thief or a slaver?"

"That is gossip no one truly believes. That is still better than the truth."

"Which is?"

Redfern swallowed hard. "That Michael ruined us in a welter of debt and dishonor and then blew out his own brains." There, he had said it. He felt his blood growing cold with a mixture of relief and apprehension.

She did not reply for a long moment. Redfern could feel his pulse, pounding light and fast. Her glance was quick, full of her old fire. "Oh, Nicholas, I'm sorry. I knew something had gone terribly wrong, something had changed for you."

"Someday, if you want me to, I will tell you the whole of it. It is not a pretty story."

"I begin to see," she said, hesitating before she looked him in the face. "Are you still, as you say, hired out?"

"Yes."

"That is where you are getting your money?"

"Yes, but I have made legitimate investments. I have recouped most of the fortune Michael squandered."

"Is what you do honest?" She ducked her head, the movement making her earrings glitter in the elusive light.

"It is for the Crown." He lowered his voice until it was barely audible.

"I see," she said. "So I cannot complain that you sacrificed me to save your family, because the method you chose was patriotic."

"You can complain, and all I can do is bow my head and take my medicine. Because I was able to help others does not mean I did not hurt you. I will regret that until I die."

Tears slid from her eyes onto her cheeks. "A few words might have saved me so much grief!"

"Silence is the only thing that guarantees our lives. I set a high value on your life."

"You might have trusted me!"

Redfern grasped her shoulders, holding her at arm's length. "I trust you, but I do not trust others. I should not be telling you any of this, even now. This is truth that kills. Lord Bedford has already paid the price."

Helen began to tremble. "Was he one of you?"

"Yes, and he died before I could speak with him. I don't know what he meant to tell me."

"The note . . ."

"The note might have been his undoing. If someone saw him write it, he was betrayed."

"Nicholas!" Helen moved close, her body warm against his. He held her, folded her in his arms as he had longed to do so many times when he could not—in the

Indies, in the Americas, in Waring's prison of a drawing room. Drinking in the scent of her hair, he prayed he had not made a losing gamble with their lives. Yet, at least now she understood why he had left. If he brought her into his confidence, maybe he could mend the rift between them.

"I will keep your secret," she said, her voice muffled against his shirtfront. "I will not forgive you for the rest."

"Then you will leave me in purgatory."

"And why not?"

Redfern heard a trace of amusement in her voice, a softening that lifted his heart. He wondered what was coming next. "Pray, why do you refuse to take me back into your good graces?"

She lifted her head. Her face looked worn, and he saw what his revelation had cost her feelings. Now she shared his burden, and he blamed himself for the sorrowful look in her eyes—and she only knew one small filament in the elaborate tangle of plots, lies, and death.

Helen smiled, a tentative, teasing gesture. "Take you back? Absolutely not. After the trials and tribulations I have endured at the hands of you viscounts and earls, I think I would rather marry the fellow who keeps the earl's grouse."

Redfern felt the first warm breeze of a thaw in his soul. "The gamekeeper?"

"Yes," she answered, straightening. She seemed to be recovering a little, finding her poise. "He isn't genteel, but his family has been on the estate every bit as long."

"A strapping and energetic lad, content with a kind word and a full tankard?"

Helen frowned. "There is something to be said for a serene nature."

Redfern lifted his eyebrows. "Perhaps you should marry one of the grouse. They seem happy enough."

Helen shook her head. "Things get a bit dodgy for them in the fall. All those bloodthirsty gentlemen with guns."

"Sounds like my life. Always someone after my tail feathers."

She ran one finger down his nose, a gesture he remembered from long ago. "I adore your tail feathers," she said. "They are so entertaining to tweak."

"How very forward of you." He found himself almost giddy. He couldn't help himself. They were talking, teasing each other as they had during the height of their love.

"It may not always seem like it, but I know what I want. Perhaps a bird of parts and fortune shall be the answer to my prayers."

"Then I wish you joy. I want you to be happy."

To his complete surprise, Helen took his mouth with hers, a sweet, soft pressure that salved his soul like balm. That kiss was only the first, and she grew demanding, tasting, pulling, drinking him in. Redfern felt nothing but delight. He met her lips and returned each kiss with interest.

Why hadn't he simply told her the truth long ago? The flood of reasons washed through his mind. They had all seemed important at the time, and might yet again, but not now. Nothing except Helen, so long absent from his arms, was of any consequence right then.

"Does the fact you're holding me indicate a willingness to at least toy with the concept of forgiveness?" he asked, easing an elaborate ivory comb from her hair. He dropped it to the carpet and set to work on the myriad hairpins securing her coiffure.

She turned her face away and the motion released her long coil of hair. It fell like a living thing, springing over his hands and falling in a warm curtain of gold. Redfern buried his hands in it, cupping the delicate curve of her neck, turning her head so she looked at him once more.

"I don't know," she answered simply. "At least we understand one another a little. We can talk now. We can touch each other. It's a beginning."

Redfern closed his eyes against a wash of panic. It was clear he had more work to do, and he had already played his trump card—he had told her his secrets. There was only one weapon left in his arsenal.

He dropped his mouth to the curve of her neck, working the satin skin with feather-soft kisses. As he felt the fragile arc of her collarbone beneath his lips, a fine heat sprang to life in his stomach and groin. Helen arched against him, her breath coming swift and light. Her hands slid up his back, nails pressing through the wool of his coat.

"I had almost forgotten you had this talent," she gasped in his ear.

"Mea culpa. I will rectify that at once."

His lips touched the tender curve of her breasts where they rose above the edge of her dress. They trembled with her intake of breath as she gasped at his kisses. As he straightened, his tongue lingered along the column of her throat, tasting the salt and sweetness of her skin. The need to claim her was a fine, dizzying ache.

At the shoulders of her gown, he found the tiny buttons that fastened the gold-laced bodice. Helen made a noise, part desire and part shock.

"No!" She put her hands over his. "Please, no. We are nowhere near that."

Slowly, Redfern dropped his hands, blood singing in his ears. It took all his will to discipline himself. "I apologize."

Helen lowered her eyes. "And so you should. We have both changed, and we can't go back to where we were when I agreed to be your wife. For one thing, there is a great deal of difference between a girl of eighteen years and a woman of twenty-three. I am more cautious."

Redfern looked away, unslaked desire souring to frustration. "Again, I am sorry. I overstepped . . ."

"The fault is mine," Helen interrupted. "I act before I think of the consequences."

"Even if you are a cautious twenty-three," Redfern said dryly.

"Sometimes because of it. I may be cautious, but I am also growing impatient."

"With what?"

Helen lifted her hand and dropped it in a gesture of helplessness. "Time. Constraints. People. Inaction. I am impatient with my brother. I treasure him and wish him every success, but I see him forgetting to love because he is so eager to win the approbation of cynical men. For reasons I have made abundantly clear, I am impatient with you to the point where I have resorted to banishing you."

"Your brother needs those men to succeed in his political career," Redfern offered, ignoring his own part in her litany.

"What for? What can James really need that he does not already have? He has wealth, a beautiful wife, and a healthy son, with another child soon to follow."

"The earl can secure his future."

"The earl is despicable."

The words startled Redfern. "Indeed?" Relief and pleasure swirled through him like brandy.

Helen froze, blinking, confused. "I said that, did I not?" She looked around her, as if suddenly realizing she was in Waring's house.

She went on, searching for her words. "These last weeks have been a whirl, and I confess I've been acting a bit of a fool. I've let the earl court me. You see, I have tried to like him for my brother's sake."

Her sentences picked up momentum. "I will grant he has his redeeming points but, on the whole, he is a toad. For one thing, he finds himself far too amusing. For another, I do not approve of his choice of books. If it is possible for a man to be foppish, sinister, and self-congratulatory all at once, he accomplishes that task. I cannot tolerate that, even for my brother."

Redfern took the necklace from his pocket, holding it up by one end. It glittered as it swung, a bright serpent in the fugitive light. "He also sought to control you with this."

"My necklace," Helen murmured. "Why do you have it?"

Redfern wavered. There was no way he could tell Helen about the League without sounding ridiculous. "Think of your brother's actions since he met the earl. Think of your own since Waring gave you this."

Helen pressed her hand to her mouth for a long moment, a gesture of acute revulsion. The expression on her face said she remembered everything. "All right. What are you saying?"

"Waring's evil is like nothing I have ever encountered. He seeks to control you and your brother with some sort of sorcery."

"Sorcery?" Helen exclaimed, wrinkling her nose. "A man like the earl? Why?"

"He needs money. You are the children of a wealthy banker."

"Sorcery?" she said again. "I can hardly believe that. There are tales and rumors, but no one ever encounters it!"

"Call his tricks what you wish, but mark him as dangerous. Consider this: Waring was feeding you tidbits from his fork tonight, and you seemed to be enjoying it. I took the necklace from your throat, and now the thought of him turns your stomach."

Helen shuddered. "I will grant you this much—he had some hold on me, and he has unnatural influence on James."

For a moment, Redfern's thoughts stalled as he looked at Helen, reveling in the life that seemed to radiate from her every pore. Hair falling down to her elbows, she looked like the girl he had known years ago. Large, gray eyes dominated a face equally capable of fervor and frivolity. He thought of the many times he had seen that same watchful gaze at a window, following him as he left for months or years at a time. The wrongness of that image staggered him.

"Nicholas?"

Redfern blinked, feeling foolish as his thoughts returned to the dire matters at hand.

"Nicholas, what are we to do?"

"Trust no one but me." He told her a little of what he suspected of Waring's plans to help the French. "However much you long to tell James, say nothing until we can free him from the earl's power.

"You are right, of course," she said with reluctance.

"And I must behave as if I am still under Waring's sway," she said. "That will be a heroic task all on its own."

He saw tears on her cheeks. She was frightened. Redfern's heart tightened at the sight, and he drew her into his arms again. "Perhaps when this is all over, the king will give you a medal."

"Given that he has already flirted with madness, he just might. Promise me you will get rid of that necklace. After what you have told me, looking at it nauseates me."

"I will promise you anything," Redfern said, his fingers twining in the long tendrils of her hair. He had to touch her, to close the distance between them.

Helen lifted her hand to his face, her fingers drifting along his jaw. "Thank you for bringing me to my senses. Still, after all that has come between us, I don't think either of us is ready for your promises."

He stiffened, drawing away.

Her mouth quirked, a smile that failed to thrive. "Please know I am relieved you are back home, Nicholas. I hope this time you stay. I am terrified of what might happen to me."

Chapter 14

Once back in her room, Helen waited while Violet undressed her. *Let the girl make what she will of the state of my hair,* Helen thought with defiance. *If the worst that comes of this episode at Arden Hall is a rumor or two, then I will be doing well.*

When the maid was gone, she collapsed into bed, burrowing gratefully into the soft, cool sheets. She left her candle burning and watched its flame sway in the currents of air, a dervish gyrating on a pillar of glistening, sweet-scented wax.

Weariness warred with anger and fear. There was too much to think about—Nicholas's stories of spies and French agents, his own secretive missions, his brother's suicide and ruin. Then there were the fantastic tales of sorcerers and the magic necklace that had held Helen in Waring's thrall.

In truth, she would have dismissed Nicholas as a madman except for the last. Her experience with the necklace and with Waring *had* happened. When she thought back, she remembered the slow, steady change in her brother's manner once he had met the earl. Ambition and poor judgment were always James's weaknesses, but could not account entirely for the cold, dull way he now viewed the world. After the few short months since making the earl's acquaintance, her brother was not the same man. He was Waring's familiar.

She sat up in bed. *Waring gave James a watch chain!* Had that, like the necklace, been a means of control? She had no idea how these things worked. She would take the damnable thing from James at the first opportunity.

Then again, maybe the chain had no significance at all. Maybe she was falling into whatever brain fever plagued Nicholas. Everyone heard gossip of men and women who lived by casting spells and making potions, but she categorized such information along with fabulous medical cures and visitations from the grave. Not impossible, but more likely a hoax.

Not this time, she thought. Something had really happened to her. Some of her memories were missing—there were hours, even days she could not remember. Since Waring gave her the sapphires, she had only patchy recollections, and what she recalled gave her no pleasure. She had suffered headaches, sickness, and a floating numbness that separated her from all vitality and feeling.

Worse, she had done whatever Waring had asked of her without question. What displeased him, she had avoided. What he liked, she had embraced. The effect had been more insidious than if she had been a shackled slave. Somehow, the necklace had made Waring's wishes her own. She had kissed him, she had let him whisper in her ear, and she had believed it had been her own desire.

I am going to make him pay, she thought with fury. *His bit of Italian petticoat will seem biddable and innocent next to the subtleties of my wrath!*

Thank God for Nicholas. Like some wandering hero from a nursery tale, he had returned from afar and restored her with his kiss. Never mind that his touch nearly stripped Helen of her wits all over again.

She shivered, lying down again and pulling the covers up to her chin. The shadows in the room hovered, the darkness soft and waiting. What was she going to do with him? He seemed to still love her and, yes, he had shared his secrets—but they terrified her.

If the French landed in Ireland, the war on the Continent would come to England. It would no longer be a matter of newspaper reports and drawing-room chatter— it would be blood in their own lanes and villages. *And Arden Hall is at the center of the plot.*

Nicholas was here to stop Waring. Her own dark-eyed, taciturn, music-loving Nicholas was a spy. *He always did take the unexpected road.*

Her mind wandered a moment, thinking over the last few days. She had been with the earl almost every moment. Had she seen Waring say or do anything Nicholas should know about? One incident occurred to her. She had been out walking with Waring when a messenger had come. She remembered Waring's satisfied smile when he received the letter.

If something gave the Earl of Waring that cat-with-the-cream expression, it had to be suspect. Nicholas needed to know about the letter.

Nicholas needed the letter.

I can get it far more easily, she thought. *A shawl wrapped tight will hide the fact that I am not wearing the necklace. I can wander about with a vacant eye like some poor wretch far gone in laudanum and no one will be the wiser.* Still, she preferred not to be caught pilfering the earl's correspondence. Unlike La Gianotta, her acting skills were purely amateur.

She knew Waring stayed up well into the night. Helen determined her best opportunity to slip into his study would come just before daybreak.

Fueled by her fury at the earl, she forced herself to stay awake. At the first lightening of the sky, shivering with fatigue, Helen rose and dressed herself. Violet was a fine maid, but too flighty to be trusted with a secret.

Splashing her face with what cold water was left in her water jug, she squinted at the pink thread of dawn outside her window. It was so early, even the birds were still quiet.

The hallway was dark, but she could not risk a candle. Relying on her memory of the house, Helen felt her way along the wall, her slippers silent on the carpet. Every sense strained to catch the trace of another body moving through the darkness. As she passed the doorway to the drawing room, she heard the brush of straw on stone and the clank of tools. The housemaids were already cleaning the fireplaces. A tingle of fear coursed over her skin. She had less time than she thought.

Holding her breath, she pushed open the earl's study door. No movement, nothing but the stirring of air as the door swung wide. It was safe. She hurried through, closing the door silently behind her. She was oppressed by the knowledge Waring slept only a few rooms away.

With cautious steps, Helen made her way past the unfamiliar furniture to the window. She propped the curtain open with a stack of books, allowing just enough light to work.

Where do I begin? A desk stood on the far wall, its drawer open. There was a lot of paper inside, and a woman's scarf, but nothing looked similar to the letter she had seen. She wondered briefly why he had the scarf, but quickly turned to a pile of books and letters that lay strewn on top of a cabinet that sat next to the desk. Nothing.

I have so little time! She had to think. She flipped through the stack of books, searching for something stuck between the pages. There were too many volumes to be thorough.

The fourth or fifth book she reached for had no title on the cover. It was bound in plain black leather, the pages written by hand. She paused, taking the merest second to scan the text. It was a genealogy, a record of the descendants of several of England's great houses.

One page was marked with a slip of paper. Her gaze flicked down the page.

In 1732, the Earl of Leyland bore a bastard son by Emma Barrett, the daughter of the blacksmith at Howe. They named the boy Peter.

Helen snapped the book shut in shock. This was the genealogical information Waring had been talking about! She lifted the book's cover again, this time reading the frontispiece.

An Accounting of the Families of England and France Belonging to the Bloodlines of the Circle: their descendants and heirs, direct and indirect.

Helen swore under her breath, stuffing the book back where she had found it. So the Circle, magicians or whatever else they fancied themselves, did in fact exist. They existed and were looking for mates descended from magical forebears.

She grimaced in disgust. Waring wanted her, not just for her money, but to bear him little sorcerers. *Not while I have one breath left, my lord.*

She looked around the room, wondering where to search next for the earl's letter.

A feeling of hopelessness flooded her. There had been plenty of opportunities for him to burn it. He could have put it in a locked chest with his family treasures or hidden it in the cellar. There was no way to know.

Refusing to quit, Helen rifled through more piles of books and papers. She perched on the edge of a large reading chair as she worked. A silk smoking robe was draped over the back, smelling of tobacco and Waring. It made her feel slightly sick, and she cringed every time her hand brushed the soft fabric. There was something obscenely intimate about contact with the garment, however remote it was from its owner.

A maid rattled her scrub pail in the hallway, and a lump of fear jammed in Helen's throat. Whether or not she had found the letter, she had to get out of there. Starting for the door, she brushed against the robe and it slithered to the floor. Impatiently, Helen tossed the limp garment over the chair back. As the skirt of the robe hit the wooden leg of the chair, she heard a faint papery crackle.

She dove for the pockets of the robe. Sure enough, the letter was there. Within seconds, she had it hidden in the pocket that hung beneath her skirts. Helen paused by the door, conscious that she had to run the gauntlet of the hallways. She could hear more activity now, footsteps rushing to and fro. As she reached for the handle, her fingers shook.

Once outside the study, she could see the sun had almost fully risen. The air still held the gray cast of early morning, but now there was enough light to move about the halls with perfect ease. So could the army of household help.

What now? Her bedroom lay at the opposite end of the house. In a moment of inspiration, Helen found a stairway that led down to a side entrance to the out of doors. Like many young ladies seeking rustic charm, she would go for an early-morning walk. With damp shoes and pink cheeks, she could return to her room unremarked.

However, it was cold, and Helen had a light shawl and indoor shoes. She quickened her pace to stay warm, but made it only as far as the corner of the house before she turned around to go back inside. Already, her feet and the hem of her dress were soaked with the morning dew.

Helen felt the slide of her pocket, heavy with the letter, against her leg as she walked. Impatient to read it, she could barely wait to get back to her room.

As she passed the study, a thrill of alarm came over her. She had left the curtain propped open. It would be folly to try to close it now. Still, she could not help but look in as she walked by.

Helen jumped back, startled. Waring was standing by his desk. As if he could feel her presence, he turned, but she quickly moved away. Cowering out of sight, Helen felt the full weight of her guilt and fear. *Did he see me? Was he watching me?*

Fortunately, there was more than one door into Arden Hall. Helen crept in the opposite direction, away from

Waring's window. When she was finally inside, she ran up the stairs to get back to her room.

She hid the letter in the lining of her trunk. She did not dare take the time to read it now in case she was interrupted by Violet coming to wake her. She stripped off her wet clothes and huddled in her bed, half expecting Waring to come crashing through the door.

Fortunately, the Earl of Waring seemed to be otherwise occupied. This was the morning he was to host a breakfast party for his guests and neighbors. The highlight of his country vacation, it was put on with a view to garnering political support for the upcoming elections. Calculated to impress the important and intimidate lesser mortals, no expense was spared. There were many notable men in the area who held sway in those boroughs Waring sought to control.

This was all irrelevant to Helen, whose thoughts revolved around finding Nicholas and giving him the letter. It was midmorning by the time she could dismiss her maid and retrieve the missive from its hiding place under the satin lining of her trunk. Refreshed from her bath, Helen curled up on the end of her bed, at long last alone and secure. She quickly unfolded the cream paper, brushing away a few crumbs of wax that fell from the broken seal.

A wave of consternation and disappointment swamped her. The letter was complete nonsense, a string of characters carefully written in pale brown ink but meaning nothing. She had risked so much for this? Helen smacked the letter against the counterpane in frustration.

Of course, it had to be in code. She glared at the paper, as if a stern look could rearrange the writing into something of use. She could spend hours trying to decipher it, and she never had been any good at word games. Though it would be wonderful to deliver a piece of intelligence to Nicholas that he could actually read, he undoubtedly had contacts used to dealing with secret languages. From a positive viewpoint, at least the code proved the letter was important.

She would find Nicholas at the garden party. Helen dressed and hurried out onto Arden Hall's carefully clipped lawns. A series of tables had been set out, the largest of which held refreshments. Or art. Helen was not sure which it was.

She had seen sculptures of ice before, but entire animals composed of fruit and vegetables were new. She contemplated a pig with a strawberry snout. Was one supposed to eat these creatures? Who would want the berry after it had been a nose? Although it was de rigueur to have a foreign chef these days, she had heard it was becoming increasingly hard to get plain food in some fashionable households. Apparently, this was one such case.

A footman with a long-suffering expression was filling glasses from a burbling fountain of champagne. The task looked difficult to accomplish without getting wine down one's clothes.

Helen took tea and a biscuit and set about looking for Nicholas. She had not seen him so far, but guests had been coming and going and the crowd was dense. She sat on a stone bench while she drank her tea, watching eddies of people passing before the lush backdrop of the garden.

To her surprise, she saw Laura Gianotta, dressed in a dark cerise gown of the latest cut. Her hair was curled in an elaborate fall at the crown of her head. Over her shoulders she wore a magnificent silk shawl, so transparent it appeared to be nothing more than mist. She looked like the figure from a cameo, perfect in her olive-skinned beauty.

Helen thought of the foolishness with the orange, and shuddered. It was going to take her decades to recover her composure from that escapade.

She rose and began a slow circuit of the garden, stopping and making polite conversation whenever she could not avoid it. Nicholas was definitely absent. It was possible there was some other crisis brewing.

He is a man who is inevitably otherwise occupied! Helen thought, starting to feel cross. She had so much to tell him, she surely would burst.

Eventually, she found her way to where the Italian actress stood. La Gianotta regaled two society matrons with tales of the theater. Helen stopped a little way off, curious enough to listen but not wanting to join in. There was fruit on the property, and she had no intention of experiencing the combination of La Gianotta and produce ever again.

Still too far away to hear properly, Helen moved to the other side of a yew tree. There, she was screened from their view but able to eavesdrop. As she listened, she looked around. Still no sign of Nicholas.

La Gianotta was speaking. "The character of Desdemona is strangled by her husband. It is a difficult moment to play, for one has to die gracefully and not look like one is being throttled by a street thug. Unfortunately, my last Othello was little better than a butcher. I had bruises for weeks." The ladies tutted sympathetically.

"I would die of terror, to feel a man's hands around my throat," one said. "Even in the name of art."

Helen shifted so that she could watch the women through a tiny bare patch in the branches of the yew.

"When I perform in the play, I prefer to use a scarf. It looks better from the balconies. It is easier to see," said La Gianotta. She pulled the wispy silk confection from her shoulders, twisting it into a rope for demonstration.

The first of La Gianotta's audience shuddered in horror, but the other gave a sly smile. "And, scarves have many uses in the bedroom. Desdemona might not have known she was going to die until Othello went too far. A little death can be a livening thing."

La Gianotta gave a husky, low chuckle, but the other woman looked confused. Helen's mind flashed to the scarf in Waring's desk. The images that conjured made her squirm.

"What you say is true," the Italian replied. "There is a precarious balance between pleasure and death. I feel both every time I step onto the stage."

"What do you mean?" the first woman asked.

"The audience can make me feel like a queen, or the lowest crawling thing. Every night is a test. After this long, I cannot resist the excitement of the experience."

"Of the risk?"

"Yes. Performing before a large house is as good as having a man."

From her listening post a few steps away, Helen rolled her eyes. She had the impression, if the actress was not actually in the theater, she would draw an audience simply by being outrageous.

"What about having a man on the knifepoint between pleasure and death?" asked the bolder of the women. "Is that not better than a night on the stage?"

"My death or his?"

"Either way."

"His, then—hmm—I must think on that."

"Are you saying you actually put the scarf around the neck of your . . .?" The first woman trailed off, finally catching the meaning of the conversation.

"Yes, my dear, it gives some people a thrill," said her friend. "But it's important to stop before it's too late."

"That's appalling! I never heard of such a thing!"

Helen knit her brow. Outdoor parties, with larger space and the illusion of privacy, were always enormously informative. She now had unwanted insight into the marriages of two prominent couples.

"If I tried that, I would be tempted not to stop," the second woman said dryly.

"When the moment comes, use wire. It works much faster." La Gianotta snapped her shawl tight between her hands, the silk vibrating with sudden tension.

The women laughed nervously. Helen froze. James had told her Lord Bedford had been strangled with a wire. Nicholas had found actor's face paint on Bedford's clothes. Laura Gianotta, Waring's mistress, was an actress. She was the killer.

Helen gulped, her stomach suddenly in rebellion. She felt nervous sweat prickling down her sides in a sudden, clammy surge of panic. Her eyes scanned the lawn, searching the clumps of guests for Nicholas's tall form. Where was he? She saw a judge. Should she tell him? No. The murder of Bedford led straight through the Italian to the Earl of Waring, and there was no telling who at this party was loyal to the Hellfire League. The judge might be in Waring's pocket.

Her eyes lit on a head of auburn hair. Hanson! He had seemed kind—she would be safe with him. She took a step forward, thinking it was strange he was not at the actress's side. He was infatuated with her. He would be crushed to learn what she had done.

The red-haired man turned a little, and she saw who it was. It was not Hanson, but his double in the *Comedy of Errors*, Andrew Coleman. Yet another male who wavered somewhere between La Gianotta's lover and servant.

With foreboding, she saw he was watching her with unfriendly eyes. Helen realized he could see both sides of the yew. Had he seen her terrified reaction and guessed its cause?

Coleman began walking toward her, his expression stormy. He was coming for her! She turned and went the other way, thinking fast. She could go to the most crowded part of the gathering and hope for the best. *Where is Nicholas?*

Coleman kept coming. Walking slowly enough that she did not attract attention, Helen passed through the thick of the crowd in the main garden. She did her best to become lost from view in the throng and then made for the lane of poplars that led to Arden Hall's extensive orchards. She would hide there a while before slipping back to the relative safety of the house.

As she reached the edge of the garden, she stole a glance over her shoulder. Coleman was not in sight, and somehow that was worse than seeing him on her heels.

Unnerved, Helen kept going, hurrying down the secluded lane that ended in a little wrought-iron gate. Beyond was a shed where the gardeners stored their tools. It was the size of a small cottage, with a thatched roof that reached halfway down its rough stone walls.

She let herself through the gate and hid from view between the last of the poplars and the side of the shed.

Surely she had lost Coleman! Still, she listened for a pursuer's footfalls on the soft earth. There were none.

Instead, she heard sounds coming from inside the shed. She sank down, kneeling in the weeds and grasses. Thumping from inside the shed's walls indicated something large was being moved. Then the weathered door opened, the wrought-iron hinges giving a low groan.

To her complete astonishment, her brother emerged, followed by the Earl of Waring. Both were brushing dust from their clothes.

Chapter 15

As Helen watched, openmouthed, the two men began walking toward the lane of poplars.

"I am thoroughly impressed," Barrett said to Waring.

Helen's heart clenched when she heard the slur in his words and saw the numb heaviness of his gait. Only yesterday she had labored under the same druglike miasma. *Just a little while longer, James! Nicholas and I will help you just as soon as we are able.*

"I knew you would be interested," said Waring, opening the gardener's gate. "It took my father years to build."

"How many miles of tunnel are there?" Barrett asked, and then their voices were lost in the trees.

So here was another entrance to the tunnels Nicholas had described. Helen hurried to the front of the shed. She tugged on the old iron handle, pulling open the door just enough to admit a shaft of sunlight.

The perimeter of the flagstone floor was piled with barrels. Most likely, that was what she had heard being moved. *There must be a trapdoor beneath.*

"Are you finding what you seek?"

Helen started, nearly leaping into the air in her fright. "Lord Stephen!"

The man lounged against the corner of the building, arms folded. He was dressed with impeccable taste, his linens pressed to perfection, but the puckering red scar on his face spoiled his looks.

"I see you are not wearing your sapphires," he said, shifting his position so that he could take a step closer.

Involuntarily, Helen touched the locket she wore. Beneath her skirts, she felt her knees quake but refused to allow the panic to reach her voice. "One cannot wear the same jewels day in and day out. The company would think I had no other ornament."

Layton gave a low chuckle that made Helen's skin creep along her flesh. "I think rather that Waring overestimates the efficacy of his charm. He makes some foolish moves. Allowing his obsession with the League to distract him from his political guests is one. Thinking you a fool is another."

She took a step back, calculating the distance between them. "Who are you to comment on my relations with our host?"

Layton fluffed his lacy cuffs, then fixed her with a predatory glance. "Do you know of the Circle? Of the Hellfire League? If you don't, you soon will."

Helen's jaw began to tremble with apprehension. She didn't know how to answer. Was it safer to confess she did, or to deny all knowledge?

"Hmm," he grunted. "Your look says that you know more than you like. You carry a drop of their blood in your veins, you know. That, combined with your wealth and beauty, makes you damned near irresistible. Waring is not the only member of the Circle interested in the role of your suitor."

This time he drew near her, showing his long, narrow teeth in a lupine smile. "In fact, the competition is quite fierce."

"Back away, Lord Stephen," Helen said, her throat tight and hoarse.

"I have a mind to stake my claim to you, Miss Barrett. There is more than one way to advance one's suit. Even Waring would have scruples about taking another man's leavings."

Anger and revulsion spiked through her fear. Lifting her head, Helen stared at Layton with contemptuous incredulity. "Oh, for pity's sake, I have had outside of enough with you men! Why can't you simply speak to my father like anyone else?"

Layton's face went slack with surprise. It wasn't the reaction he expected.

Neither was having the heavy oak door of the shed slammed into his temple. He reeled backward, tripping over his own feet.

Helen scrambled away, running back through the poplars a few dozen yards until the lane forked. Panting with alarm, she swerved right, looking over her shoulder. She could see no sign of Layton.

Relaxing a little, she slowed, exchanging speed for silence. Hopefully, he would think she ran back to the garden party and would look for her there. Her aim was to return to the house and find Nicholas. If she followed this narrow path, she would reach the main road that ran outside the grounds of the hall. From there, she could bypass the lawns and enter the house from the side. The route was shorter, and she could escape notice.

Soon she reached the road. Falling into a businesslike stride, she felt her pulse drop to a normal rhythm. It was sunny but not too warm, actually a pleasant day for walking. If only she had not been trying to evade a demented suitor, she might have enjoyed herself. As it was, she glanced behind her every dozen steps.

A minute or so later, Helen heard horses. Cautiously, she moved to the side. From the sound of it, the beasts were moving fast, too fast for the narrow road. As she turned to look, the vehicle raced into view. Four black horses with nodding plumes pulled an old funeral coach. Helen backed farther to the side, sure the driver was going to capsize the boxy vehicle.

It began to slow. Now that it was closer, she could see the gilt trim and gold-painted panels. They bore the design of a moth on the side—most unusual.

The vehicle was old, but kept in wonderful condition. Who had died? she wondered. Helen had heard nothing of a passing, and news like that traveled quickly in the countryside. Suspicion nagged at her.

The horses were just walking now, blowing and working the bits in their huge mouths. The coachman in the box wore a tricorn and cloak, black with gold trim to match the vehicle.

"Whose funeral is this?" Helen called to the man.

He hauled on the reins, stopping the horses. She shaded her eyes to see the coachman better, but he remained as he was, looking straight ahead. Puzzled, she thought for a moment of an automaton.

Then the head of the coachman began to turn. Helen's mouth went dry as dust. Between the high collar and the tricorn was nothing, just darkness.

"Run," it said.

Her nerves, already badly frayed, snapped. With a horrified shriek, Helen bolted, hauling up her skirts and using her long legs to eat up ground. She heard the crack of the carriage whip behind her, the creak as the old wheels lurched forward. The rocky surface of the road was brutally hard under the soles of Helen's fine leather shoes and seemed to roll and pitch at every step.

Terror pushed her on, pounding through her muscles like a potent elixir. The road wound on and on, an endless terrain of dust and rocks. The horses galloped behind her, like a nightmare never slowing but never quite overtaking her.

Fatigue shredded the breath from her lungs. She was used to riding, not running.

She looked back. The coach was gone. In its place was Lord Stephen, cutting across the field at a flat run toward her.

The sudden impact of Layton's body on hers threw her into the dust. His grasp slipped as she kicked away. Helen rolled, tangling in her skirts and falling into the scrub at the side of the road. She got to her feet, conscious of bruised flesh. Layton was standing, his hands on his trim waist.

"Come, Miss Barrett, don't make us work too hard. The end's all the same, anyhow."

"Damn your eyes!"

That made him blink. "Such language from a lady!" he said, mocking her.

Helen backed away so that a little dip of land lay between them. She wouldn't waste breath on words. After a last look at Layton's sneering face, she plunged into the trees that ringed the orchards to the south. Helen darted to her left, quickly crossing the line of bushes that shielded a grove of apple trees. It took but a moment to find what she wanted—a full-grown tree thick with summer leaves. She was up in the branches before Layton made it past the bushes. Tiny apples shuddered on their stems, a few hitting the ground with muffled thumps. Helen bit her lips to stifle her panting. She could still climb, even in a dress, but she did not have the wind of a teenaged girl anymore.

Layton looked around, scanning the lawn, every line in his body speaking his puzzlement. Helen's arms, bracing her weight in an unfamiliar position, began to shake. A cross thought about the cost of her ruined dress flitted through her mind.

Will he not go? Helen willed herself to stay still, for her muscles to lock in place. She gambled on the fact he would not look up, would not expect to find a society miss in the trees. For the deception to work, she had to remain perfectly still.

A dog barked in the distance. Layton took a last look around and walked back to the road. Helen's head drooped, and her long, gold hair finished falling loose from its pins. Only when she could no longer see Layton's figure diminishing along the road did she lower herself to the ground.

Redfern gaped in astonishment as Helen burst into his room. She did not greet him, but stood, swaying slightly, before she spoke.

"Why did you not come to the garden party?" she cried, distress thick in her voice.

She was filthy, her dress in shreds, and some sort of leaves were tangled in her hair. What sort of a garden party had it been?

"Are you hurt?" he asked. The knife he had been honing fell to the table, slipping from slack fingers.

"No, but I have a lot to tell you." Helen tossed her hair out of her eyes, her chin jutting forward with a stubborn expression.

He took her in his arms, picking a bit of green from the tumble of her hair. "What happened? Did you walk through the house looking like this?"

"I did," she said into his chest. "Thank Heavens for back staircases."

She looked up from their embrace, craning her neck. "Why were you not at the garden party?" she asked again.

He shook his head. "I thought I would learn more exploring the house while everyone else was out of doors. I did not think I would learn as much of value talking to the earl's guests."

"Bollocks." She swore for the second time that afternoon. "I learned plenty."

"Helen!" His amazement at her language was compounded as she began fishing down the front of her bodice. "Helen?"

She pulled out a folded piece of paper and pressed it into his hand. It was warm from her body.

"I have a lot to tell you, but I will start with this. It came to Waring. I stole it from his study." She sank into his chair and toed her ruined shoes off her feet.

Redfern opened the letter and blinked at the scrambled text. "I've not seen this code before. I will have to pass it on to another with more expertise."

What she had said suddenly registered with him. "You stole this from Waring?"

She nodded. "I am in a great deal of trouble."

He set the letter down and knelt by the chair where she sat. "What happened?"

"I was chased by Coleman, then by a funeral coach. Then I was attacked by Lord Stephen. It sounds like the members of the Hellfire League are in some race to wed me at any cost. It seems I am related to some illegitimate son of the Circle." Helen started to tremble, and Redfern grasped her hand. It was cold.

"A funeral coach?" he asked, remembering the night Bedford had died and then his vision of Michael.

"Yes," Helen replied, her gray eyes round and filling with tears. "And then there was La Gianotta."

Her trembling became more violent. Redfern realized she was descending into a kind of shock now that she was out of immediate danger.

He stroked her hand, trying to calm her. "I saw she was here."

"I heard her all but confess to killing Bedford. She talked about strangling a man with wire!"

Redfern digested this for a moment. Helen had done so well, he was put to shame. "How did you find all this out? Between us, I am the one who is the spy."

"If you had gone to the garden party, you would have!" A single tear slipped down Helen's dirty cheek.

Redfern wiped it away with his thumb, leaving a smudge. Her skin was coated with dust. "If we catch Waring, I will have to give you half the reward. You are quite the mistress of espionage."

Helen sniffed. "I just want you there next time. I had to climb a tree to get away from Layton."

Angry as he was, he could not stifle a chuckle. "So I see."

Wrinkling her brow, Helen looked at him. "You should at least offer me a basin of water to get clean."

Redfern stood and pulled her to her feet. "Come with me."

Taking her by the hand, he led her to his dressing table. Dipping a cloth in the basin of water, Helen wiped the grime from her face. Redfern watched, fascinated by the graceful, quick motions of her hands.

Drying her hands on the towel, she turned to face him. She used his comb to tidy her hair, and the long, fair tresses fell over her shoulders. With her hair down, she looked very young.

"I think I will have bruises in the morning," she said, bending her elbow to study the scrapes along her forearms.

Redfern came closer, circling her waist as he bent to examine the damage. She smelled of his soap. "Such a blemish only adds to your perfection." He kissed her ear.

The kiss made her jump. She tensed in his arms for a moment, and then turned to huddle against him. Redfern felt his mouth go dry. If she felt vulnerable and full of need, suddenly he did as well.

"Hold me," she whispered. "I need you to be close."

"You have had a terrible ordeal." He tightened his embrace, holding one hand to the back of her head and stroking her hair as he would a frightened child's. Only a shred of her story was enough to rouse his protective instinct. He could not bear to think about how much he did not yet know.

"I need you closer," she said, her fingers sliding up his back. "As close as you were in the library."

He dropped his hands to her shoulders, pushing her away enough to see her face. "Helen."

"What?" Her fingers traced his jaw. "I need you. For once, just be here."

The rebuke silenced him. He dropped his mouth on hers, giving everything in that kiss. "I am yours."

She surged against him, turning her head to find a better angle. Her lips parted and she took his tongue into her mouth, her fingers roving through his hair.

His breath was starting to come hard, but he forced himself to slow his caresses. "Your dress is covered in dirt," he teased. "You're rubbing it all over me."

"Then get rid of it," Helen replied, her eyes dark and full of challenge.

Redfern needed no prompting. The bodice fell away to reveal small, perfect breasts resting above her stays. He fumbled with the ties of her skirts until the dress slipped to the floor. The nimbus of her petticoats swelled, cloud-like, around her. Soon, they fell, too, and then her stays, leaving nothing but the thin wisp of a chemise clinging to her limbs.

Helen kissed him again. "I remember you have always had talented fingers. No one could play Scarlatti quite so well."

Untying the ribbon at the neck of the chemise, Redfern slid his hands under the muslin to cup her hot flesh. "I will remind you of all my repertoire and introduce you to a few passages I have held in reserve."

He circled her nipples with his thumbs and felt her shiver with pleasure. Gently, Redfern took her hand. They sat down on the edge of his bed, her white chemise startling against the dark blue of his counterpane.

Helen's fingers twined in his hair, catching him firmly. He could not move, had no choice but to move along with her as she slowly reclined. She kissed him fiercely before she let him roll free.

"Take off your coat," she demanded. "You have the advantage of me." In a deft motion, she grabbed the end of his cravat, pulling the knot loose.

Redfern hastened to obey, removing his waistcoat as well. Her hands found their way beneath his shirt, exploring, tracing over the raised flesh of a scar.

"That one is recent," he said, reclining on the bed and pulling her down onto his chest.

"I do not know your geography," Helen said softly. "I was always the model of decorum."

"And now?"

She shifted to look at his face, her long hair falling around her. "Everything that has happened lately has made me afraid to leave my happiness to chance. Maybe we have waited too long to lie together. I want it to be you I give myself to."

Redfern pulled her close. "Have you forgiven me?"

She studied him. "Almost. Prove you want to be with me."

The words humbled him. Redfern rolled over so she was trapped beneath him. "I want you." He ached, burned, his blood heavy with need.

She looked up at him, the light catching the moisture in her eyes. "I know."

Raising himself on his forearms, he took in the gentle curve of her chin, the long line that scooped from shoulder to hip. Such immaculate beauty.

Impatient, he rose and shed his own clothes. When he lay down beside Helen once more, her eyes were round.

"I have never seen . . . ," she said, words lost beneath his lips.

"A man in a state of desire," he murmured. He lowered himself inch by inch, feeling the press of warm flesh as their bodies met. His hands traveled back to her breasts, then down to her hips, inching the fabric of her chemise up over her hips. "Are you sure you want this?"

In reply, she grasped him, the pressure of her hands making him start. "Have a care! The Earldom of Whitford depends on that!"

Helen giggled, the soft vibration of her laugh sending shocks of desire through his body. He could barely see through the urgency of his need. Resting his hand on the soft mound between her legs, he felt the sweet, moist slick of her craving. Her thighs parted as he slid his fingers inside her, urging her toward pleasure.

Helen bucked under his touch, gazing at him through slitted eyes. Mastering his own urgency, he searched out the secrets of her body. She surged under him, nipples peaked under the film of muslin.

"Mercy!" she whispered.

"Not yet."

Redfern barely kept control, withdrawing his fingers and thrusting the tip of his manhood into her. She moved herself against him, greedy to take in more. Pushing gently, he thrust against the barrier of her virginity. She gave a faint cry as he burst through, but surged up to meet him.

He had wanted this for so long. Redfern found the ancient rhythm of possession, working, pushing, making Helen his. His fingers found her hair; his hands traced the delicate architecture of her ribs. Somehow, he wasn't sure how or when exactly, they managed to get rid of the tangling obstruction of her chemise.

At last, hot, wet spasms wracked her. When ecstatic

oblivion finally came, Helen was naked beneath him, long limbs sweat-slicked and brilliant in the afternoon shadows of his bedroom. As she muffled her cries of release against his shoulder, he finally let himself go, pouring himself into her. As he fell away, spent, he saw the look of wonder on her face and treasured it away.

He felt like a battered ship that had finally made it home. They lay touching, panting, the cool air prickling at their flesh. He put his hand on her belly, dark on light, and traced the midline of her form until his hand strayed to cup one breast. Redfern lifted himself on his elbow to look down on Helen, her face framed by the spreading tendrils of her hair.

She is mine, he thought. In that moment, nothing else mattered.

Chapter 16

Mourning each article of clothing as it covered the firm, pale beauty of her flesh, Redfern watched with fascination as Helen dressed.

"Marry me," he said. "Forgive me."

She turned, tossing her unbound hair from her eyes. "With my brother's current devotion to Lord Waring, I doubt my family would permit our marriage. You might have to take me barefoot in my shift."

He smiled. "I think that is already a fait accompli."

She gave him a disgusted look before she grinned. "You are an impractical man."

"No, I am completely practical. I have at last learned what is of value, and I mean to keep it close."

She looked up from adjusting her skirts. He could see a faint spray of freckles across her nose where the country sun had touched her face.

"Marry me, Helen," he said again.

"If I agree once more to marry you, promise to actually wed me. The entire arrangement works far better that way."

She gathered her hair and began twisting it into a knot

at the back of her head. By the set of her jaw, he could see the light tone in her voice was a mask. Right now, he could easily hurt her with a thoughtless word.

"I will marry you. Somehow, I will find a way to stay with you."

She pushed the last of her hairpins into her neat roll of hair. Her chin quivered a moment. "Find that way, Nicholas. I will give you an answer then."

Redfern's gut twisted. She was not as much *his* as he had thought. The meaning behind her words was clear: No longer a mere girl, Helen kept her independence. Bedding him did not mean she had surrendered control of her life. She would marry him only if he could give her what she needed.

"Very well," he said softly. "I will not disappoint you."

He felt like a gambler with everything he had on the table. Winning was the only acceptable option. Waring had to lose so that Redfern could live.

Blinking hard, Helen faced him. The maelstrom of emotion they both felt shadowed her large, gray eyes. "If we are going to get through this, we need to address things in their proper order. We need to save James. You need to find a translation for that letter. We need to stop the earl."

From his position on the bed, Redfern looked her up and down. "First, you need to return to your room and change your clothes."

"And what are you going to do?"

He stretched out on his back, his hands behind his head. "I am formulating a devious plan. I have discovered from chatting with the stable master that Lord Bedford— who had an eye for a fine jumper, apparently—kept a house not far from here. It might be worth a short walk to see if he left anything behind that might shed light on what it was that he meant to tell me the night he was killed."

Helen threw his shirt at his head. "Let me go with you. I want to know everything you learn."

He pulled it off his face. "It might be dangerous."

"I would feel safer facing danger with you than fending off Waring and Layton on my own."

She had a point. "Wear walking shoes this time."

As Helen finished changing, she looked out the window of Lady Waring's bedroom to see Nicholas on the path below, talking to the gardener. The servant was nodding and pointing at the horizon. As he replied, Nicholas smoothed back his dark hair with one hand. Helen knew the gesture. She had seen it a thousand times. Fondness welled up in her, a giddy, unsteady wash of affection.

Beware, she chided herself. *You have felt this before, and it brought you nothing but pain.*

Yet, he had told her his secrets, let her share a little in the risks that clouded his future. He had changed.

That is too simple an answer. Perhaps it suddenly occurred to him he had lost me. It would be like a man to want something simply because he could not have it.

The last time he left, she was standing in the music room. He kissed her, left her a bouquet of tulips, and said he would be back in the autumn. He had not come as the leaves drifted down on her father's estate, nor as the snow drifted over fields of dry stubble. He had lied. The memory should serve as an antidote to treacherous sentiments.

Helen's giddiness gave way to sober thought. She felt the wood of the window frame steady beneath her fingers, but her inner self was seasick with turmoil. Random impressions flickered through her mind: the warmth of the morning sun, the way Nicholas's hair lay on the top of his head. She had never noticed that before, but then she rarely saw him from this perspective. Her mind felt frozen, unable to make sense of her emotions.

At last, Helen recognized her feeling as fear. Did their newfound understanding have real substance, or was this another sad and beautiful dream that would vanish when Nicholas walked away once more?

Was I right to give myself to him? Will it be enough to make him stay?

They had loved each other so much before their engagement. She wanted nothing more than to recapture that feeling of complete love and trust. If only he would always look at her as he had an hour ago!

How much anguish will this cost me?

Helen folded her arms. Nicholas was still engrossed in conversation with the gardener, who was now leaning on his spade. It must have been an amusing tale, because Nicholas gave one of his rare grins, a flash of white teeth that recalled the schoolboy. Helen could not help smiling herself just to see it. She wanted to hold him, to see him grin at her that way.

He is worth the risk.

She turned away from the window and picked up her shawl. Without telling her maid where she was going, Helen went outside to join Nicholas.

They had agreed to leave separately, meeting out of sight of the house. He was waiting for her where the drive met the main road when she caught up.

"Nicholas!" she called, hauling up the skirts of her sprigged cotton dress so that she could run the last few yards. Despite the exertions of the day, it felt good to be free and out of doors once more.

His dark eyebrows lifted, mocking. "Did you call, madam?"

She stopped, the soles of her short boots slipping in the soft dust of the road.

"I expected to see you back at the main gate. I thought you had gone, leaving me behind once more. How could you?"

Helen hadn't actually been worried, but enjoyed ribbing him.

One corner of his mouth turned up. "And so you ran me to earth."

He took her in his arms and gave her a lingering kiss, as if they had not been together barely an hour before. When they broke apart, Helen felt her body ache in places that had only just learned pleasure.

"Indeed, my lord, I have been far too forgiving in the past. I have decided to keep you on a short tether for the time being."

"It is as much as I deserve." Nicholas's eyes met hers with a smile. "Let us be gone quickly. It is already midafternoon."

Helen slipped her arm through his. "Then lead, and I shall follow."

"The gardener gave me directions. Bedford's house is but two miles distant."

They walked, sometimes talking, sometimes in silence. Light dappled the road through overhanging oaks, flickering with the light breeze. Birds peeped in the branches and in the bushes beside the road, rustling into flight as Nicholas and Helen passed.

Rising in a gentle slope, the road curved around a

stand of trees. Soon they stood on the crest, looking down into a broad depression crisscrossed with white paths and hedgerows. It was growing hot, and Helen folded her shawl over her arm.

Nicholas pointed to an old house that sat in the center of the little valley. Though spacious, it looked like a large, comfortable farmhouse. "That is Bedford's dwelling. It's not his main residence, but I think he may have used it if he was watching Waring."

"The place looks deserted," Helen replied. Every house of consequence had servants and, even more common, animals. There were no people, chickens, horses, or dogs in view. No smoke came from the chimneys.

"That may well make our task easy," Nicholas said, but there was doubt in his voice. Helen understood. If the house was locked up, they would have to find a way to force a door or a window.

Wanting to remain inconspicuous, Nicholas insisted they approach the house from the side, avoiding the lane that ran almost to its door. Circling around to the side garden, Helen followed him through a neat forest of bean poles to stand at the side of the stone building. Though the house looked deserted, there were few weeds. Someone had tended the vegetables not long ago.

The garden ran up to the foot of the wall. Patches of herbs alternated with wallflowers and carnations, a jumble of the useful and the pretty thrown together. A casement window looked over the herb bed. Helen stepped carefully between the flowers, her shoes sinking into the soft, well-tilled earth. Pulling the strings of her bonnet loose, she took off her hat so that she could press her nose to the panes of the mullioned window. The breeze felt good in her hair.

Nicholas bent next to her, his shoulder brushing her arm. Closing her eyes for a moment, Helen enjoyed his nearness, the feel of the sun warming her body. She could smell thyme where their feet were crushing the leaves, the savory scent mixing with the spice of the carnations.

She was alone with the man she loved on a hot summer's day, with a perfectly good deserted house at her disposal. Despite the potential danger of their situation, romantic possibilities nudged at her imagination.

Nicholas's hand rested on her back. "I think we're too late."

Disturbed from her fleeting dream, she turned to look up at him, squinting against the sun. "How so?"

"By the condition within," he said, nodding toward the window.

Obediently, Helen shaded her eyes and really looked at the room. It was a study, and it had been ransacked. Papers were scattered across the desk, a chair was overturned, and pictures hung askew on the wall.

"To state the obvious, someone has been here before us." Nicholas took out a knife and slid it between the casements, lifting the latch. The windows swung outward without protest.

Helen watched, mildly scandalized. "You do this frequently, don't you?"

With a bland smile, Nicholas tucked the knife away. "I want to take a quick look around. I won't be a moment. Stay here and call out if you see anyone."

He pulled himself up, swinging one leg over the sill in the same motion. Lightly he dropped to the floor inside and walked immediately beyond Helen's line of sight. A moment passed.

Helen gazed out at the beans and flowers and felt the

beginning prickles of irritation. Hitching up her skirts, she hauled herself through the window. She hadn't spent an entire childhood climbing trees for nothing.

As her shoes hit the floor, Nicholas spun in the doorway, his body tense until he saw it was her.

"I grew bored," she said, her tone curt.

Though silent, he had the decency to look contrite. For a moment, she thought back to the night at the Apollonian Rooms and of the conversation she had there with Waring about climbing apple trees. The memory irked her. Even at his most thick-skulled, Nicholas was an infinitely better man.

She looked around the study. It was small, with a low ceiling crossed by heavy, dark beams that forced Nicholas to duck his head as he moved about the room. Like the garden, it had seen the care of a servant not long ago. Despite the chaos of overturned chairs and strewn papers, there was only a day or two of dust on the dark wood table. The hearth was clean. Some daisies had wilted in a silver vase, but the petals were not dry.

Nicholas rustled through the letters and bills on the desk. Walking past him, Helen paused to look at a book open to an engraving of insects. In the top corner of the page was a picture of a moth just like the one on the panel of the funeral coach's door. Like the one hanging on Waring's wall, she realized with a start.

"Look at this."

"Pardon?" Nicholas looked up, holding a bundle of letters.

"This moth." She turned the book so he could see it right side up. "I've seen one like it in Lord Waring's collection."

He looked as if he had tasted something foul. "It is the device of the Hellfire League."

The faceless driver appeared in her memory. "It was on the door of the funeral coach." She shuddered, setting down the book. "I wonder where Bedford saw the design. He was obviously trying to identify the insect."

Nicholas frowned. "Now that I am looking for traces of the League, I see the moths everywhere. One would think we were investigating an old wool carpet."

A new voice entered the conversation. "Bedford saw the moth on the seal of a letter. He drew it for me one night as we were at cards. I think you saw his drawing in my makeup case."

Both Helen and Nicholas spun toward the door. Thomas Hanson leaned against the squat door frame, a pistol held loosely in one hand. He looked pale, his eyes bruised with fatigue. "I seem to find you snooping everywhere, Lord Redfern."

"It is a bad habit, I admit." Slowly, Nicholas reached for his sleeve, where Helen knew he had secreted a knife.

Hanson shook his head in mock consternation. "I am disappointed with you. Really, you should ensure Miss Barrett stays safely at home. Thievery is such dangerous work." He hefted the pistol in his hand, raising the nose an inch. "I would not want to accidentally harm a lady."

Like a trick of the eye, Helen saw, but did not see, a flash of silver streak through the air. With a sharp cry of surprise, Hanson dropped the pistol. Blood welled through the slash in his sleeve where Nicholas's knife had struck.

The pistol fired as it hit the floor, shattering the leg of a chair. Hanson feinted, starting for the doorway but turning just as Nicholas dove for him, driving his shoulder into Nicholas's chest. The latter staggered back, breath wheezing from his lungs.

Helen inched around the table, wondering if she should run or join the fray. She was strong, but not strong enough to win in a contest of brute force. Picking up a pewter candlestick, she kept moving. The heavy weight in her hand was less of a comfort than she had hoped.

Recovering his footing, Nicholas grabbed Hanson's sleeve, dragging him to one side as he swept the actor's feet out from under him. Hanson went down hard, landing on his injured arm. He yelped, rolling his body to shelter the wound. Before Hanson could get his knees under him, Nicholas placed a foot on the man's back, forcing him flat on his stomach. The fight had taken but moments.

Mesmerized, Helen drew nearer, still holding the candlestick. Even though they were now still, the two men radiated a kind of animal fury. Nicholas was breathing hard, his eyes bright and angry. Helen heard her pulse in her ears and she gripped the candlestick more tightly to stop the tremor of nerves in her hands.

"You would draw a gun on a woman?" Nicholas asked, his voice quiet but full of menace. The words cut the air as surely as any blade.

Hanson wheezed, turning his face away from the carpet. His gaze searched upward, trying to look at Nicholas. "Lord Bedford may be dead, but his property should be respected. Surely a banker's daughter has enough bibelots, she doesn't need to take up housebreaking?"

"But we are no thieves!" Helen exclaimed, unconsciously lifting the candlestick as she spoke.

"Then what are you doing in Bedford's house?" Hanson said, writhing so hard that Nicholas dropped to his knee to keep him pinned.

"You tell us your business first." Nicholas grabbed a handful of the actor's long, auburn hair, forcing him to lie still.

Hanson's face was squashed against the floor, his handsome features distorted. The actor closed his eyes, skin pale and moist with pain. "You said Bedford was murdered. I came looking for some clue as to what the killer wanted so desperately."

"Did you find one?"

"No. Someone tore the place apart before I arrived."

"Who?" Nicholas reinforced his grip on the actor's hair.

"I don't know for certain. The house has been shut up and unguarded for months while Bedford was in London."

"But the house and garden are cared for," Helen put in. Her voice felt thin and shrill, as though she was choking on her own agitation.

Hanson kicked ineffectually. "The caretakers live in the village. Let me up, please!"

Relenting, Nicholas released his hold and stood back, but drew another knife. Hanson flopped over, cradling his arm. Blood ran down his hand and wrist, soaking the front of his coat. The sight sickened Helen. Setting down the candlestick, she knelt to help him sit up.

"Let me bind your arm," she said.

Hanson swallowed hard, closing his eyes. "You would help me even though I was most unconscionably rude?" The apology held an edge of anger.

Nicholas moved closer, protective. Helen was grateful.

"I will forgive you the pistol if you help us." With stern efficiency, Helen pulled his arm out of his coat sleeve. She knew enough basic nursing to at least stop the bleeding.

Hanson took a hissing breath through his teeth as the fabric passed over raw flesh. "Help you? How can I assist? Do you need help packing up the valuables?" His green eyes were sharp with mockery.

Nicholas nudged him with the toe of his boot. "If you are telling us the truth, we are on the same errand as Lord Bedford. Mind you, I have seen you lie. You're very good. I doubt I will believe anything you say."

Hanson turned his face to Nicholas, doing his best not to look as Helen tore the fabric of his shirt sleeve away from the wound. The cut was not deep, but it was long and bloody.

"I should sew this up," she observed. If possible, Hanson grew even paler.

The actor licked his lips. "The same errand? You are looking for something to lead you to Bedford's information? If you think to take on the Hellfire League, you haven't a clue what you are dealing with. You haven't a chance against them!"

Nicholas folded his arms. "And how would you know of the League?"

The air was thick with tension, and Helen was glad to have a practical task before her. Lacking a needle and thread, she contented herself with wrapping her muslin fichu around Hanson's arm. The fabric was too light and the lace edging looked ridiculous on a bandage, but it was the best option at hand.

She bent her head as she tied a knot to hold it in place, not wanting to meet Hanson's eyes. Without the extra fabric at her neckline, she felt exposed. Finishing her bandage, Helen released the actor's arm.

"Thank you," he said, and cupped the wounded arm with his other hand, saying nothing more for a long moment. His thoughts seemed to turn inward as his expression grew blank.

"How do I know of the Hellfire League?" Hanson repeated. "I would ask, rather, how do you?"

"I learned of its existence while trying to solve Bedford's death. What do you know of it, and why did you disappear from London?" asked Nicholas.

At those words, Hanson seemed to come to himself, his face growing hard. "I left London because I was following Waring. I regret leaving the Ash Lane short an actor, but what could I do?"

"Why were you following the earl?" Helen asked.

The actor looked from her to Nicholas. "I have an idea of what Bedford found out. I am not welcome at Arden Hall, but I hoped to watch from this distance and learn enough to put an end to my cousin's treachery."

Helen's heart leaped with eagerness. "What do you know?"

Nicholas put away his knife, finally appearing to relax a little.

The actor dropped his gaze. "Some. I've seen Frenchmen coming and going from his lands, men I'm sure were soldiers—officers—by their bearing. The first time I saw them, months ago, Bedford was with me. He seemed to recognize the men and warned me to stay out of their way. The same thing occurred to both of us: What would Waring have to do with the Frenchies when we're at war with them? These weren't politicians, these were men of battle."

"Then you, too, believe the earl is a traitor?" Nicholas replied, his voice a fraction less chill than before.

"I would wager money on it." Hanson gestured around the room. "No roving thugs did this damage. I think Waring searched this house before I got here. He knew Bedford suspected him."

"How?" Nicholas righted one of the upturned ladderback chairs and sat on it.

"I'm not sure how but, that night at the Apollonian Rooms, I saw the two meet. Waring had gone to fetch some wine and almost ran headlong into Bedford coming out of the games room. There was so much anger in the look they exchanged, I thought the ice buckets would boil. Waring told him to keep his distance. I did not catch all the conversation, but it sounded as though Bedford had been writing one of the king's secretaries, Sir Alaric Fitzwilliam, about Waring's unofficial transactions, and somehow the letter had been intercepted. Waring had caught him tattling on his activities."

"By transactions, do you mean selling political influence?" Helen asked.

"I'm not sure, but it sounded as though whatever Bedford had caught him at was especially bad."

Helen thought of the note Bedford had passed Nicholas. Bedford had said he had been discovered. Now she knew it was Waring he feared.

Hanson went on. "We left the Apollonian Rooms at the same time. Bedford was nervous and couldn't wait to be gone. I was going to have dinner with Laura Gianotta. I left him at the corner and we walked down opposite streets."

"And did she meet you?"

"No, I'm afraid not. She did not keep our appointment." He grimaced. "That's not unusual for her. It is a great tragedy to love a diva. One ends up eating a lot of meals alone."

Should I tell him his lady love was the killer? Helen thought, but hesitated. If he became defensive or upset, he might say nothing more, and he seemed to know so much.

Nicholas ran his hand through his hair in the same meditative gesture Helen had seen earlier that day. "And what of the League?"

Hanson drew his feet under him and stood up slowly. "Bedford was an outsider. He died in part because he discovered its existence. The Circle merely guards its secrets, but the Hellfire League kills to preserve silence. Beware."

"There is one thing I do not understand," Helen interjected. "How exactly will the Hellfire League help the French?"

Hanson gave a wry smile. "They use the natural forces they are able to control. Bedford said they will hold a ceremony to draw down the darkness."

"We will literally be plunged into darkness? An eternal night?"

"No." Hanson shook his head. "Nothing that literal. It will come as blight, chaos, fear, and unrest. The French armies will stroll across a land consumed by its own nightmares and wrest the crown from an administration crumbling in confusion. That is the nature of the darkness they will call. It is the darkness of doubt."

Helen and Nicholas were silent for a long moment. Hanson was completely still, waiting out their mixture of incredulity and horror.

"How do you know this?" Nicholas said at last. He had

the tone of a man grasping for something simple to wrestle with.

Hanson shrugged, favoring his injured arm. "I am Waring's cousin. I grew up in the Circle, and the League, just like him. Do you want proof?"

He snapped the fingers of his uninjured arm and a flame, pale as ice, flared along his palm. Just as simply, he closed his hand, and it was gone. "Is it any wonder I chose a life on the stage? There is no need to hide. I can be who I am, and it is considered clever entertainment."

Nicholas had turned pale. "'Sblood!"

Helen nails were digging into the muscle of Nicholas's arm. "Can all the Circle do that?" she breathed, somewhere between wonder and terror. She had seen the flame, but she still did not quite believe in it. Was a spoonful of that magic really in her blood?

Hanson leaned against the wall, as if the brief demonstration had taken the last of his strength. "No. Some of us are adept at changing the weather, others at controlling weaker minds. A few of us can speak to the dead."

"But you are not of the League?" Nicholas asked, his voice still heavy with doubt.

Hanson grimaced. "I am not a good man, but I am not insane enough to court that kind of chaos."

"How can we stop them?" Helen asked.

"Since you have no power to command, brute force will work quite well. It is hard to wreak havoc, sorcerous or otherwise, with a broken skull. The trick is to get close enough to land a blow."

At that, Nicholas almost looked cheerful. "I can break heads. Will you stand with us?"

Hanson gave his catlike smile. "If you refrain from poking me with knives, I think we might manage an alliance. I am barred from entering Arden Hall, but I can watch the roads from here until I am needed."

Nicholas pulled out the letter Helen had stolen from Waring and unfolded it. "Since you watch the roads, do you know who delivered this? It arrived yesterday."

Taking the paper, Hanson studied it. "I saw nothing come yesterday." His eyebrows drew together, his lips moving slowly.

"Can you read it?" Helen asked.

"More or less. It's an old code the Circle uses." He sat down at the desk, picking up a pencil and printing awkwardly with his left hand between the lines. Obviously, his wounded right hand was his dominant one.

When he reached the bottom of the page, he sat back. "According to this, the Frenchies are arriving at any moment. The League is going to perform the ceremony on the full of the moon."

"That's tomorrow night," said Nicholas. "Can you take Helen to a place of safety until then?"

"If I am gone, they will suspect something is amiss!" she objected.

Nicholas opened his mouth to speak, but Helen silenced him with a glare. "I am well able to manage. We must look as if we suspect nothing."

The actor reached into his coat pocket and pulled out a tiny knife that closed into a handle no more than four inches long. "If you are determined to stay, keep this, Miss Barrett. It is silver—silver will always break through magic. It will protect you from enchantment and serve equally well in more mundane emergencies."

"Thank you. I will take good care of it." Helen turned the folding knife over in her hand. It looked well used, the etching on the handle worn smooth. She reached through the slit in the seam of her skirt and dropped the knife into the pocket that hung beneath. It seemed too light even for its small size, as if it were made of something other than metal.

"I hope you shall not need it." Hanson's eyes were sad. "The Circle once protected Christendom. Those at its core still believe their gifts are meant to keep the world at peace."

"Is that what you believe?" asked Helen.

"I am not an idealist—but there is no excuse for this Hellfire League madness. If either of you need help of a—*special*—nature, light a candle in the east-tower window. I will come to your aid and bring any of the Circle I can muster."

Nicholas extended his hand. "Thank you for your help. If you do not think me a thief, and I hold you innocent of murder, there is every chance we can work together."

With a lingering air of caution, Hanson extended his uninjured hand and shook Nicholas's. "I am not convinced that I like you, but we are fighting toward the same end. That is adequate common ground. And, hating my cousin is an enduring virtue in a man."

Nicholas's dark eyes twinkled, though the smile did not reach his face.

"Are you well enough to return to your lodgings, Mr. Hanson?" asked Helen.

His expression was full of charm. "Thank you, Miss Barrett. My horse will take me. I am not hurt so badly that I cannot ride."

Nevertheless, Nicholas went outside and saw him safely mounted. Helen watched from the doorway, noticing the shadows of the bean poles showed the afternoon was wearing on.

"I'm sorry I hurt him," Nicholas said as he returned. "Nevertheless, he was a bit too ready with that pistol. You are too dear to me to risk."

He took Helen's hands and kissed them one by one, first the backs, then the palms. His dark eyes were lit with the excitement of the last hour, the color high in his cheeks. Cupping his face in her hands for a long moment, Helen studied the features she knew so well. They were soft with affection, just as she remembered from long ago.

Why can't it always be like this between us?

She slipped her arms around his neck and leaned into his chest, feeling the heat of his body. The strong beat of his heart comforted her, easing the sore tension from her neck and shoulders.

Helen had been too focused on Hanson to dwell on her own comfort. Now she saw her skirt was covered in his blood. It would be hard to hide and harder to wash out, but she still preferred perilous adventure with Nicholas to anything else. He made her feel alive—even if she had ruined two dresses in one day.

Lifting her chin with his fingers, Nicholas covered her mouth with his. His tongue was hot and strong, teasing, tasting, claiming her kisses. Helen's breath began to quicken as a slow, melting hunger quivered in her belly.

What if it could always be like this? Do I dare to hope?

Chapter 17

Nicholas and Helen returned to Arden Hall in the late afternoon. Winding their way across the side garden, they escaped the notice of the other guests, who were taking tea on the back lawn. The two stopped at the edge of the maze, standing in the same spot where Nicholas had seen Lord Fairmeadow and the peacock. The sun was almost directly overhead, sparkling on the fountain. Tired from her long walk, Helen reveled in the gentle splashing of the water.

Nicholas drew her close, his arm firm around her waist. "I will join the other guests on the lawn and tell them I have been on a long ramble. You had best go in alone and change your clothes. You have Hanson's blood on your skirt."

"I would rather stay here and soak my feet in the fountain," Helen replied, resting her cheek on the wool of his jacket. The sun was warm and good, and she was weary. The physical exertion of the day was catching up with her.

"While I find that image delightful, I am sure James would think it below the proper level of Barrett dignity."

Nicholas kissed the top of her head, and then, ever so lightly, her eyelids.

"Even before he met the earl, I thought my brother's dignity could withstand some deflating on occasion. There are times he reminds me of a great frog, puffing up so that his fellow frogs believe he is king—but it is all just air." She ran a hand under Nicholas's jacket, sliding it between the satin lining of his open waistcoat and the soft cloth of his shirt. Firm contours of muscle and bone moved as he shifted to pull her still closer.

"That is the way of political men. Puffing and counter-puffing."

"You defend him?" she said with mock horror, but her heart was heavy. James was in trouble, and their jesting was only a means of facing the situation before them.

"Barrett is my friend. I think it is my duty to protect him from his irresponsible, irrepressible sister."

They kissed again, drinking each other in. The breeze felt benevolent on Helen's flesh, soft as fleece. Her senses were filled with the sound of the leaves and the faint scent of the hot stones beneath their feet. Most of all, her world was filled with Nicholas. She had forgotten what it was like to be this happy.

Their embrace ended, and she rested her hands on his shoulders, reluctant to break the contact of flesh on flesh. She could see her own delight mirrored in his eyes.

"I will see you in an hour," she said.

He touched her cheek, a smile lurking at the corners of his mouth. "Try to be invisible on your way in. Be careful."

He turned and walked toward the far lawn, where the Earl of Waring and his guests lounged in the sun and played a game of bowls on the smooth, perfect grass.

Men had it far too easy, Helen decided. Nicholas could simply walk into the crowd and say he had been for a stroll. She had to look as fresh and neat as if she had done nothing but lie about all afternoon.

She almost made it to her room undetected. She stood in the short hallway in front of her door when her brother grabbed her by the elbow.

"Where have you been?" Barrett asked, his voice slurred but still sharp with reproach. "I came upstairs to ask you to join the other guests three times, but you were nowhere to be found."

Helen shrugged him off, opening her door and walking into the Countess of Waring's bedroom. She saw Violet had laid out her afternoon dress on the bed, a spill of pink skirts against the white counterpane. "I was in the garden."

"What's that on your clothes?" Barrett forcibly turned her to face him, his gaze fastened on the splotches of Hanson's blood. "Lord save us, are you hurt?"

"No, I'm unharmed," Helen pulled away again, moving backward a few steps. "I came across one of the servants, who had cut his hand."

James narrowed his eyes. His face was lax, all the life drained from it by Waring's control. Where intelligence should have shone, suspicion made him look dull and brutish. "Is this true? This would have nothing to do with Redfern's sudden appearance? I saw him walking across the lawn. Were you together? Was that why you were gone?"

Helen ran out of patience. "What if I was? He is a guest here and so am I. We met outside and talked a long while. There is nothing strange in that."

Barrett swore, turning away from his sister with clumsy steps. "Are you mad?"

"What is mad about taking a walk with an old friend?"

"You were engaged to be married, and he as good as jilted you!" Barrett's face was red, his eyes wide with anger.

He is irrational, thought Helen. *This will end with my brother having an apoplexy!*

"Yet we can still enjoy a civil conversation," she said in calm tones, trying to soothe him.

Hiding her own annoyance, Helen sat on the edge of the bed. She was frustrated that her brother had caught her sneaking into her room. She felt like a truant child. It was mortifying.

"What if the earl had seen you?" Barrett asked in a low, tight voice.

"What if he did?" *I am doing a terrible job of pretending I am under Waring's spell.*

"What would he think of you?"

I don't really care, she thought silently. Helen met her brother's eye, but kept her peace.

Despite her reticence, Barrett's face flushed an even deeper shade, the veins in his neck bulging above his cravat. "You abuse his hospitality and goodwill."

"I do not. I went for a walk and had a civil conversation with another guest." *Is that precisely a lie?* she wondered. *I cannot believe I am hiding from my brother!*

"The Earl of Waring is my future."

"Then that is your affair," Helen retorted before she could stop herself.

Barrett's hand worked, alternately clenching a fist and wiping his palm on the leg of his breeches. Helen did her best not to see the shadow of violence in the gesture. She refused to be afraid of her brother.

Barrett made a sound that was close to a snarl. "It is Redfern, isn't it? He encourages your unreasonable temperament. All was well until he arrived and breathed new life into your pathetic, forlorn passion. How many times will you make yourself ridiculous before you understand that he does not love you?"

She felt the corners of her mouth twitch down. *I will not give in to his rantings. He can't help himself.*

She arranged her features into a passive expression. "I will not marry Nicholas. It does not matter if he longs to marry me, if he longs to marry another, or if he sells camels at the foot of the pyramids. I have set Nicholas free to wander the world as he pleases."

"I think you still admire him."

Helen snorted. "That must be why I sent him packing. Here, your watch chain is all tangled."

She reached for her brother's waistcoat pocket, wishing she had Nicholas's dexterity. She fiddled, but the watch chain was anchored securely and she could not remove it undetected. *Bother!*

Helen gave one last, desperate tug, pulling the watch from James's pocket. The chain snagged on his waistcoat button.

"What are you doing?" He snatched the timepiece back.

"The seals on the chain were all back to front," she said in her best imitation of a fussing female. "I was going to turn them around."

"Leave off." He stepped away, repairing the damage to his valet's handiwork. "Leave off, and leave me alone."

Barrett left the room. A deep sense of foreboding crept into Helen's bones.

In spite of a general sense of unease, Redfern found the outdoor gathering mildly pleasant. With events unfolding so quickly, attending a party was a waste of precious time. Still, it was less of a hindrance than any suspicion generated by his absence. Since he had avoided the breakfast gathering, an hour of idle pleasantries would establish his role as cheerful guest. The charade was not as difficult as he anticipated. There was food and drink, and a chair in the shade afforded a view of all the entertainment. In between nibbling at ratafia cakes and candied almonds, Lord Fairmeadow declaimed upon the ill effects of fresh air on the complexion, and the marchioness chased a loudly shrieking peacock with her walking stick when it tried to eat the hem of her gown. On the whole, there was plenty to amuse.

After the time spent with Helen, he felt contented. She had embraced him, invited him into her gentle secrets.

Leaning his head against the back of the chair, he gazed into nothingness. It was a moment of pure creature satisfaction. He relished the gentle scents of the garden and the cold weight of a glass of punch where it rested on his thigh. He could hear Fairmeadow laughing, a snorting, high-pitched sound. It was pleasant to hear people being merry, even if at least some of them were thoroughgoing villains.

His eyes focused on the corner of Arden Hall. From his vantage point, he could see the south and west walls, the reflection from the leaves of nearby plane trees dappling the walls a pale green. Above the tall first story with its pedimented entrance, many-paned windows marched with rigid symmetry along the second floor. Small, square towers sat on the corners of the building, making a partial third story. With idle fondness, he wondered which pair of windows belonged to Helen's room and whether she could see him sitting there.

I thought sparing her my burdens was for the best for both of us, but I was wrong. She is as strong as I am and deserves my confidence. If we do not trust, we risk not loving, and that is worse than any other gamble we might make.

His thoughts were sleepy, half-formed. They were hardly profound or new to humanity, but they were his and established the basis of his plans. Before long, he would catch Waring at his treasonous games. Then, he would win his freedom from the Master, save his family, save Helen, and live out the rest of his days in gentle afternoons like this one. Redfern's eyes drifted to half-mast, lulled by the balmy afternoon sun. He would save England from the twin scourges of the Hellfire League and the French Republic just as soon as he gathered the strength to move.

His reverie was cruelly shattered. He felt a hand on his shoulder, grabbing a handful of his sleeve and roughly hauling him from his chair. Redfern cursed as the glass of punch spilled down his leg. He shot to his feet, surprised to see that his attacker was Barrett.

Redfern looked at his old friend, puzzlement battling with annoyance. "What do you mean by this?"

Releasing his hold of Redfern, Barrett looked around. Lord Fairmeadow was watching with open curiosity. "I would speak with you in private. Follow me."

Redfern signaled for him to lead on. Barrett started toward the rear of the house, going past a stand of trees that separated the lawn from an expanse of ornamental gardens. Redfern followed, his eyes fixed on a point between Barrett's bulky shoulders. Instinctively, he began to worry for Helen. Something had gone wrong. Confirmation of his fears was only moments in coming.

Once they were in the privacy of the garden, Barrett wheeled to face Redfern. "I found Helen creeping into her room with a bloodstained dress and filthy boots."

A pause followed. "And?" Redfern prompted.

Barrett leaned forward, belligerence plain in his face. "What have you done to my sister?"

Startled by the vehemence in Barrett's words, Redfern frowned. He wondered how much Barrett knew about the day's activities. "I have done nothing to her." *Nothing she did not want.*

"You have turned her against us." Barrett's voice held the raw edge of paranoia.

Redfern felt a lurch of unease, sensing the argument was about to grow worse. "I don't think any man can turn Miss Barrett where she does not wish to go."

"Not long ago she found the strength to be rid of you and accept the attentions of a man worthy to have her. Now she has set her mind against him. How did you convince her to transgress against her own interests?"

Despite mounting irritation, Redfern kept his voice civil. "I cannot claim to have changed her mind. Whatever course your sister has set, she decided it for herself."

"She says she will not wed you, but she lies. I know her. I am her brother, after all."

Redfern could not help but feel a leap of pleasure at those words.

Barrett let fly a neat, powerful cross-punch, his fist narrowly missing Redfern's jaw. Redfern ducked, raising his fists to protect his face. He did not want to hurt Barrett, but he would not submit to a pummeling, either.

"Calm yourself!" Redfern snarled.

"You have done worse than defile her body. You have stolen her future and mine." Already breathing hard, Barrett dropped his fists. The spell he labored under seemed to rob him of his vitality.

"He will grow angry with her defection," he gasped. "You have ruined us."

Without asking, Redfern knew his friend spoke of Waring. "Are you so desperate for an alliance with the earl that you would purchase it with Helen's happiness?" Redfern said with contempt.

Barrett matched and raised Redfern's derision. "That is the way of the world. Beauty, wealth, and position pool their favors to build strong dynasties. Stay away. Leave this place. I would keep Helen honest for her bridegroom. She is not your light o' love."

For a moment, anger robbed Redfern of sight. "You compare your sister to a whore?"

Barrett gave a short, choking laugh. "What should I call a woman who would dangle after you for so long? You treated her like a country cottage, visiting for a holiday and ignoring her between stays. Yet she still welcomed you back time and again, taking the dust sheets off her hopes and affections."

"I want to stay with her," Redfern protested, hoping against all odds that he could make Barrett see reason. "You know I mean to marry her. I always have."

"That will never happen. Not while I live." Helen's brother folded his arms. "I remember our conversation after the night Bedford died. You knew about the League. You were plotting against us then."

Us? A new alarm quickened Redfern's pulse. "But you knew nothing about Bedford's death or the League!"

"I did not then. I had not yet earned my benefactor's trust. Now I know his mind and his plans."

And his desires, Redfern thought, his stomach rolling over with disgust.

Barrett stepped closer. "I will lock Helen away where you cannot reach her."

Redfern felt his dismay transmogrify to a hot core of wrath. "I will not stand for that."

"You have no choice." Barrett reached beneath a flowering shrub and pulled out a long-nosed pistol he had obviously hidden before he had lured Redfern away from the crowd.

"I think it is time for you to pack your things and go, Lord Redfern."

"That would be most inconvenient," said Fairmeadow, who emerged from behind Barrett to stand in his path.

Fairmeadow stood on the balls of his elegantly shod feet, quivering like a terrier defending its bone. Barrett was forced to step back, crowded by the smaller man. For the briefest moment, Redfern felt heartened and a little amused. As the Master had promised, Fairmeadow would try to defend him.

"Lord Redfern is my traveling companion," Fairmeadow shot back. He drew a lace-edged handkerchief from his sleeve and fanned himself violently. "I cannot do without him."

"You would do well to be more careful with whom you travel," Barrett growled. "You might find yourself entirely dependent on that person for society."

"I do not fathom your meaning, sir!"

"Lord Redfern is an annoyance. The earl does not

receive annoyances. He does not receive the friends of annoyances. They do not exist for him."

Fairmeadow pressed the handkerchief to his lips for a moment, as if repressing an exclamation of horror. "Egad, Redfern, we have ceased to exist! Have your man post our obituaries straight away."

Fairmeadow waved his handkerchief, and Barrett's gun flew into the flower beds as if it had been struck from his hand. Barrett cried out, diving after it. In two steps, Fairmeadow caught up and threw himself on top of his foe, smashing him into the dirt with the full weight of his body.

"Go!" cried Fairmeadow. "Get out of sight so I can calm this fool!"

"I am gone," Redfern replied, not a little impressed with Fairmeadow's flamboyant support. *Too bad he can't teach me the trick with the handkerchief.*

He brushed past Waring on his way to the house, one man refusing to give way, the other refusing to change his path. Schoolyard politics, thought Redfern, but his pride would not let him waver.

Stalking toward the house, Redfern did not at once see Helen. She had washed and changed into her pink dress, her hair coiffed by her maid. She looked soft and delicate, her fair coloring as subtle as the inside of a seashell. When she came down the steps, she balked at the look on Redfern's face.

"What happened?" she asked immediately.

"I'm leaving," he snapped, the words out before he realized what he had said.

Her eyes flew wide with hurt, their gray translucent in the bright sun. "What?"

"Your brother has all but thrown me out. He drew a

pistol on me. There is no way I can continue on as a guest. He is so far out of his senses, I cannot think what sort of scene he will cause."

"What nonsense!" she cried. "You can't go! We just . . ." She trailed off. "We just made our peace. Don't leave."

Redfern touched her arm, his skin dark against her fair complexion. The color had gone from her face, leaving it a pasty white. Redfern squirmed inside. *Is this how much distress she has always felt when I leave? How did she manage when I vanished for months—years—at a time?* Redfern kissed her hand, his throat too full to speak.

"If you are not able to watch Waring, what can I look for in your stead?" she asked, her eyes glistening. "I want his head."

"Don't." Redfern made a warning gesture. "Don't meddle in his business. Stay safe."

"I have courage enough."

"But you only have one life, and I want a share in that." Redfern felt sadness pulling at him. An exquisite vision of their future had seemed so much closer but a few minutes ago. He bent close, breathing in the scent of her hair.

"I'm not going far," he whispered in her ear. "But I must look like I am leaving. I will return. In the meantime, don't accept any rings—or any other jewelry."

Relief filling her eyes, Helen tried to smile, but it twisted into a grimace of frustration and worry.

"Helen!" Barrett was surging toward them, his face a storm.

"Good-bye," Redfern murmured. "Look for me in the shadows. I love you."

He turned and burst through the doors of Arden Hall before she could reply. This time, he thought, he would fight against the forces that kept them apart.

He ran up the stairs to his room, calling for his valet. Not long after, he heard a disturbance down the hallway. He looked out his door and saw a turmoil of hat boxes and trunks in front of Fairmeadow's room.

Fairmeadow popped out of the doorway like a puppet in the Punch and Judy shows. "I have ordered the carriage to be made ready immediately. This is shocking! And damned inconvenient."

"Did Sir Alaric not warn you that I am uneasy company?" Redfern asked in a low voice.

The little man waved an airy hand. "Oh, yes, but he did promise that time spent with you would be entertaining. I am not in the least put out. Really. I just hate hurrying to pack."

Fairmeadow gave a brief shrug and looked at the brilliant, brocaded waistcoat in his hand. "Besides, what care I for Lord Waring's hospitality, or his approbation. He has no imagination in his wardrobe. That fad for dark colors won't last. It's too somber. There are no new interpretations of black."

With a roll of his eyes, the man and his waistcoat disappeared back inside his room. Redfern glumly returned to his own room to help his valet pack. The sooner he was gone, the better.

They left in the late afternoon. No one came to bid them farewell. Redfern studied the windows for a glimpse of Helen's face, but saw nothing. Barrett was probably keeping her at his side.

As he climbed into the coach, the sunlight was slanting low through the trees, bars of gold angling over the deep green lawns. The air was losing its heat, making the stuffy carriage almost bearable.

They rolled away. Redfern, thinking, stared out the window. The outcome of this assignment so far was nowhere near anything he had expected.

Helen had been a complication. It was the only way he could describe it—a complication that he relished. He had shown his love and shared his secrets, drawing her into his mission. But, she was not a professional spy, and her shift in alliances had been detected. Fortunately, she had been caught by her brother. In another context, she might have been killed.

The thought flitted through his mind, rousing an urge to leap from the carriage and run back to Arden Hall immediately. This farce of exile was costing him precious time. He had to go back at once!

No, he had to wait until dark, at the very least. To be caught sneaking onto Waring's grounds would be folly. That kind of miscalculation would be the iceberg that wrecked the mission.

What was left of it. He had been thrown out of Arden Hall like a drunken servant. He had failed Sir Alaric. He was farther than ever from his goal of living free of the Master's yoke.

Redfern bit his thumbnail, chewing it because he did not have Waring's flesh to rend. It was ironic that permitting love had compromised its survival. Wooing Helen had cost him the easiest means of snaring the earl.

He had to recover from this. He had to have the earl's head and Helen both. One or the other was unsatisfactory. He had gambled too long in the game of spies to quit play after one bad throw.

*   *   *

"Come with me, I want to show you something."

James walked up the steps of the hall and Helen followed. Nicholas had been right—her brother was half-mad with fury. Their earlier conversation must have caused his black mood—but to threaten someone with a gun? This was not like James at all.

She watched him carefully as he began mounting one of the servants' staircases, his feet shuffling heavily from step to step.

He walks like an old man, Helen thought, appalled. Cautiously, she followed a few steps behind, keeping distance between them. She did not like this one little bit.

The stairs went higher and higher, finally opening on a small landing flanked by a pair of bedrooms. She realized they must be inside one of the square towers that sat at the topmost corners of Arden Hall.

"Look," James said, pointing to the window. "From up here you can see the bend of the Brackendale River."

Obediently, not wanting to cross him, Helen looked. They were high up and the view was magnificent, rolling green between stands of lush trees. She could barely make out a slash of silver reflection on the horizon. "Yes, I can see it."

"That is the edge of Waring's property. You could be mistress of all this." His eyes flicked up and down her face so quickly it made her giddy.

"So I could," she said, keeping the emotion out of her words. She had to convince James that nothing was amiss.

"You are not wearing your necklace." His tone was quiet and grim, as if discovering she had incurred great shame.

Muscles stiffening, she remained utterly still, suddenly too alarmed to make the slightest noise. All at once, he seemed to be too close for safety.

"Helen?" Barrett squeezed her upper arm, clumsy fingers crushing the flesh. "Helen, what have you done? Why have you turned away from our benefactor?"

With an excruciating grip, he marched her through the door to one of the bedrooms. Helen cried out, her vision going blank from the pain in her arm. The floor was polished wood and her slippers had no traction. She twisted but could not find enough purchase to wrench herself away.

"James. James! Let me go!" She stumbled, unable to get her balance. She skated, tangling her feet in the edges of the bedroom carpet.

Barrett gave a final heave, tossing her backward with a strength she had not known he possessed. As if no more than a doll, she flew through the air. She landed on the bed, but the mattress was still not enough to completely break the force of her fall. The bed creaked as she hit it, loud enough she thought it might collapse.

Is my arm broken? She clutched it with her good hand. The skin was hot and sore, the nerves of her fingers tingling wildly. *Not broken, but, oh, it hurts!*

Shocked, she pulled air into her lungs with a frightened wheeze. "What do you think you're doing?"

"I don't trust Redfern to stay away. I'm keeping you shut up tight until I can throttle the man with my own hands. He has turned you against us."

"That is nonsense!"

"I think not. I'm preserving you for Lord Waring."

"Preserving me?"

"You are going to be *his*!" He shouted the last word.

Helen struggled to sit up, the strain of anger aching in her neck and jaw. Outrage barreled over caution.

"If you force me, I will play my own games. I will whisper in Lord Waring's ear, stroking, teasing, and insinuating until he turns against you and brings your house down around your ears. If you force me into a marriage that is a rape, I will have retribution!"

Rage made Barrett's eyes stretch wide. "How dare you speak to me in such a fashion!"

Helen felt a fine, white anger. "I dare because you compel me to it!"

A long moment passed. Helen began to shake with mounting anxiety. *I think he will strike me!*

But Barrett backed away first, resettling his coat on his shoulders with the same air as a cat turns away from a standoff. He had not won, but refused to concede defeat. "Don't plan to leave Arden Hall until this matter is resolved."

Helen said nothing, unable to believe that this was her brother. He walked toward the door, pausing at the threshold. "I will leave you to think on your situation. Tidy yourself. The earl may visit."

"Perhaps I should lie upon a platter with an apple in my teeth?"

"If it increases your attraction, do it." With that, Barrett left, and he locked the door.

After dark, Redfern crept into the house through one of the library windows. Fairmeadow had pressed on to London to relay everything they had learned to Sir Alaric Fitzwilliam. Whatever else happened, at least the Master would know his suspicions about the Hellfire League had been correct.

First, Redfern checked Helen's room. She was not there. The maid, Violet, was in the adjoining chamber but had not seen her mistress for hours. This, combined with the unexpected appearance of a persona non grata, threatened to reduce the girl to hysterics. Inwardly cursing, Redfern did his best to quiet the maid with a liberal dose of brandy and hurried on. The fact that Helen had not been seen since midafternoon was the worst possible news.

He climbed to the next floor and sought out the long hall that ran along the west side of the building. The rooms here were empty, even with a large party of guests in the house. Redfern sat down in one to think.

He had to find Helen and make sure she was safe. He had to hide until the ceremony. When it started, he had to be ready to strike. As plans went, it was simple and all-encompassing. It just lacked most of the necessary detail, such as how to avoid death or enchantment or possession by whatever demons the Hellfire League called on to perform their dark magic.

He sighed. The visit to Arden Hall had been a very strange journey. At least, Redfern thought grimly, he wouldn't have to sleep over the kitchen one more night. He was heartily sick of the smell of burning bacon.

It was not much, but he would be grateful for whatever mercies the gods allowed.

Chapter 18

Oddly, being locked in a tower came as something of a relief. Helen was grateful not to have to lie and smile and pretend to adore the Earl of Waring. In contrast, the solitude of a prison held appeal. As darkness came, she sat in the bed, covers pulled up over her knees, and resigned herself to a fit of brooding. There was not much else to occupy her time.

What am I going to do? She had already established the obvious—the door was firmly locked, the windows opened to a fatal drop, and there were no hidden panels or trapdoors through which she could escape. She was well and truly caught.

Helen picked at the embroidery that ran along the edge of the bedsheet, flowers and vines worked by some woman's patient needle. The moonlight cast a silver glow over the bedclothes, making a landscape of shadows and folds. She smoothed the crisp sheets, her mind working furiously.

A door slammed on one of the floors below, making her jump. Even such a small start set her nerves jangling, bringing back all the tension of the last hours. For an instant, the shadows seemed menacing, the huge wardrobe a hiding place for lurking evil. Helen took a deep breath. The room was unfamiliar, and she had experienced a trying day. By force of will, she calmed her racing pulse. She thought of kissing Redfern, wishing back that feeling of happiness they had shared. It helped a little.

Gathering herself, Helen slipped off the bed and went to open the window, hoping a dose of country air would make her sleepy. At this rate, she would still be wide-awake come dawn, and she needed all the strength she could muster.

Curling up her toes to avoid the cold floor, she pulled apart the curtains and pushed up the sash a few inches. Cool air rushed in, smelling of some night-blooming flower. She crouched by the sill to catch the fugitive, sweet breeze. The night was clear and starlit, the moon flirting through the topmost branches of the trees. The moment was beautiful, a fleeting comfort Helen could not bear to let go. She pulled her shawl from the chair, wrapping it around her shoulders, and gazed out into the night.

Resting her elbows on the sill, she braced her chin in her hands, letting her mind drift for a long while. There were many subtle variations in the darkness. Night was not simply black, as so many claimed, but a rich tapestry of shades and shapes, movement and deceptive stillness. Small creatures went about their business, invisible except to the patient watcher. Helen lingered, immobile. She was finally calming down.

Then her interest was drawn by a shifting shadow, a long caterpillar of darkness that merged with and separated from the trees. She blinked, at first wondering if her eyes were overtired. Then she saw the shape of a hat, the nose of a horse. A party of men approached the house through the woods.

A meeting in the middle of the night? This must be what Nicholas had been waiting for! She crouched down, making herself as small as possible, only her nose and eyes above the line of the sill.

Wide-awake again, she felt her heart pattering with excitement. Her eyes strained, searching out the horsemen. For a long, frustrating moment, she thought they were gone. Then, she heard a bird flutter up from the low bushes nearer to the garden. They were there, moving noiseless and swift.

Why do I not hear them? Helen listened closely. The sound of their approach should carry, even this high up. She could hear the wind and the distant gurgle of the fountain. Then she caught the muffled creak of leather, weight shifting in a saddle. They moved like ghosts, but they were solid enough.

Now they drew close enough to count. There were four—no, five. The men sat ramrod straight, with the confident, proud bearing of cavalry officers. She remembered Hanson's story about seeing soldiers on Waring's lands. These had to be the same men, or their colleagues.

Details began to emerge from shadow. The hooves of the horses were bound with rags to muffle the noise of their approach. If the light had been better, Helen was sure she would find their harnesses wrapped to stop the jingle of metal. Stealth was apparently of prime concern.

Unconsciously, she bit her lip, her chest aching with tension. Despite her precautions, she felt conspicuous, as if a thousand lights were shining on her face, exposing her to the eyes of these dangerous men.

Her fear of discovery was doomed to increase. As the

horsemen drew closer to the house, they dropped below her field of vision. She had to rise from her crouch, showing more of herself in order to keep them in view.

The breeze coming in from the window was growing colder. Discomfort began to dampen her excitement. She was chilly now, trembling not just from fear.

The horsemen stopped at the edge of the garden, staying in the shadow of the trees. Two dismounted, and Helen thought she heard a few words exchanged. One of the horses snorted, pawing the ground. Its rider soothed the beast, patting its neck and offering it a treat from his pocket.

The two men who had dismounted walked toward the house. Helen ducked, crawling to the side of the window and peering out at an oblique angle. They stopped at one of the small servants' doors some yards to the left of Helen's window and sheltered by a narrow stone overhang. The door, she assumed, led to the cellars. Or the tunnels? *This is no wine delivery,* she thought grimly.

Using the curtain as a shield, Helen eased up the wall. If she ducked behind its heavy velvet, the material provided a bit of warmth as well as disguise. From beneath the thick fall of fabric, she held back the edge of the curtain with her fingers. With one cheek resting on the plaster wall, she could peer out and just see the cellar door. She allowed herself a quick self-congratulation for resourcefulness. So far, her surveillance was going well.

The shorter of the men knocked at the door, two quick raps. Helen waited, breathless. The men stepped into the shadows, out of Helen's view.

Come back where I can see you! She waited, her heart missing a beat, until the cellar door swung open. A hand with a shuttered lantern emerged, spilling a thin band of light. The men advanced, and now she could see their clothes—the dark, nondescript coats and breeches of the merchant class. At once, they looked respectable and invisible. It was only their air of command that set them apart and said they were no shopkeepers.

Now a third horseman was walking across the lawn. No, thought Helen, he did not walk. He marched. He strutted. Even though he was dressed in identical fashion, this had to be the leader of the little troop.

He stopped a few feet from the door and bowed, a brief, jerky movement. The figure who had opened the door set down the lantern and stepped forward to take his hand. Helen pressed her lips together. The man at the door was the Earl of Waring. Of course.

At least it isn't James, she thought. She had seen enough of her brother's guilt for one day.

The men shook hands; then the first two horsemen bowed to Waring. The leader bowed again, then embraced Waring and kissed him on both cheeks. The ceremony of polite greetings took some time.

Definitely French, thought Helen.

Waring opened the door to the cellar and the three men followed him into the house. The other two horsemen stayed at the edge of the garden, watching the horses.

Now thoroughly chilled, Helen waited some time before crawling into her bed to get warm. She saw nothing more. Whatever action was taking place was deep under the house.

What are they doing? Helen wondered. Who exactly were these Frenchmen? Most importantly, by what means could she find out?

She was helpless, trapped. Seething with frustration, Helen tossed in her bed. She got up several times to peer out the window, waiting to see them leave in case she learned something more.

The clock struck three when two of the men finally emerged from the cellar to join their fellows and melted into the darkness of the trees, leading the fifth horse. Helen felt ragged with fatigue. Their meeting had lasted close to four hours.

One of the men was still in the house. Who was he? Where was he?

She pulled the covers up to her chin, staring at the window from where she lay. The first false light of dawn was fading the stars. What should she do? Obviously, Redfern needed to know about the meeting as soon as possible. He said he would come back. How long would it take him before he realized she was locked up here? Would he rescue her in time to learn what she had seen? She rolled onto her back, her mind whirring like a spinning wheel.

Waring's house party provided a perfect alibi for the earl. To the casual observer, there was no time when he could have met with foreign agents. It just would not seem possible—he was always in the company of his guests.

The plan was almost perfect. Normally, not a soul would be awake in the dead of night. No one would see the visitors—except Helen, who was too upset to sleep.

Helen rolled over, trying to mound her pillow into a more comfortable shape. *It never pays to cross a woman. She will always find you out.*

The first thing Redfern had to do was locate Helen. If she was missing, there was a good chance she was being held near the heart of villainous activity. Find her, catch Waring. Perhaps that was merely an excuse to make her

welfare his priority, but Redfern refused to argue with any
logic that brought them together more quickly.

He rose from his chair in the empty bedroom. The
chambers along the west hallway were eerily silent.
There was no light but the moon through the many-paned
windows. Like ghosts, the furniture sat shrouded by dust
sheets, humps of white and gray in the murky darkness.
Carpets lay in rolls, wrapped up against the ravages of
moths. Everything smelled faintly damp, like wet ashes
and the first flush of a creeping mold.

When he had sat down, he had thrown the dust sheet
from that chair to the floor. He picked it up, planning to
replace it before leaving the room. There was no point in
drawing attention to the fact someone had been in the
abandoned rooms.

"I expect all women wish their men were so tidy. How
lucky the banker's daughter would be to get her heart's
desire. It is so sad that she will not." The voice was female and all too familiar.

Redfern dropped the sheet. It fell with a rustle to the
dusty floor. He had heard no one moving down the hall,
not the rustle of a skirt, not the tread of even the lightest
slipper. The hair along his neck bristled.

He looked up. Laura Gianotta stood in the doorway,
one hand on the frame. Shadows hid her face, but he
knew her voluptuous form. He knew the butter-rich accent that made every phrase something more than mere
words.

"Madam," he said. "So, you have found me out. What
now?"

She dropped her hand from the door frame and took a
step forward. Like something living, the soft silk of her
gown clung and caressed her legs as she moved. It was

tight under the breasts and topped with a layer of transparent material stitched with tiny gems. As the moonlight caught her dress, it reflected a cloud of subdued glitter.

Redfern's mouth went dry with a mix of apprehension and arousal. He couldn't help the latter. He was a man, and she was like something out of an opium dream.

"What now? Now I finally have you to myself. I did not think you would stay away." She looked at him from under the veil of her dark lashes.

She had drawn close enough that she laid a hand on his chest, smoothing the lapel of his coat. Her arms were bare and slim, their rounded flesh as perfect as those of Bernini's marble nymphs.

Redfern gently pushed away her hand. "I came back for purposes other than dalliance, madam."

"And if you chose to dally, it would be with someone other than me? Is that not your meaning?" She turned her back so quickly, her skirts swirled around her feet.

"I would not be a gentleman if I misled you."

She chuckled low in her throat. With a purely animal instinct, Redfern felt himself reaching for the knife in his sleeve. Something in that laugh was pure malice. The sound made him want to run and run until he was safe in blessed sunlight. La Gianotta was beautiful but terrifying.

She grasped the edge of the dustcover shrouding the bed and began pulling it off, hand over hand, as one would haul in a rope. The drop sheet began slithering over the mattress with a dry, rasping whisper.

Without turning his back on the woman, Redfern edged toward the door. The combination of beds and La Gianotta was not one he cared to explore. What Hanson saw in her was an utter mystery.

"No, no," she waved an admonishing finger. "I did not give you leave to go."

Redfern's feet froze to the floor. It seemed natural to stop, as if it was the only proper thing to do.

La Gianotta had bared the bed. It lay like a white tablet in the fugitive light, a blank page waiting for the stroke of a pen. It did not bear thinking what the words would be.

"There are many ways to stop your interference in our little ceremony," she said. "Ah, yes, do not pretend ignorance. Barrett has told us you suspected the Hellfire League from the beginning. Someone out there has a sharp nose, because you are not the first agent deployed against us, nor the first I have had to discourage."

The Master. Bedford. The garrote of wire. Thoughts chased themselves through Redfern's mind.

"One circumstance eludes me," she said. I could never understand why Lord Bedford's body was found in the park. Coleman and I killed him in an alley. Poor Bedford never suspected a pair of actors strolling home from the theater would murder him."

I was to meet Bedford. The coach brought him to me. Why? Justice? A warning?

The woman drew close, so close he could smell the spicy scent from her skin. His own flesh warmed, as if his treacherous blood rose to meet her nearness. Instinct told him to pull back.

I cannot move! His mind raced, frantically commanding his limbs to push her away, to flee, but he could not stir so much as one toe.

La Gianotta repeated her low, intimate, bone-chilling laugh. Redfern was a prisoner, his mind shrieking against the inanimate clay of his body.

She pushed against him, winding her arms around his

neck. His flesh, now independent from his mind, responded with a rich, impatient aching.

"I think you will have a different end from Bedford. I don't trust your corpse to stay where I put it, and too many dead men may prove inconvenient."

He struggled to protest, to give voice to his outrage, but his tongue was no longer his own.

She slid her belly against his aching flesh. His breath caught with a hiss.

A half smile curled her lips. "There, you see, much better than a quick end. I can make this quite literally last forever."

She licked the length of his jaw. "One taste of me and you will not be able to abide the touch of another. I can keep you all for myself. You are so pretty and you could be so useful."

La Gianotta pulled him to the bed, and he followed like a willing dog. His fingers fumbled with the metal hooks that clasped her bodice, a treasury of soft flesh beneath the gossamer veil of her gown.

She wore nothing beneath. Redfern's reason began to drown, subsumed by the raging glee of his desire. His hands could barely remember how to work and the urge to rip the dress away began to take over.

"Here." She undid the last hooks herself, letting the gown drift soundlessly to the floor. Her breasts fell free, the nipples already swollen, waiting to be taken.

With mindless greed, Redfern pushed her down on the bare bed, trapping her with his body. She laughed, kissing his lips, his jaw, his throat. He burned as if he was himself melting into hellfire.

Confusion blotted out his thoughts. The beauty that dazzled his eyes belonged to a monster. That knowledge counted for naught with his mounting need. His body crushed against her, obeying the demand for surrender.

I am lost! He had never understood the dread of damnation until that moment. This was it. He was drowning where there was no shore. His life, his love for Helen, would sink to black, bottomless depths.

He felt the pressure of her teeth against his throat, her tongue tasting him in quick, tentative flicks. The bite became painful, threatening to break through his skin. *This is no woman, this is a beast!*

Revulsion welled up in him, gagging, retching, finally gorging him with enough disgust to rip through the spell.

He flung himself off the bed with a roar, cold perspiration coursing down his temples. "Get away from me!"

She rolled onto all fours, her naked body as lithe and sleek as a panther. Anger, and perhaps hunger, crumpled her face, lighting her eyes with feral hate. She hissed, a long rattle of fury.

It quenched all suggestion of desire. As quickly as it had been taken, Redfern's body was his once more. He backed away, feeling sullied by her touch.

But as he retreated, he stepped into a cold, still pool of hair. The hair on his arms rose, as much a response to the sensation of magnetism as of temperature.

The air was thick with portent. He felt wind ruffle his hair, like a stirring of breath. Something was behind him, watching. He heard his own voice giving a wordless cry of consternation.

He threw himself to the side, trying to pull away from this new threat as well as the creature by the bed. La Gianotta was up now, stepping into her dress. Her eyes stayed on Redfern, cruel and angry.

Redfern put his back to the wall. Fear hovered at a lit-

tle distance, where he had pushed it long enough to think.
His gaze roved from the bed to the doorway, where the
nameless cold hovered. He could feel it against his right
side, radiating like the chill from a block of ice.

Black on black, some of the darkness broke away,
curling and spiraling, gathering itself until it was more
solid than the shadow around it. Redfern's lips parted,
forgetting for a moment everything but the mystery before him.

The cold intensified. La Gianotta hissed again, her fingers clenching. She sounded afraid, and that made everything worse. What could frighten her?

The coachman stood in the doorway. Redfern's eyes
strained for some semblance of his brother, but there was
no face where there should have been features. There was
only darkness.

He heard the same whispering exhalation he had heard
in the tunnels. It came from everywhere and nowhere,
perhaps only in his imagination. A smell like old, rotting
leaves filled the room.

Without visibly moving, the thing seemed to come
across the threshold. It was hard to tell its size, for it
seemed to stretch to the high ceiling and yet be no taller
than a man. La Gianotta cowered against the bed. She
seemed to be the one the coachman wanted.

She whimpered, the cry of a cornered beast. Nature
prompted Redfern to help any creature in distress, but he
knew she would turn on him with the ferocity of a hungry serpent the moment danger was past.

Crouching, she bared her teeth. They were sharp, almost too pointed to be those of a woman. The apparition
of the coachman wavered before her, its black form shifting and wavering like a trick of the eye.

"Go." The word formed in Redfern's mind. Unlike the time in the tunnel, there was no voice, just the thought. Disappointment tugged at Redfern's heart. He wanted to hear it speak.

"Michael?" he whispered, as if he might destroy the spirit with the sound of his words.

"Go. Hide yourself until sunrise. Do not let yourself sleep until dawn walks the sky. It is not safe in this house."

Again, he could not identify the voice, as if it lived as much within him as without. Redfern burned with the ache to know what soul lurked in that dark form.

As if it read his thoughts, it replied. "Do not question me."

The coachman raised his arms, the caped coat flaring out like the shadowy wings of the black moth. Redfern could not tell if it faced him, or if it faced Laura. It was a mass of fearful shadow, looming larger and more menacing as scraps of darkness seemed to break away from the corners and float toward it. Towering, ragged, the coachman grew until it loomed like a mountain of fluttering blackness. La Gianotta gave a yowl, somewhere between a snake's rattle and the night-shriek of a cat. The sound was pure, frustrated fear.

The doorway was clear. Redfern ran.

Chapter 19

Helen slept the better part of the day. Though she had been terrorized and terrified, she had been awake for nearly forty-eight grueling hours. Her body needed to rest, so rest it did.

When she finally woke, the light indicated it was the middle of the afternoon, probably about three or four o'clock. A black lacquered tray sat on the stool at the foot of the bed. She threw the covers off and crawled across the bedclothes to examine it. There were jugs of both water and wine, bread, cheese, and fruit. The sight and smell of it reminded Helen she had not eaten since the garden party the day before. Hunger cramped her stomach.

But can I trust any of this to be free of drugs and poisons? She sniffed the jug of water. It smelled clean. She poured a little into a glass and touched it with her tongue. There was no taste. Fine, she would drink that and leave the wine. In the same way, she chose to eat the bread and leave the rest. She had heard too many nursery stories about maidens and lethal apples.

She ate and tidied herself as best she could. Her arm

where James had gripped her was sore and bruised, and she felt stiff from an unaccustomed bout of sprinting and tree climbing. Simple movements were suddenly a source of discomfort.

Just as she finished her meager toilette, she heard the lock of the door rattle and grind as a key turned the old iron mechanism. Her back to the window, she faced the door as the Earl of Waring entered and closed the door behind him. As he slipped the key into his waistcoat pocket, her breath left her body, driven out by apprehension.

Tidy and perfectly groomed as ever, Waring wore a dark gray coat over a pale blue silk waistcoat. A bloodred ruby was pinned into his cravat. He looked dressed for an afternoon concert.

"Good afternoon, my dear Helen," he said affably. "I hear you have lost the necklace I gave you. Your brother suspects it might have left Arden Hall in Lord Redfern's pocket."

He stopped between the door and the bed. The room was small enough that it was the only real place to stand.

"Have you come to tell me how I shall be punished for its loss?" Helen replied, in no mood for pleasantries. "I am sorry, I am sure it was an expensive gift."

"We both know its value was greater than the price of the gems. Do not be coy, Helen. The time for games is done."

He folded his arms, looking her up and down. "After all, perhaps the necklace has served its purpose. What is gone, is gone. If I cannot control you with sorcery, locks and bolts will do equally well."

Helen clasped her hands behind her back to hide the trembling in her fingers. Waring did not deserve the pleasure of her fear. "It depends on your goal, sir. If your aim is to keep me as a captive audience for your escapades, I am clearly at your disposal."

He laughed, the same mellow chuckle he used during all their banter. It was as if this was but one more skirmish of repartee. "Do not think I am going to regale you with a catalogue of my prospective villainy. That is the stuff of low farce, and you will find out what I have in mind when events have ripened."

Despite her pretense of courage, she gulped. How could he be so composed? "Then why are you here?"

"I am here primarily to make sure your brother did not hurt you."

Helen felt a start of apprehension. "You believe he is so far under the influence of his own necklace—the watch chain or whatever you gave him—that he might do me harm?"

Waring leaned against the edge of the dressing table. "I did not use the same enchantment on him as I did on you. As you might have guessed, my control over James grew more slowly and went deeper than it did in your case. I need him to work on my behalf in many delicate situations. I cannot risk the spell being broken by something so trivial as the loss of an item or an old passion being rekindled."

He gave a slow smile that stopped Helen's blood in her veins. "The only thing that will break my hold on Barrett is my death. That will not be easy to achieve."

Which is not to say that I will not try, Helen thought with fierce desperation.

"In your case, all I needed was your cooperation for a time. The necklace was good enough for that. We have been seen in society as a courting couple. No one will marvel if we marry. It is a pity that you have lost your freedom of movement, but I have you at Arden Hall where I want you to live. We will wed here. Your dowry, as you might have surmised from our earlier conversations, is not your only charm. The families of the Circle are dwindling. You can give me heirs worthy of the Waring title."

His matter-of-fact tone, as much as the scope of his plans, curdled the blood in her veins. Helen found herself stammering. "W-why not change me as you did my brother?"

Her obvious fear kindled an unpleasant light of interest in his expression. "It's not completely healthy and, as you shall be the mother of my children, I do want you in the best condition."

Weakness robbed the strength from her legs. She sank to her knees, her pink dress pooling around her.

Amusement flickered in his blue eyes. "Go ahead, give your thoughts voice. I am a monster. You will feel better for hurling insults at my head."

"And they would all be true," she said, but her words felt lame.

"Quite probably." He straightened from his slouch against the dressing table. "I'll have your maid bring up your things later. I think she can be persuaded to share your confinement with you, and I am sure the company will be a comfort."

Waring took the key from his waistcoat. "Though it might be a week or so before she is completely ready to assume her new duties. As you saw in your brother's case, the permanent alteration of a subject's mind does not take place immediately. Good things take time."

"Oh, Violet!" Helen burst into tears. She couldn't help

herself. It was one thing to be brave on her own account, but her maid was a silly, innocent girl.

"Come, come, we have avoided high drama so far. Your stern resolve is what I admire most in you. You have held up amazingly well, even if your erstwhile lover did abandon you in the end."

Helen kept her eyes down. *This is a trap. He is waiting for me to deny it, to say Nicholas will rescue me. Then the earl will know whether there was a plan for him to return.*

After a pause, Waring left, locking the door behind him. Helen remained on the floor, hugging herself. He had scattered the seeds of doubt, but she struggled to brush them aside.

Nicholas will come. He promised.

As soon as he escaped La Gianotta, Redfern indeed began searching the house for Helen, working his way through Arden Hall by way of the back staircases. He meant to follow a basic grid, working his way down each hallway in turn before moving to the next floor. It should have been simple.

It was not. He was distracted by the scene he had just endured. What was Laura Gianotta? Was she even human? He wondered for a long, cold moment about Hanson. Was he in her thrall? Had they been safe to trust him, or was he bound to La Gianotta by more than the bonds of a casual liaison?

I fell into her web so easily, Redfern thought, his spirits as black as the coachman's coat. *She is more dangerous than I would have dreamed possible.*

He stopped walking, thoughts of the actress fading in

the light of a new problem. He appeared to be losing his sense of direction.

The floor plan of Arden Hall was straightforward— four hallways formed a rectangle on each level. Still, as he turned from the east hall to move south, he found himself back at the beginning of the same row of rooms. He went up a stairway, but found himself arriving at the story below.

Redfern paused again, realizing with a rush of frustration that he was wasting time and energy. Perhaps he was overtired and becoming lost because he could not think clearly. Perhaps the same forces that had made the tunnel entrance disappear had followed him up from the maze beneath Arden Hall. The last thought made him prickle with cold sweat.

Determined to outwit whatever was leading him in circles, he took out his pocket handkerchief and tied it around the handle of the last door of the east hallway. There would be no mistaking this door for another. He turned into the south hall.

The row of dimly lit doors came into view, each with a handkerchief tied to its door handle. Redfern cursed roundly. He traced his steps backward, taking his handkerchief from what he believed was the correct door.

When he went forward again, all the door handles were empty. There was no way to know where he had been, or where he was going. *I'm trapped,* he thought desperately, and he was right.

Frantic, Redfern continued on, around and around the same halls and stairs. Corridors seemed to stretch for miles, steps seemed to double and triple in number. Exhausted, he had to push on, but could never gain an inch of ground until he heard the clock on the landing strike four.

Only then did he go up the staircase and actually ascend to another floor. As in the old legends, dawn broke the dark spell.

When he finally achieved the upstairs landing and saw the different carpet and different doorways, he nearly shouted for joy. With breath heaving loud in his lungs, he slumped against the wall and cleared his head to make new plans. He had just enough time to get out of sight before the servants set to work. The house had kept him away from Helen all night. He would have to lie low until the morning flurry of household activity was done. When that quieted, he could resume his labors.

He found a room filled with old furniture, abandoned trunks, and other detritus of a great house. The ceiling sloped, showing it was right beneath the roof. From the window, he could see the pale light wash the garden from black to gray. With great gratitude, he watched dawn bleach the stars from the sky. Birds began to stir. Redfern sat on the floor of the lumber room, letting the first rays of sun touch his face. It felt as powerful as armor, as healing as balm.

Calmed by the warm sunlight, he silently thanked the coachman. Whether it was Michael or some other wandering spirit, it had saved him from Laura Gianotta.

Exhausted, Redfern fell asleep where he sat. Like a watchful mother, the sun kept him resting safely until it was time for her to go.

Helen watched the light fade. It left first in the corners, angling away from the sharp edges of the floors and walls to leave tangles of shadow like dust kittens waiting for the broom. Then the darkness seeped out of the cracks around the floor, a stain that spread and merged to rivers and streams of night. As she watched, continents of light shrank to islands, then paled, finally surrendering to a blue-gray dusk that drank the warmth from the room, leaving her alone and cold.

Nicholas had not come.

She considered weeping, but somehow she had gone beyond the release of tears. Her emotions battled with more than distress at her personal plight. Tonight the Hellfire League would work its magic for the French enemy. She did not need to cry, but to blast Arden Hall from its foundations.

She got up and looked out the window. The shadow of the hall stretched like a cloak on the lawn before her, a sharp, inky silhouette. Beyond, tips of light still greened the highest hilltops.

I am in the eastern tower, she realized with a jolt. A candle in one of the windows of this tower was their signal to Hanson to send help.

She looked around with new purpose. There were two four-armed candelabra on the dressing table, ugly porcelain affairs covered with painted roses. Eager, she grabbed one and set it on the wide ledge of the window. The candles were still long, with a satisfying amount left to burn.

These would be grand if I only had the means to light them! Helen put her hands on her hips, her sense of accomplishment short-lived. She had no matches or flint or fire. *Perdition!*

She thought enviously of Hanson's trick with the flame in the palm of his hand.

Absorbed in thought, she did not at first detect the

faint smell of decay that filled the room. By the time it disturbed her concentration, she had started to shiver from an unexpected gust of cold air behind her.

She turned around, thinking someone had opened the door unheard. A faint cry of surprise escaped her. The door was closed, but Nicholas stood in the room, his features faded in the growing darkness. His form seemed a shadow on a shadow.

"I have brought you light," he said, but the voice was wrong. The timbre was similar, but not the same.

Now that she guessed it was not Nicholas, she could see the figure was an inch or so shorter, his shoulders more heavily fleshed. Yet his stance, the set of his head was the same. Who was this man? A creeping sense of unease pebbled the flesh on her arms.

"Thank you," she said, her words careful. She was not even sure of his meaning. If he brought light, where was it?

The candles beside her sprang into flame. Helen jumped, skittering sideways away from their eldritch brightness. Their flames were pale, almost colorless for a few seconds, sputtering madly before settling into an ordinary yellow glow.

"Do not fear me," the man said.

She barely had time to look away from the candles before he vanished. The room was undisturbed. The door had not opened and closed. He was there, and then not.

Her heart thundering in her breast, Helen grabbed the wall for support. Her knees were wobbling. For one instant, she had seen his face. Her head swam with shock.

She had met Michael Saville on only a handful of occasions, but she knew his face well enough to know she had been visited by a dead man. A dead man who had brought ruin and shame upon his family.

What did this mean? What did it mean for Nicholas? Weakness made her lean against the frame of the window, drawing close to the comforting light of the candles. But then she sprang upright, an involuntary squeak leaving her lips. Something cold had brushed her hand!

An iron key sat on the window ledge. She grabbed it with both hands. *Thank you, Michael!*

Racing across the room, she slid it into the lock. It turned with perfect ease. She gave a soft crow of triumph.

Escape from the tower was paramount. Next, she would find Nicholas. Failing that, she would leave Arden Hall and run for help. She would take whatever opportunities came her way. Without a weapon, she did not have many choices.

Helen lit one of the candles from the second candelabra and headed for the tower stairs. She started down, sheltering the candle flame from the currents of air in the stairwell.

And arrived on the next landing only to find herself back where she had started. Helen stood a moment, doubting herself. She had been at the top of the stairway before. She was at the top of the stairway again. She descended once more.

Once again, she was at the top of the stairs.

This is not the time for games, she thought crossly. *There must be some magic meant to keep me from breaking free.*

She fumbled for her pocket and felt a tingle of relief when her fingers touched the shape of Hanson's folding knife. He said silver would break enchantments.

She unfolded it and, holding the knife ahead of her in

one hand and the candle in the other, proceeded down the stairs for the third try. This time she reached the landing below.

Aha! Helen thought.

The knife gave a decided tug to the left. She frowned. The knife was meant to break enchantments, not to be enchanted itself. Was this the sign of some latent talent passed down from her grandfather, another helping hint from a ghost, or a trick? She wasn't even going to try and puzzle that one out. She turned left. She was lost in this part of the house, anyway. She may as well follow its lead.

Folding the knife and tucking it in the sash of her dress seemed to work just as well as holding it. She could still feel which way it wanted her to go. Following the knife to the north side of the hall, she could hear people moving out of sight down the long corridors ahead. She tread as softly as she could, shielding the candle flame from sight with her hand. The voices grew louder and she hurried down a back stairway before she could be seen.

These stairs went all the way down to the main level, the last flight ending in a door to the back garden. Helen slipped out, blowing out the candle. The full moon washed the night in a luminous glow.

Helen crouched low beside a rosemary bush, calculating the best way to reach the edge of the park. She thought she could remember the way to Bedford's house. With any luck, Hanson would be there or on his way to Arden Hall in response to the light in the east-tower window. He would provide her with safety.

On the other hand, she could attempt to find an entrance to the underground tunnels. Armed with her trusty silver knife, could she find a way to stop the ceremony?

Helen wavered with indecision. *After all, Nicholas might need my help, and there might be an opportunity to free James.* But how, realistically, could she hope to do that?

A dozen yards away, the side door of the house creaked open. Helen shrank into a tighter ball, cursing the pale color of her dress. She felt conspicuous and vulnerable. Trying to quiet her breathing, she gulped a mouthful of the rosemary-scented air and held it.

Waring stepped out the door, followed by James and Layton. James came out last, shutting the door behind him while Layton stretched luxuriously, wandering in a circle on the lawn. By contrast, Waring was all business, consulting a large book he carried. They started in the opposite direction, following a path down the side of the house. None of them took any notice of Helen.

At the sight of the trio, she flushed with rage. These men were monsters, and they had made a monster of her brother. A cold, still logic took possession of her mind. Closing around the hilt of the knife, her fingers flexed to take a better grip. If they caught her, she would fight. She was angry and frightened enough to lash out.

The sight of her adversaries settled Helen's mind. Waring and Layton had to be punished. She, personally, would march James right back to his family where he belonged. There had to be a way to stop Waring's madness.

Willing herself invisible, she rose and ghosted behind them along the path. After a few dozen yards, Waring stopped at the door to one of the kitchen storerooms. Helen dove behind a jog in the wall, remembering this was where Nicholas had found the entrance to the tunnels. One by one, the men disappeared through the door. *It's started,* thought Helen. *The ritual, the darkness.*

My God, it's begun. She looked up at the stars, panting with fright.

I can't follow them. If I do, I'll run into one or the other around some bend. At the least, she'd lose the advantage of surprise. At worst . . . she could not even contemplate that.

A less obvious route might let her get close without being seen. She would enter the tunnels through the trapdoor in the gardener's shed, and creep up on them from there.

Chapter 20

Redfern jolted awake, horrified that he had slept so long. He had meant merely to rest a little, out of sight of the servants bent upon their morning chores. Precious hours had been lost, but he felt clearheaded and energized, as if it had been more than ordinary sleep.

He looked out the window, cursing the late hour. The sun was down, the dusk fading to true darkness. Tonight the ceremony would take place. Time for new tactics. Now, with the ritual so near, the first step to safety—his and Helen's—was dousing the flames of the Hellfire League. Nothing could be accomplished until the League was stopped. He felt a flutter of nerves, half anticipation, half dread.

Redfern waited a few minutes until the concealing darkness had thickened. Cautiously, he climbed out the window, lowering himself to a gable roof. From there he reached the branch of an overhanging plane tree and made his way to the ground. There was no point in risking a repeat of the previous night's fruitless wanderings, going over and over the same ground, when he could take another route to the tunnels beneath the hall.

He dropped out of the plane tree, his boots hitting the grass with a soft thud. Late though it was, the air still held the last kiss of warmth from the day. The scent of the garden was musky-sweet with evening blooms. Redfern headed for the deepest shadows next to the house. He ran, quick and silent, until he found the entrance he had used before to reach the tunnels.

It was hard to move the heavy barrels off the trapdoor, but Helen was not in a mood to be discouraged. She had run all the way to the gardener's shed, startling with every hoot of an owl. By this point, she was brimming with enough nervous energy to compensate for lack of brute strength. A mere physical obstacle did not stand a chance.

A ladder led from the trapdoor down to a flagstone floor. The air here was damp and chilly and had the same scent of old stone as a crypt. Helen shivered, wishing she had kept her candle. As her eyes adjusted to the increased darkness, she could just make out the tunnel walls. There had to be light coming from somewhere, however faint. She took three steps, her arms stretched out to feel her way along.

Her toes stubbed against a ridge, and the flagstones gave way to bricks. She went a little farther, listening to the echoes of her footsteps.

The tunnel turned sharply, and the light increased. Far ahead of her, someone had lit a sconce on the wall. The silver knife urged her toward it. Faster now that she could see where she was going, Helen complied.

As she hurried along, she began to notice the occasional stone with the black moth design set into the floor. Wall lights appeared at regular intervals, just often enough to navigate through the gloom. Occasionally, she could see where water had leaked through, blackening the bricks with streaks of dirt and mold. In one place, a tree root had crumbled the side of the tunnel. Waring needed to see to the maintenance of his chambers of doom.

No wonder he needs my dowry, she thought dryly. *His games room is falling to ruin.*

Without the knife, she would have been hopelessly lost. As it was, it still took some time before she began to hear voices.

Helen's pace began to slow. It would not do to run headlong into the earl. The voices fell silent. She stopped, withdrawing into the mouth of one of the unlit tunnels.

Far to her right, she heard a shuffling, like the movement of many feet. Then she heard one man speak, his voice echoing.

"In balance, the light and the darkness are praised." Helen recognized Waring's voice.

A group of voices, male and female, responded. "In pairing the dark and the lightness are equal."

"Where dark is alone find the void and the power," intoned the earl.

"Where dark is alone find destruction," responded the others.

"Lo, let the power of darkness be praised," said Waring.

"Let the power of light be forgotten."

Helen felt her brows knitting together as she struggled to believe her ears. It was one thing to hear about the League's ceremony, another to actually witness its beginning. A mixture of fear, outrage, and disbelief beset her.

Somewhere in the mix of her emotions, she was faintly embarrassed. There had to be something of the schoolboy in anyone who would gather with friends to chant doggerel verses in underground tunnels. It simply was not adult behavior.

Which did not mean the League was not dangerous, just lacking in good taste.

Helen heard one set of footsteps and the rustling of cloth. Then there was the fall of more feet, then more, and more swishing of fabric. A low, droning chant of male voices began, and Helen realized they were coming toward her. She retreated farther into her hiding place. Female voices joined the men, and she realized they were now singing the verse she just heard as they processed through the tunnel.

Not only bad poetry, she thought, her fear more comfortable as sarcasm, *but wretched singers, too.*

Waring passed the mouth of the tunnel first, wearing a gray-hooded robe and a bloodred tabard emblazoned with the moth. He carried a book and seemed to study it as he walked, chanting to the darkness, one deliberate step at a time.

Nerves made Helen want to giggle at the sight.

Then came Layton and another man. They carried spears draped with tall, narrow banners showing the moth on a field of flames. After them was a figure she did not know, small and dark and looking uncomfortable. Helen wondered if he were the Frenchman she had seen arrive the night before.

Two by two came the rest, fourteen in all, including the marchioness and Lady Gray. All wore the same hooded gray robes as Waring, though only he had the blood-colored tabard.

They all are part of the Hellfire League! These are the traitors who would bring the war to our doorstep!

The procession moved on, slow and solemn. They

chanted, finishing the verse and starting again, each iteration gaining in urgency. Dark emotion thickened the air and made the shadows draw around, noose-tight.

Last, his head bowed and hands clasped before him, came James.

At the sight of her brother, a tear slid down Helen's cheek. *He is lost to me forever,* she thought, surrendering to hopelessness as she watched him disappear from sight.

"You should not spy if you will be upset by what you see," said the silky voice of Laura Gianotta.

Helen glanced up, her heart skipping wildly at the woman's sudden appearance. "Hush!" she replied. "They will know we are here."

The actress's full lips lifted in a predatory smile. "Oh, they know I am here already. There are a handful of us whose task is to prevent interruption from intruders like you. Now, I would be very interested to know how you got past my wards."

"I walked."

"It was not Redfern who released you?"

Nicholas came back! New life flooded Helen's heart. "I let myself out. A lady can wait only so long before boredom sets in."

"Ah." Laura Gianotta shifted her weight from one hip to other, the movement sending a glitter down the front of her jewelled dress like the iridescence of scales. "Well, he must not have reached your lofty tower once he—most unchivalrously—left me to fend for myself last night. Nevertheless, I did keep him occupied for a time. Quite an ardent man, once properly motivated."

Helen's eyes narrowed. "I do not believe you."

The Italian tossed something at Helen's feet that skittered and bounced off the wall of the tunnel. It was a man's coat button. "I ripped it from his clothes as he writhed on top of me."

Helen had no idea if it belonged to Nicholas. Unlike Fairmeadow, he was not prone to wildly distinctive garments. The button could have come from anywhere.

Still, as much as she loved Nicholas, there were misgivings five years of waiting had made. He was used to freedom. Why wouldn't he take advantage of a lovely woman who offered herself?

Helen pressed her lips together, angry with her own uncertainty.

"You doubt me," said La Gianotta, her voice rich with amusement. "You doubt him."

"Why spread poison this way?" Helen asked, forcing her voice to be calm.

"It creates *balance*." She said the word with derision, echoing the chant from the ceremony. She obviously thought no more of the poetry than Helen did. "You took the earl from me. I take your man from you."

"I don't want the earl!"

"But he wants you. You can give him heirs. I cannot. You will displace me from his side."

La Gianotta took a step forward. There was such menace in the simple movement, Helen began to panic. Tension gathered around the actress, her body seeming to coil like a snake about to strike.

"Then let me leave!" cried Helen, wanting nothing more at that instant than to flee the woman. "I will run far away where the earl cannot find me! He will be all yours!"

She fumbled at her waist for the knife. It had slipped and tangled in her sash, hiding in the folds of satin.

"No, no, dear Helen. If you have a tongue left to tell

tales, I'm afraid the earl cannot sleep soundly. If he does not rest well, then neither do I. Such is the price of devotion my lord commands."

Helen's fingers touched the metal of the knife hilt. Warm from her body, it felt like something living as her fingers drew it out and unfolded the sleek silver blade.

Laura stopped with a hissing gasp, equal parts surprise and laughter. "You think to stop me with such a little thing?"

Stop her from what? The hair on her arms rising, Helen began to back into the adjoining tunnel where the Hellfire League had passed. "Stay away!"

"I think not."

La Gianotta made a snatching gesture, and Helen felt her limbs jerk. Her body froze for an instant, but the sensation faded, leaving behind a bruising pain.

What is this? She can drag me to a halt with the crook of her finger? Helen shook with fear, her feet clumsy as she tried to run backward. She held out the knife like a shield, praying it was enough to ward off the woman—if that was even what she was.

La Gianotta's teeth bared, sharp and white. "Is that a little silver trinket you have? It will slow me down, but cannot stop me altogether."

Laura flicked her wrist, as if batting a fly. Helen felt the knife slip, and she grabbed it with both hands, pulling the hilt close to her body.

Slowing La Gianotta's magic might be enough to gain the upper hand. Growing up around her older brother and his friends, Helen had scrapped all her childhood. She had the advantage of height and reach on the actress. A physical fight didn't frighten her, if she could just get past the woman's unnatural powers.

Helen's mind now was utterly clear, aware of every placement of her foot, every winking gem on La Gianotta's dress. Like a bad card player, the actress signaled everything, the glittering cloth announcing the least shift in posture.

Do your worst, you vain hag. I'll be there one move ahead of you. Without looking, Helen was aware she had reached the junction of the tunnel. The increased echo and movement of air meant more room to maneuver.

With an annoyed frown, the actress began to circle, the motion driving Helen's back closer to the wall.

She's trying to trap me. Helen took two long steps back, avoiding her reach.

Then La Gianotta made a thrusting motion that threw Helen flat on her back. Her back cracked on the bricks. Pain shot from her tailbone to her teeth.

That was not all. The knife had twisted as she fell, cutting through her dress and dragging a long scratch along her thigh. It was not deep, but still she felt the hot kiss of blood. Whatever silver alloy the knife was made of, it took a sharp edge. Helen swore, anger and pain overtaking fear.

Laura sniffed delicately, her dark eyes seeming to fill her face. "First wound goes to me."

With another curse, Helen struggled to rise, her feet tangling in her skirts. The actress lifted her hands again, ready to deliver another magical blow. Freeing one foot, Helen kicked La Gianotta's ankle. As the actress jumped back, Helen scrambled into a crouch and threw herself forward, slamming into the woman's legs. The combined motion of their two bodies knocked La Gianotta to the ground.

Helen grabbed the actress's hair and pinned her head

to the floor, one knee on her stomach. She touched the blade to La Gianotta's throat. "What will happen if I cut you with silver? Will you dry up like a bug? Turn into a bat and fly away? Or will you just bleed out your life in this sorry pit?"

The actress bucked with rage, but stopped when the point of the knife dimpled her skin. Tilting her head back, away from the blade, she glared through lowered lashes.

Helen was thinking frantically. She did not actually want to take a life, but there was no virtue in letting La Gianotta go.

"Roll over," she demanded, shifting the knife from Laura's throat to the ticklish flesh beneath the ear. "Slowly."

Helen shifted her weight off the actress's midriff and tensed as she started to move. With relief, she saw Laura was obeying to the letter, turning over with great care so as not to brush against the knife.

I know what you're afraid of now, Helen thought with triumph. Taking a deep breath to tamp down her own fears, Helen untied her sash with one hand. When the length of pink silk came loose, she knelt on the small of La Gianotta's back, using all her weight to pin the actress to the ground. Holding the knife in her teeth, Helen tied her adversary's hands with the sash, then looped it around La Gianotta's throat with elaborate care. The more the woman struggled, the harder it would be to breathe. The knots would not slip easily.

For good measure, Helen tore a strip out of her petticoat and gagged Laura. She would have preferred to decimate the actress's clothes instead, but there was not enough sturdy cloth to work with.

After making sure her captive wasn't suffocating,

Helen rose. La Gianotta squirmed, but stopped the moment she felt the sash's pressure on her throat.

"My apologies for such rough usage," said Helen, hefting the knife in her hand. "I'm growing short-tempered. The earl's hospitality has plenty of élan, but it lacks warmth of feeling."

They were brave words, but she felt hollow and forlorn. Too much had happened in the last few days, and now the ferocity of the fight had shaken her. Barely holding on to her courage, Helen crept down the tunnel, following the direction of the Hellfire League.

Tracing the path he had taken earlier, Redfern found the same chamber with the black-and-white mosaic on the floor. It was empty, the bloodred marble pillars shimmering in the lamplight. Like far-distant summer thunder, he could hear chanting deeper in the tunnels. He studied the arched entrances that led to the unknown warren of chambers beyond. Torches flickered somewhere down the corridors, giving the archways the look of gates to hell.

Hellfire! he thought, then decided the curse was all too apropos.

Swallowing a lump of anxiety, Redfern chose one of the tunnels and started down it. The air was thick with the pungent tang of incense. He went down one passage, then another, feeling the grade of the floor dip while the ceiling remained level. The tunnels were growing larger and more imposing.

Finally, the bricks gave way to natural stone. Redfern stopped, stunned with momentary awe. The passage opened into an enormous underground cavern of black, shining rock. From where he stood, he could look across at the entrance to another tunnel perhaps twenty yards away. Eight tunnels in all emptied into the chamber, some high up the inky walls, some at the level of the floor. The chanting was growing louder, echoing up and down the stone like a living thing.

Wooden platforms ringed the pit, forming a series of galleries. Flights of stairs, some wooden, some hewn from the rock, zigzagged down from the tunnel mouths.

Most remarkable was the cluster of thick beams that projected from the top gallery over the cavern, each anchored by heavy chains spiked into the cavern ceiling. The beams formed a nine-armed star, each with a row of lamps hanging along its length.

Redfern's courage wavered. Despite this star of flames that shivered in the draft from the tunnels, the shadows of the underground abyss devoured the light. No natural rock was that particular polished-jet hue. No natural shadows were so absolute. This was the home of darkness.

He inhaled a long, shaking breath, secured the grip on his knife hilt, and peered over the wooden railing that rimmed the gallery. What he saw below did nothing to comfort him.

Unlike the smaller chamber he had seen first, this had no decoration. There was only a cube of veined, liver-hued marble at the center. Around the periphery of the cavern, tall iron tripods held lamps or dishes of incense. This was a working room, not a place for show.

The chanting was louder now, the low vibrations rolling through the air. *They are coming this way, but from below.*

Redfern closed his eyes, steadying his nerves. Without

pausing to review his folly, he ran down the nearest staircase.

There were crevices and folds in the walls, and he found an easy hiding place behind a lip of rock. Redfern settled just as they entered, Waring first, then Layton and another carrying banners, then pairs of robed figures. Anywhere but in that chamber the hooded costumes would have looked ridiculous. There, they added solemnity to the bizarre scene.

Waring stood to the east side of the cavern, about a dozen feet from the center. Layton placed the spear that held his banner in a holder to one side of Waring and stood to Waring's left, just in front of Redfern's hiding place. The second spear-bearer did the same and stood opposite Waring.

As the Hellfire League filed in, each pair brought an object with them and placed it on the marble slab, turning it into a makeshift altar: candles, jewels, roses so dark they looked black in the uncertain light. Redfern gaped when he saw the marchioness and Lady Gray leave a human skull. *I will never again underestimate older women.*

The last to enter was Barrett, who bore no offering. He stood beside the marchioness, feet apart, hands folded before his waist.

The chanting suddenly stopped. Silence reigned with the hush of a snowfall. Waring drew a long sword from beneath his robes and held it, point up, before him.

"With this sword, I describe the circle thrice."

He lowered the point to the ground and walked clockwise around the periphery of the group three times. Sparks flew from the tip as the steel made a grating noise that crawled under Redfern's skin.

When Waring stopped, Layton stood forward. "With salt, I seal the circle."

Taking a dish from the altar, he trickled salt along the circle that Waring had drawn. As Layton finished and set the dish down, expectancy hung over the League.

"The circle is closed," they said in unison.

Redfern felt a shudder, as if a gigantic door had slammed. He looked uneasily at the cavern roof. Now he could feel the weight of *something* before him, a solid presence around the League where before there had been none.

How powerful could a ring of salt be? What touchstones of science could be relied on in this dark realm beneath Arden Hall?

Now Waring was walking the same circle, but in the other direction. He had one of the dishes of incense, and was swinging it to and fro like an altar boy. "With this fire, I ban the light; with this cloud, I call the night. With this scent, I call the grave: What eternity lost, what mortality gave."

He stood, his back to the altar of stone, and faced the east. "I banish you, denizens of light and air. Bring no more the merry laugh, the brilliant flash of wit. Bring no more the dawn."

"Begone! Begone! Begone!" cried the League as one.

Waring turned to face Redfern's hiding space. Redfern squashed himself deeper into the curl of sheltering rock, concealing the pale skin of his face in the crook of his dark sleeve. He couldn't see Waring, but could hear him all too well.

"I banish you, fires of passion, fires of rage. Like the fleeting comet, may the wake of your passing be filled with night."

Was it Redfern's imagination, or could he feel a damp chill begin to creep through the rock, leaving a slug's trail of discomfort behind it? He shuddered, suddenly numb with cold.

Waring turned again and continued on. Redfern could not wait another moment. He peered around the rock, judging the distance between his knife and Waring. He was too far away. Praying to whatever beneficent spirits were left in the cavern, he crept to the shelter of a stalagmite closer to the east.

Finally, Waring was done speaking. Now an olive-skinned man walked to the center of the circle at the same time as Layton. *Could this be the French representative?* Redfern wondered.

Layton spoke first, drawing out a small, horn-handled knife. "The balance that holds the light and dark in harmony must be overturned. Demons of the League, we summon you."

He stretched the man's wrist over the slab of dark red stone and cut through to a vein. A trickle of blood spilled over the candles, the roses, the jewels. It ran down the skull, licking over the empty eyes and straggling teeth.

The man had his eyes closed, his teeth bared from the pain. With his other hand, he held up a fat purse. Slowly, he upended it on the bloody stone, gold coins clattering against the skull and bouncing from the altar to roll along the inky black floor.

"The payment is made," said Layton. "Blood for life; gold for honor. Neither life nor honor can hold us now. The darkness, my French friend, is yours to take."

"I claim it," said the man, his voice trembling. He was clearly unhappy, as if this horrific scene was not what he had expected at all. "I claim it for the glory of my general."

Waring walked forward to join them. "The light is paid and released. Let the darkness take its place."

He lifted a decanter and goblet of smoke-dark glass from the altar and began pouring the contents of one into the other. "Let the darkness fill the void as this wine fills this cup."

The company began to chant again, a wild, wordless howl that slowly rose higher and higher in pitch. The sound froze Redfern's flesh like the touch of filthy November ditch water. Once again, he crept to a new hiding place, this time directly behind Waring. He peered over top of the boulder, risking detection for a good look. He could see Waring's back, a tempting and open target.

Redfern wiped the palm of his hand on his knee and took a fresh grip on the knife.

The chant rose to a shriek and suddenly stopped. Silence hung, razor-edged, waiting for what came next.

It was then that Redfern saw Helen, white-faced and wide-eyed, in the tunnel mouth directly across the cavern.

Chapter 21

Redfern jerked, barely stopping his first instinct to leap from behind the boulder and run to her. That would expose them both.

What is she doing here, now? He had to get her away before Waring and the others saw her!

Helen vanished. Was it only that she pulled back to avoid detection? Anxiety and relief warred in him. If he could not see her, then neither could any of the League. But, if he could not see her, he could not know that she was safe.

Damnation! Redfern had a clear shot at Waring. He would throw the knife and run for Helen. Now was the time to end this.

Alas, he had delayed an instant too long. The darkness began in earnest, melting all the remaining light to an ash gray haze. For a moment, he thought he was losing consciousness.

What is happening? Waring was barely visible, and there was no way to take aim. Alarmed, Redfern looked around.

The Hellfire League craned their necks upward, arms

stretched out in supplication. Roiling and indistinct, the shadows were swirling down from the roof of the cavern, blotting out the lamps of the nine-armed star. A rotten smell overpowered the incense, a pungent bitterness that caught in the back of Redfern's throat. The stink conjured the horrors Hanson had described: war, famine, and chaos. Redfern could well believe it was the putrid essence from which evil flowed.

The shape of the cloud looked almost like a moth. He felt his blood pounding with some emotion that went beyond terror. It was primitive awe.

"It hungers!" cried Waring, and there was fear in his words.

The marchioness pushed Barrett, and he drifted forward with automatic obedience, an unwitting morsel to appease the darkness.

"No!" Helen's voice shrieked from across the dark cavern. The echo rang, silvery and bright.

All heads turned in her direction, hounds catching a scent.

No. There were only so many ways this could end, none of them bearable. Redfern sprang from where he hid and ran forward until he could clearly see Waring's robed form in the dim light.

With the force of a fist, the salt line of the circle repelled Redfern, throwing him back. He staggered, groping for support. His skin tingled as if he had stood too long in the sun and wind. The protective circle was as impassable as a brick wall.

The earl turned, astonished at the intrusion. Recovering, Redfern took careful aim and threw his knife. Waring made a dismissive gesture and the weapon skittered uselessly to the floor.

With a sneer, Waring turned away.

What now? He had another blade, but would throwing that one be any more effective? Redfern groped for his lost knife on the floor, barely able to see his own hand. His mind raced, seeking alternatives. He had lost the essential advantage of surprise.

The darkness was thickening, funneling down over the altar. All the air seemed to be sucked away, leaving only the putrid stench to breathe.

Redfern squinted, not sure what tricks his eyes were playing in the near-blackness. He thought he saw the tip of the cloud extend a hand and caress the objects on the altar. It fingered the skull, exploring the eye sockets and creeping over the jewels, fondling, stroking, seeking blindly. Redfern's gorge rose at the sheer obscenity of the thing.

With relief, he felt his hand close on the hilt of his knife.

At that moment, the figure at the western point of the circle produced a globe from beneath his robes. Redfern saw the movement only as a shifting of shadows, but almost at once a faint glow sprang to life at the heart of the orb.

Waring cried out in consternation, a wordless bark of outrage and denial. The figure with the light raised his hand, palm outward, warding off interference.

The members of the League surged forward, but in a heartbeat the figure raised the crystal globe and spears of blinding radiance burst from its core. They shrieked, the marchioness throwing herself to the floor to escape the brightness.

The light shone clear as dawn, hot as fire, pure as

moonlight, sharp as the sparkle of northern snow. All the light the League had banished seared forth.

Redfern threw his hands over his eyes, scorched by the intensity. He felt more than saw the darkness, cringing like a thing wounded and afraid, suck back to the cavern roof.

The force of the salt circle diminished. The weight Redfern had felt dissolved to nothing, restoring the sense of openness to the cavern. The spell was broken. Dazzled, he blinked, trying to restore his vision.

The altar cracked with the resounding *boom* of a cannon, shards of rock and debris scattering in a shower of dust. Redfern ducked behind the boulder that had been his hiding place and watched pebbles skitter past on the floor beside him. For a moment he could hear nothing but ringing in his ears, and then a gust of fresh air brushed his face. The stifling stench was lifting.

His ears popped. His hearing returned enough to perceive a low, wrenching moan and the confused sound of many people running. Redfern shook his head in an attempt to clear it. His first thought was of Helen's safety, his next of Waring. Redfern clutched his knife and scrambled to unsteady feet.

The members of the League were running away. A first look at the wreck of the altar told Redfern the moan he had heard was the Frenchman's last. A shard of rock protruded like a dagger from the man's neck. At least he had died quickly for his misdeeds.

Redfern lifted his gaze from the sprawled body to the figure with the orb. His mind froze with astonishment. The figure had pushed back his hood. It was Sir Alaric Fitzwilliam.

"Come, come," said the Master, smiling at Redfern's

expression. "Surely you didn't think reading reports was my sole occupation? A little field work was in order."

"But how . . ."

"With so many dark rooms and hooded robes, it was easy to take the place of the poor fool who lies unconscious somewhere in this subterranean maze."

Helen rushed out of the tunnel to Redfern's right. "James! Nicholas!"

Redfern caught her in his arms, glad of her warmth. With a wrench, he saw her face was tear-streaked and dirty. There was blood on her dress, which was now missing its sash. What *had* she been doing?

Then she turned to her brother. James stared about him, lost and stupefied. Waring's hold had slipped, but not enough to restore Barrett to himself. Her face crumpled when she saw his dazed expression. "No! Surely the spell is broken? Are we not safe now?"

"Not quite," said the Master.

Helen turned, her eyes round with astonishment. "Sir Alaric!"

He bowed slightly. "A histrionic evening, wouldn't you say, Miss Barrett? The next time I am invited to attend a dull night of cards, I will accept and be grateful."

"Why are you . . ."

The Master lifted his hand to silence her. "Now I am obliged to go chasing after our host. Restoring your brother is of the first importance, and we will need Waring's presence for that. Perhaps his death."

"Where did he go?" Redfern said, sheathing his knife.

"He ran," said Sir Alaric. "They all scuttled away like spiders, and I am going to scuttle after them. Secure Barrett and come find me. I have men in the woods. There is much left to do this night."

He set the globe, still glowing, on the rubble of the altar and hurried away, his gray robe billowing around him.

No sooner had the Master left than a footfall sounded on the wooden gallery above. Redfern heard someone descending the stairs.

"Do not move." The voice was familiar.

He heard the quick intake of Helen's breath. "Layton!" she whispered, fear thick in her voice.

And La Gianotta was beside him. They stood barely a dozen feet away. Her maleficent stare was aimed at Helen, who glared right back.

The actress was holding a feminine, silver pistol, the hammer cocked and ready. It was pointed at a spot right between Helen and Redfern, ready to pick off either target.

A sound made Redfern look across the room. The actor, Coleman, was there with a weapon of his own. They were pinned between the two.

"I said, do not move." Layton narrowed his eyes. "Yesterday, you led me on a merry chase, Miss Barrett. I didn't like that at all—and this evening I stumbled upon the lovely Laura whom you tied up and left in the passage. You are no end of trouble."

Redfern couldn't help stealing an admiring glance at Helen. No one replied. In the cavernous ceiling high above, gusts of air from the tunnels sighed through the stalactites and the maze of wooden beams. It sounded like the moaning of a ghost.

"Throw your knife to the side, Redfern." said Layton.

He hesitated, fingers shifting on the handle.

"Put it down or Miss Barrett dies like a dog."

Slowly, he set it on the floor and kicked it away. The

blade spun as it slid, coming to rest near the spot where he had been hiding earlier.

Redfern cursed to himself. He tried to calculate the odds of disarming one of their opponents before the other could shoot. They were not good. Still, he worked his fingers up his right cuff, straining to grip the hilt of his second wrist-knife.

Then, at the periphery of his vision, he saw another shadow move. A figure balanced on one of the rafters, running toe-to-toe along the narrow beam like a rope dancer. He dared not look up, afraid to give their rescuer away. He prayed no one else noticed the intruder.

Crouching into a ball in the shadows, the figure stopped just above Coleman. It was Hanson.

"Are we going to simply stand here?" complained Laura Gianotta. "There is no time to waste!"

Redfern thought he saw Hanson flinch, and felt a pang of pity for the man. He knew the pull the actress could have.

The knife slid into Redfern's palm.

Hanson dropped from the ceiling, smashing Coleman to the floor. They rolled, crashing into the wall. Hanson leaped up, only to fall again on his nearly identical opponent. Coleman struggled, flinging feet and fists with desperation. Hanson went down and the two wrestled, the sight like good and evil twins from a morality play.

As Hanson fell from the ceiling, Redfern saw Laura Gianotta recoil but recover at once. Before he could act, she took careful aim and fired, the small pistol making a sharp, echoing crack. Redfern threw his knife, dim light and distance making a precise aim impossible. The knife missed Laura Gianotta by inches. She whirled as it went by, her stomach arching away from its path.

At the same time, Layton was advancing on the Barretts. Cat-quick, Redfern dodged behind him, wrapping his arm around the man's throat in a choke hold. Layton struggled and sputtered, clawing at Redfern's arm. As his opponent's knees began to buckle, Redfern forced him to the ground.

Layton wormed out from under Redfern's weight, groping for the pistol he had hidden under his robes. He managed to pull it out, but Redfern seized his wrist, taking the pistol for himself. The movement released his grip on Layton's throat, leaving the man red-faced and gasping.

He grabbed Redfern's ankle. Redfern kicked with his other heel, aiming for his opponent's kneecap. It connected, but Layton wrenched away, twisting Redfern's foot in the process. Pain spiraled up his leg, making his mind go white with shock. He flung his body wildly. The motion slipped him out of Layton's grip, but the pistol flew from his hand. Redfern lurched forward for the weapon, Layton a beat behind. It was too far away, so he grabbed Layton's hair, thumping the man's head to the floor. Layton went limp at once.

Instinct overcoming his trance, Barrett pushed Helen to the floor just as La Gianotta fired her pistol. Barrett flung up his arms. His body jerked and fell like a marionette suddenly cut from its strings.

"No!" Helen screamed, scrambling to her feet.

She knelt beside Barrett, running her hands over his body to see where he had been hit. He was facedown, the injury hidden from view.

"Oh, God!" she cried. "Oh, God! Somebody help us!"

Helen looked wildly around. The others were grappling on the floor, Nicholas and Layton fighting one other for a pistol. A despairing sob escaped her throat.

Coward! she scolded herself. *This is no time for weakness.*

Layton was unconscious. Redfern limped over and crouched on the other side of Barrett, but looked around nervously. There had been two pistols to begin with, but only one shot. Where was the other?

Laura Gianotta had run away, but Coleman and Hanson were still fighting. Then Redfern saw Coleman raise his weapon, the barrel pointed straight at him.

A sudden blankness filled Redfern's soul. He was about to die. With a mercurial quickness born of panic, he spotted the pistol Layton had lost, grabbed it, and shot the man dead.

Time hung suspended for a moment. A quake of nerves shivered along Redfern's spine. He lowered Layton's weapon and it fell from his hands to the stone with a clatter. A cold feeling, like the water from melting ice, seemed to flow from his stomach to his veins. He had shot men before, but it was never easy.

At the very edge of his perception, he could hear Hanson groan and Helen curse under her breath.

At least we are alive, Redfern thought dully. Then again, he wasn't sure about Barrett. He leaned forward, bracing his hands on the floor to steady himself.

Hanson was running toward him. With an effort, Redfern sat up.

"You took care of the other one as well?" Hanson said, his face flushed with exertion. His arm, still bandaged from the other day, was bleeding again. He stood for a moment, scanning the room, then picked up the knife

Redfern had been forced to toss aside. "No, it looks like your man has flown."

Redfern raised his eyes and came back to himself, like a swimmer breaking the surface of a lake. He twisted his head around. Layton was indeed gone.

He swore with whatever vigor he had left. He should have slit Layton's throat. "We need a surgeon for my friend."

As Hanson approached and handed Redfern the knife, Helen got to her feet, moving around to where Redfern was kneeling. Slowly, he rose, the aftermath of the battle making him clumsy. As he put his arm around Helen, she began to sob.

Bending over Barrett, Hanson rolled him over, using both hands. Blood spread over Barrett's front, wet and shining. His head fell to one side, slack and open-mouthed. Gently, Hanson touched Barrett's neck, feeling for a pulse.

"Sir Alaric will have brought a medic," he said. "I will go fetch him directly."

Hanson left. With anxious eyes Helen watched him go. Nicholas stripped off his neck cloth, pressing it to Barrett's wound. Dark red blood bloomed on the white, the bleeding refusing to stanch. Helen put her hands over the cloth as well, as if their combined touch could do what his alone could not. The only sounds were their movements and the wet wheeze of Barrett's ragged breathing. Nicholas grew more and more somber.

Helen closed her eyes, just wanting to bury her face against his chest. After being enchanted, bullied, imprisoned, chased, and attacked, and witnessing dark ritual and the shooting of her brother, Helen was at the end of her strength, and what she had left was trickling away like the last blood from a mortal blow. By the time Hanson came back with the surgeon, she was falling into numb despair.

"Sir Alaric is looking for you," Hanson said to Nicholas. "He's over by the maze."

Nicholas took Helen by the shoulders, pulling her away so the doctor could work. "I need to find Waring," he said softly. "You heard Sir Alaric. Only Waring can release Barrett from the spell."

Helen shook her head, digging her fingers into his sleeve. He was speaking, but she was too exhausted and afraid to comprehend the words. "Don't go."

"I can't let Waring run free. You see what he can do," he said, almost pleading. "If I start now, he can't get too far."

"But James is hurt!" She had felt her brother slide away from her, and now Nicholas was going, too.

He squeezed her shoulders. "There is nothing I can do for James that the doctor cannot do better. I *can* catch the earl, and he can be made to free your brother. Helen, this is my chance to catch a traitor and win my freedom. Then I can stay by your side for good."

A promise was not the same as his presence then and there. Helen felt alone, an abyss on every side. She always loved him; he always left.

"Helen, please." His dark brown eyes were soft with pain.

The clamor of thoughts in Helen's head receded, leaving her empty. She had been through this scene so many times. Resignation crept over her. It was the same as always.

Of course Waring had to be stopped. It was the truth, but not the truth she needed. "Go, then."

Nicholas sighed, pulling away. "I am sorry, Helen."

Still moving with a limp, Nicholas headed for the nearest tunnel, leaving her in the vast cavern. She bent over the still form of her brother, tears falling on the bloodied front of his gray robe. Hanson put his hand on her arm, trying to comfort, but he might as well have been a ghost.

Nicholas is gone again.

Chapter 22

Feeling filthy with guilt, Redfern left in search of Sir Alaric. As the Master had said, there were men in the woods. Some he recognized as Sir Alaric's spies; others he guessed were members of the Circle. It seemed Fairmeadow had reached London in time to raise the alarm—which would have meant a grueling, nonstop journey as fast as the roads would allow. The journey back to Arden Hall would have been just as hard, but their plan had worked. The combined forces of the Circle and the Master's spies were defeating their foe.

As the members of the Hellfire League fled the hall, they were captured. If they tried to use magic against the Master's men, members of the Circle were on hand to help. Redfern saw Wilson binding the arms of the marchioness, Fairmeadow standing by with his hands on his hips. Redfern wished he had a moment to stop and congratulate the little man for a job well done.

As Redfern drew near the maze, his senses sharpened. There was something indefinable lingering there, something that made him look over his shoulder. He was reluctant to enter the twisting confusion of a maze on a night already fraught with magic. With relief, he saw Sir Alaric seated just beyond the entry, on the same bench where Redfern had met Fairmeadow.

He sat down before he realized the man was not the Master. Astonishment made him recoil. He could have sworn it was Sir Alaric. Glancing back out the entrance, he saw the funeral coach now stood there, black and gleaming. Cold crept up his neck with insinuating fingers.

Slowly, one degree at a time, he turned his head. Redfern sat facing Michael. Now he could see his brother's features. They seemed indistinct, shifting in the moonlight. Shock quickly turned to old, aching pain.

"I'm sorry," Redfern said. It was the first thing that came to his mind—not fear, but sadness. "I'm sorry I argued with you."

The form flickered. It might have been a shrug. "You mean you're sorry the last thing you said to me before I blew my brains out was the truth. What of it? I ruined the family. You took on the job of making everything right. The apology is up to me."

Redfern shook his head. "I wish . . ."

"Don't. I'm all right, Nick."

"Michael, I . . ."

"I love you, brother. It's taken years to tell you, but there you are."

Redfern blinked, recognizing an old irritation. Michael never did let him finish a sentence. "I must say this."

It might be the only chance he had to speak his heart, and he was weary of secrets and silences. "I had to atone for the way I treated you. I drove you the last inches to despair and death."

The spirit tilted its head, as if astonished. "Do you really believe that?"

"Look at our family, Michael. There is wild blood in us, sometimes cruelty. Is it any wonder I rebuked you as I did, rather than extend my hand in compassion?"

"Nonsense. You had a right to tell me to do my duty. I was just too much a coward to face ruin. Besides, I wanted money, not friendship. As I recall matters, you were to be married and could ill afford what I asked of you."

"What right had I to think of marriage when you were in such trouble?"

Redfern buried his face in his hands, feeling the hot rush of blood to his cheeks. It had been so hard to say, but he had needed to speak these words for five long years.

The shade crossed his legs, slouching on the stone bench. "Good God, Nick, for the steady one in the Saville family, you do have a remarkable penchant for dramatics. You had every right to marry. Furthermore, you didn't shoot me; I shot myself and never spared you a thought when I did it."

Redfern frowned. The tone was so like Michael—drawling, sarcastic, derisive.

"Go home, brother, love your woman, and stop trying to atone for sins you did not commit. You are absolved. It was my folly that ruined us and drove me to my untimely end. Listen carefully: my fault, not yours."

"But I . . ."

"To rephrase: This is my apology. I came back from the grave to make it. Stop trying to usurp the moment, Nicholas."

Redfern raised his eyes. The apparition had faded.

Barely an outline showed where Michael sat. Their time was almost at an end.

Redfern felt a painful mix of loss and wonder—and something like amusement. "What the bloody hell are you doing messing around in the Circle's coach?" The words came as a hoarse whisper, squeezed tight with emotion.

The answer came out of the darkness. There was a smile in the words. "It was a vessel I could use to reach you. When Bedford was killed, I moved his body to warn you. You were in danger and the coach was—available."

"Available" was the way Michael had always rationalized taking something, usually a horse, that wasn't his.

Surprised laughter choked in Redfern's aching throat. Death hadn't changed his brother one bit. But then again, it had. He had apologized—something he had never once done in life. "Michael!"

A faint rustle made Redfern jump to his feet. Waring stood at the entrance to the maze, staring off across the garden and panting heavily. He still wore his robes. As he turned, Redfern could see his face was blanched with fear. "I thought I saw that blasted coach."

In the next second, he had recovered himself enough to realize it was Redfern stepping out of the maze. "Damn you!"

"The coach is the Circle's harbinger of death, is it not?" Redfern studied the man. Waring was tired and afraid. He had spent his reserves calling the demon. "I think it came just in time for our tête-à-tête."

Wild terror flickered over Waring's features once more, but his voice was harsh. "If I have seen my death tonight, it will not come at your hand."

"Then again, perhaps the Dark Gentleman favors me to carry out his commission."

"You think you can destroy me, Redfern?"

"I am Death's brother. I owe him a favor or two."

"You have no power over me." Waring produced a small pistol. "I wouldn't even bother to waste spellcraft on you."

With the speed of a serpent, Redfern threw his knife. This time, the blade hit home, striking Waring in the shoulder and forcing him to drop the weapon. The point stuck where it hit, biting deep into flesh. The earl fell to his knees, his mouth a rictus of pain.

Redfern kicked Waring's pistol out of the man's reach. "Precision trumps brute force. Just as a hint, you'll find that principle works better with the ladies as well."

Waring struggled to his feet, his face a mask of agony, the front of his scarlet tabard wet with the darker red of blood. Sweat slicked his face. He tried to reach for Redfern, strike out one last time, but his strength was gone.

Redfern had defeated his enemy. He felt neither triumph nor regret. Both would come, but now there remained the task of taking Waring prisoner.

"Come, my lord," said Redfern with frigid politeness. "Sir Alaric would like a word. He represents the king here tonight."

Redfern grabbed Waring's uninjured arm and scanned the area beyond for the Master. His attention was caught by another figure moving in the darkness.

La Gianotta. Redfern's stomach clenched with apprehension. For a moment, things had been going his way, but no more.

"Laura!" Waring called, his voice hazy with pain.

Redfern pressed the pistol to the back of Waring's head. "Be silent."

But the actress was already coming toward them, taking long strides across the grass. Her hair had fallen loose and trailed in wild, curling strands past her waist. Her dark eyes were fixed on the earl.

"Your hold is slipping, Waring," she said, baring her sharp teeth. "It has been years since you coaxed me into your bed. They have not been altogether pleasant, and now I see a doorway to freedom."

"Laura, my love." Waring's voice was brittle with false hope.

Redfern had his hand on the earl's arm and felt him begin to tremble. At the look in Gianotta's eyes, he began to feel a cold knot of fear in his own belly.

"Your love? Your *love*?" The words were amused. "You throttle me in your spell. You use me to wreak havoc in your name and then you cast me aside for a pretty broodmare."

She stopped a few feet away. "You have the temerity to call me *love*? That is quite optimistic, even for you."

Anxiety spiked in Redfern's blood. He could not begin to guess how this would end. "Please, madam, let me take him to face justice."

She gave a delicate snort. "There is not punishment enough to mete out justice for this man."

"No, Laura." It was Hanson's voice. He came out of the darkness behind her. "He is lost. Forget him."

"He made me what I have become!" She turned on Hanson. "Thomas, I am not the lost soul you think me. I'm not sure I even have a soul anymore. He has left me with nothing but memories and a dark hunger. I come and

I go and I take other lovers, but when he calls, I must attend and do as I am bid."

"Please, Laura, no," Hanson pleaded, raising his own weapon. "Don't make me see you do this."

Apprehensive, Redfern moved to place himself between Waring and the actress. As little as he liked it, he had a duty to protect his prisoner. The move brought him unpleasantly close to La Gianotta. A smile crept over her lips.

"Fear not, Lord Redfern, I wish only to kiss the earl farewell." The words were as ambiguous as they were tempting.

Before he could resist, Redfern met her eyes. Cold paralysis slipped over him once more. Shuddering in his struggles, he tried to raise his pistol, but could not.

"Laura!" Waring whispered, terrified as a child sunk into nightmare.

La Gianotta pressed close to Redfern, trailing her fingers along his chest. Fury shook him, making her laugh. She turned away with a pirouette and continued on to where Waring stood.

Taking Waring's face in her hands, she pulled his head forward in a sensual, breathless embrace.

Hanson's shot split the air. Waring fell to the grass.

With a huge, sucking breath, Redfern ripped himself from the invisible bonds. He swiveled around, weapon raised, but La Gianotta had vanished.

Hanson had fired, but his pistol ball hit only a nearby tree. Waring was dead of a kiss.

*   *   *

Waring is dead. The treason is uncovered. I am free!
Redfern sprinted from the garden, his one thought to find
Helen.

He would never, ever leave her again.

He skidded to a stop when a stretcher bearing James
Barrett emerged from Arden Hall. The Master walked at
its side, Helen steps behind.

"How is he?" Redfern asked.

"He will live," replied Sir Alaric. "There are those of
the Circle whose skills extend to healing. What of Waring?"

"Dead. La Gianotta has disappeared."

"So has Layton, but the rest have been caught. We can
only hope this night has seen the Hellfire League's
demise."

Redfern was barely listening any longer. His thoughts
had turned fully to Helen. He hardly noticed when the
Master ordered Barrett's stretcher be loaded into the
fastest coach.

"We're safe," Redfern said, grasping Helen's arms.

She said nothing for a moment, wrapping her arms
around him. They just held each other, finally at peace
after fending off too many emergencies.

"I must go with James." She lifted her head. "I'm
afraid he will wake up and be afraid. He may not know
what happened to him."

"I understand," Redfern murmured.

The hub of activity had moved farther away toward the
carriages that had brought the Master's men. They were
more or less alone.

A tear slipped down her cheek. "I don't think I'll ever
sleep again. When I shut my eyes I keep seeing that Italian woman with the gun! I can't bear it!"

She began to cry in earnest, sobbing on Redfern's shoulder. She dissolved with a heartrending, childlike misery, messy and from the core of her soul. Redfern stood, drawing her into his arms, and let her weep. After all she had been through in the last few days, she had a right to it.

As Helen began to quiet, he gently kissed her ear, then her neck. She sighed softly, a little pleasure mixed in with the last of her sobs.

"I'm sorry," she said, ending the words with a hiccup.

He stroked the hair away from her red-rimmed eyes, thinking it a privilege to bear a little of her pain. "It's all right."

She mopped her eyes with the backs of her hands, smearing the grime on her face. It reminded Redfern of the day before—Helen dirty and full of leaves from the orchard, washing her face before they made love. He could not keep from smiling.

"What is so amusing?" she asked, prim perhaps due to a touch of embarrassment.

He pulled her to him, locking his arms around her waist. "I'm not laughing at you."

"Then why are you smiling? This is hardly a gleeful occasion."

"Because we are here together. You are more than enough reason for at least one moment of happiness each day."

She managed a tentative smile of her own. "I never thought you prone to attacks of cheerfulness, with or without reason."

"I'm not. I'm a house closed up against all optimism. It is you who opened the shutters and let in the sun."

Helen tilted her head, a little color coming back into

her face. "When houses are shut up, they tend to get rather dusty and full of mice."

"I assure you, I am in fine trim. You see, I am encouraging guests into my heart these days." With that, he kissed her.

Helen kissed him back. All the passion that had racked her with tears now poured into her embrace. Redfern felt her need, the hunger for reassurance. He touched her face, stroked her neck, softening the fierceness of her mood.

"It's all right," he whispered, soothing her as he would a frightened animal. "Everything will be fine."

She clung to him, burying her face in his neck. "I need you."

"I'm glad," he replied, keeping his tone light.

He ached for her, the distracting, heavy kind of ache that was accompanied by thoughts of a bedroom. She ran her hands down his chest, her nails lightly denting the front of his torn waistcoat.

"If I comfort you like this much longer," he observed, "I'm going to need some comforting myself."

Helen looked into his eyes with longing. "Once I am no longer needed at James's bedside, I can ensure your efforts are properly compensated."

Indeed! he thought, drawing away a little to gain some self-control.

Helen was looking at him, her face serious. "I am so sorry I doubted you. When the moment came, you saw to it everything was taken care of, including me and James. You kept your promises."

"Because I love you," he said, putting his hands on her shoulders. He held her lightly, as if she were a winged creature too delicate for the touch of mortal hands. "I am home to stay. Forever."

Helen touched his face. "Marry me, Nicholas."

A grin split his face, the one she had waited so long to see. Redfern gathered Helen Barrett in his arms once more and kissed her long and hard.

Chapter 23

The wedding of Helen Barrett and Nicholas Saville, Viscount Redfern, took place in a little church close to the country home of Helen's father.

The crowd—family, friends, neighbors, onlookers of all descriptions—overflowed the pews and straggled out the doors. It was a crisp October day, but the world shone with that special intensity only a clear autumn sun can provide.

The ceremony went forth, a variation on the usual theme. Redfern's younger sister, Panthea, held the bride's flowers. The youngest Saville brother, Randall, stood up with Redfern. Helen's father, stiff with age, gave away his daughter. It had been his ambition to bestow his radiant Helen on a man with a title, and he had achieved it. James and Constance were there, too, fully occupied with their children, the second but a newborn. A sentimental and tearful Lord Fairmeadow brought his particular friend, Mr. Abercrombie.

Hanson also attended, appearing in the character of Viscount Farnwell. Though not entirely reconciled with his family, he had made some effort to thaw the arctic chill of paternal wrath. He sat in the back of the church with Sir Alaric and Lady, smiling wistfully.

"You are melancholy," Sir Alaric observed.

Hanson looked at him, the light in his green eyes subdued. "I am. My friends say that I am young and will recover, and then they pour me more ale."

"That is good of them," Sir Alaric said with a lift of his brow.

"I'm afraid it doesn't work. I still love Laura, deceiver that she is." Hanson lifted one corner of his mouth in a catlike smirk. "It was part of her charm, until I discovered she had deceived me. I always thought, having some powers of my own, that I was immune. I forgot that a man is always prey to a beautiful face, whether or not spells are part of the equation."

The Master coughed, and it sounded suspiciously like a laugh. "I think you are at least in part enjoying your heartbreak."

"There is a part of me that finds it interesting in a scientific way. I can label and catalogue all the parts of my woe as long as it is my head and not my heart at work. If I let myself feel it, I am good for nothing. Poor Bedford. I cannot forgive her that. He was my friend."

He sounded genuinely heartbroken.

The Master studied his hands. "We continue to look for her, you know."

"You won't find her in England. That much I am sure of. Anything here would be a reminder of her servitude to Waring. Besides, I want Laura the way I thought she was. It is a difficult thing to discover the woman you love, well, may not be altogether human. I find my insouciance is not what it used to be."

"Understandable. La Gianotta is a mystery. Was she a

demon Waring coerced, or a woman he made into something else?"

"I would guess the latter. She was not entirely a monster. Yet she was enough of one that I tried to shoot her."

The Master eyed Hanson. "A sad case. However, you have many years ahead of you to find a genuine Italian female. I understand Italy is riddled with them."

Hanson looked astonished. "Fancy that!"

Sir Alaric patted Lady's head. "I might even give you an assignment there." He liked Hanson. The young actor had joined his service willingly after the episode at Arden Hall. It made the loss of Redfern less of a disaster.

From the church, the wedding party trooped to Seabright Manor, where the Barrett patriarch had thrown open his bulging vaults to furnish an exquisite feast. Nothing was spared—the best wines, the choicest meats, and gifts for everyone to commemorate the day. The crowning glory was, to Helen's dismay, a large array of sculptures composed of fruits and vegetables, including a strawberry pig. Her father had hired a French chef.

James Barrett, now almost completely recovered from his ordeal, had invited most of the county. With sincere bonhomie, he divided his time between shaking hands and chasing his son out of the duck pond. His father was getting older, and it seemed a good time to withdraw from London for a few years. Constance, the wife he now realized he had given far less than her due, agreed. There was always a need for men with administrative capabilities in county affairs. James would not be bored.

After the business of eating had concluded, the talking began. Once the party got through the usual congratulations, Hanson recited an epithalamion—a formal and flowery wedding poem much in vogue amongst the young poets—and then announced a toast.

"I give you Helen Barrett," he said. "She is a woman of amazing character, strength, beauty, and resourcefulness. And I give you her husband, Redfern. He had the good sense to want her, and the even better sense to learn how he could win her. And I give you all of us."

Hanson lifted his glass, looking around the room, waiting out the proper pause before going on. "May we all marry the paragons we ought to deserve."

"Hear, hear," said Sir Alaric, thinking they had all come away with the prize they most needed.

Then Redfern's father, the Earl of Whitford, stood up.

"To the beautiful bride," he said. "May my son protect and honor you. And to my son, who deserves all the good fortune imaginable. You have exceeded every wish a father could have for his child's character, his sense of duty, and his ability. Bless you both."

Redfern looked at the tablecloth, his heart full. He thought of Michael, whose forgiveness and apology had given him the peace of mind to fully enjoy his return to Helen's arms. It was as though a self-imposed curse had been lifted.

He did not wish Michael were there. He thought he probably was.

To Helen, it seemed days—happy, good days, but days nonetheless—before she could finally retire with her new husband. Her father had provided the best bedchamber for the bridal couple, a large, stately room hung with Belgian tapestries. By the time they walked in, it was lit with candles to chase away the growing dark.

Nicholas closed the door and touched her arm lightly, drinking her in with his eyes.

"I recall when you proposed to me," Helen said with an arch tone, "you knelt."

"I what? When?" Nicholas looked perplexed.

"The first time you proposed, I mean—you got down on your knees in a spring meadow. You fairly begged me to wed you."

"I did?"

"Of course you did. I adored you for it."

He looked uncertain. "When was that?"

"I was very young. I made it up in a story. You were wearing armor."

Nicholas grinned. "It sounds as if I was more likely wearing *amour*."

Helen pouted. "You are a beast!"

"Rejoice, now you are burdened with me forever."

"Will you kneel? Just this once?" She held his chin, gazing softly into his eyes. He would have taken her seriously but for the grin on her face.

"Does that do a woman's heart good? To see a man prostrate at her feet?"

"Once in a while. If it occurs too frequently, it poses a hazard. One might trip over one's prone lover and fall down the stairs."

Nicholas knelt in the approved fashion, his hands clasped to his breast. "Fair Helena, sweet Helena."

She burst into a fit of giggles, which only got worse as he bent to kiss her toes. But soon, the kiss became something else. He lifted her foot, sliding off the white slipper. Then he repeated the process with the other.

Sliding his hands up her ankles, he lifted his face. She could see in his eyes something serious, something dark and—oh, joy of joys—no longer forbidden. Helen dropped her tiny, beaded reticule on the floor and stripped off her gloves, one dainty finger at a time.

Nicholas searched under her skirt and petticoats, running his hands up to her knee until he found the garter. His hands were warm, gentle, playing her as if she were an exquisite instrument. She shivered, and felt the ribbon slip away from her leg. Nicholas tossed it behind him, rolling down the stocking to expose her bare foot. He kissed the inside of her ankle, his tongue finding the hollows of bone and tendon, biting a little as he found flesh.

Helen moaned, already feeling a well of heat in her belly. He began working on the other leg, reaching higher this time, his hands on the soft skin of her thigh. As she lifted her foot so he could remove the second stocking, she felt a wave of mischief.

"My turn," she said. "Or perhaps you owe me two."

Nicholas flung the stocking with a dramatic air. "No, both stockings count only as one. Women have more clothes, so it has to work that way."

Helen took hold of his cravat, wrecking the careful architecture his valet had wrought. "Perhaps I should learn what Laura Gianotta knew about scarves. I'm sure it would work equally well with any neck cloth, and men always seem to have one handy."

Nicholas lifted his chin so that she could untie the knot. "I think she had an eye to early widowhood."

Helen chuckled. "I think she and Waring deserved one another."

He took her by the shoulders, turning her around. The wedding dress was the same one her mother had worn, slightly restyled for the occasion. Encrusted with tiny pearls and gold braid, the low bodice fastened up the back. Growing more impatient by the moment, Nicholas tugged at the crisscrossed lacing.

"You could have let my maid do this part," Helen said slyly.

"If I thought it proper to wear a knife to my wedding, I could have this undone in a second."

"How can you bear to be without your blades?"

Triumphant, Nicholas pushed the bodice off her shoulders, kissing the soft curve of her neck. "I have all the weaponry this occasion demands."

Helen untied the ribbon at her waist, and the dress shushed to the floor in a pool of white satin. Her petticoats fell, one by one, a whispering snowfall of lace and muslin. She stepped out of them, feeling lighter.

She turned, and Nicholas had stripped down to his shirt. The candlelight played on the falling folds of his sleeves. He looked just as he had in her girlish imagination, when he was the pirate, and she the innocent maid.

Helen's heart began to trip, her mouth to run dry. "I am still wearing far too many clothes."

"Let me help you," he said, chuckling deep in his chest, and he freed her from the rest of her lacy underthings.

Nicholas picked her up. Helen was tall, and it was slightly awkward, but it was almost like the prince whisking the princess away in her private fairy tale. It was just a good thing they did not have to go far.

The bed was soft, the covers cool to the touch. Helen spread out her arms, feeling the freedom of its wide expanse. Nicholas shed the rest of his clothes, the firelight edging his fine, lean form. Helen held up her arms in welcome.

He knelt over her, taking her mouth, tasting her

tongue. She used her teeth delicately, catching him, teasing, biting his lips like a playful kitten tests its milk teeth. His breath was coming hard. Helen felt utterly, completely free in his arms.

She rose to her knees before her husband, cradling his head. Nicholas lowered his mouth to her breasts, circling the aureoles with his tongue, licking, sucking, raising the peaks to a new sensitivity. Helen cried out, the waves of desire almost painful.

He pushed her backward, his sex hard and urgent. She felt his fingers probe her, testing the hot, slick place between her legs.

"Come to me," she said, lifting under his touch. "Come to me now."

He stretched out above her, resting on his forearms, and gave her a long, lingering kiss. "I love you."

"I love you," she answered, her lips on his ear.

"Helen?" he said, a teasing note in his voice. He rolled to one side, stroking the velvet inside of her thigh.

"What?" Her hand roved over his chest, exploring.

"Do you forgive me?" His fingers teased her. "You never answered me."

"*Redfern!*" she growled in frustration, giving him a playful kick.

He slapped away her foot. "Do you? Now is the time to answer."

"Yes! Yes!" she cried, pulling him down on her and laughing. "Now get on with it!"

He laughed, seeming lighter, and surged over her, pinning her arms above her head. He left swift kisses the length of her, starting at her mouth and working down her body, over her breasts and belly, finishing at the wet softness of her sex.

He pushed himself inside, easing his way with gentle strokes. Helen locked her legs at his sides, rocking with him. At first it was slow, a communion, the marriage at its most bare and primal. Gently, the pressure built in her, a rising urgency that fought to become her master.

Greedy, she rose to meet Nicholas as he pushed, working muscles she barely knew. She felt the slow contractions of her desire begin to mount, growing faster and harder. She held on, making it last until she could resist no longer. She felt his hot breath, the fire taking control of his blood. He was pushing, pumping, claiming her body. Her instincts took over, matching him stroke for stroke until the pleasure exploded, and she wailed in her surrender. She was nothing but the moment, only there, only then, only the hot rush of seed inside her.

Nicholas kissed her, and she melted. He had promised himself to her, and she trusted him. He would be with her always. He loved her, and she him.

They had both sworn an oath today. They belonged only to each other. They were one, mated and married.

She ran a hand along his shoulder. "I didn't quite catch all that. Would you repeat it?"

Nicholas gave Helen a long, hot kiss. "From the beginning?"

"Yes, please."

Historical Note

The French did land in Ireland in August 1798 to support the Irish rebels. They won a battle in Castlebar, but in September they surrendered at Ballinamuck, County Longford. The Irish rebellion of 1798 came to an end.

Sir Francis Dashwood established the most famous hellfire club, the Friars of St. Francis of Wycombe. The members of this group were a remarkable collection of statesmen, aesthetes, and libertines. Club activities seem to have included political discussion, blasphemous rituals, and revelry, but no "real" magic.

The Earl of Waring's ceremony is not taken from any historical accounts or any other faith or ritual practice, but is entirely the product of my own fevered imagination.

In 1798, Napoleon was busy invading Egypt. Though the general's obsession with his own destiny is well-known, I am not aware of any reliable account of Napoleon hiring wizards. If he had, I am sure he would have chosen someone more effective than the gang at Arden Hall.

NAOMI BELLIS

STEP INTO DARKNESS

Sarah Leaford is desperate to rescue her father from the dungeons of Paris, and it seems that her success depends on one man: Gentleman Jack, the greatest thief in all of London. What she doesn't know is that Jack is already well acquainted with her father....

Years ago, Lord Carleigh framed Jack for murder, leaving him a ruined man destined for the gallows. Now Jack has a chance for revenge—but to take it, he must resist falling for the beautiful noblewoman and her mysterious, untamed magic.

Drawn together by a dangerous mission, Sarah and Jack must not surrender to the passion that flares between them. They are not simply a maiden and a thief, and more lives than theirs are in peril. So much is at risk that even the dead take notice....

0-451-21938-4

Available wherever books are sold or at
penguin.com

LYDIA JOYCE

WHISPERS OF THE NIGHT

**When four London seasons fail to find her a
suitable match, Alcyone Carter does the
unthinkable and treks across Europe to marry
a foreign nobleman she's never met. But on
her wedding night, she discovers her
handsome, enigmatic husband is not the man
he claimed to be. Rather than live a lie, she
escapes his estate into the darkness. But her
husband—ignited by his desire and pride—
risks everything to follow her from the depths
of the Romanian forests into the decadent
heart of Istanbul, where they're forced to
confront the sensual passion they've
discovered—and the dire threat that could
cost them both their lives.**

0-451-21897-3

**Available wherever books are sold or
at penguin.com**

Jo Beverley

To Rescue a Rogue

Lady Mara St. Bride has never backed down from a good adventure, which was how she wound up roaming the streets of London in the middle of the night, wearing nothing but a shift and corset beneath an old blanket. Luckily, her brother's oldest friend, the devilishly sexy Lord Darius Debenham, answered her plea for help. Now she intends to repay the favor...

Before he was wounded at Waterloo, Dare had embraced everything life had to offer. Forever changed by the war, he now believes nothing—not even the interference of a lovely young minx like Mara—can rescue him from his demons. But Mara is determined to reignite his warm smile, and enlists the help of all the Rogues to offer Dare a temptation he cannot resist...

0-451-22011-0

Available wherever books are sold or at penguin.com